STEAMBORN

Books by Eric R. Asher

Shop ebooks, audiobooks, and paperbacks at ericrasherstore.com

The Theme Park at the End of the World

The Steamborn Series

Steamborn

Steamforged

Steamsworn

Skyborn

Skyforged

Skysworn

Stormborn

Stormforged

Stormsworn

The Vesik Series
(Recommended for Ages 17+)

Days Gone Bad

Wolves and the River of Stone

Winter's Demon

This Broken World

Destroyer Rising

Rattle the Bones

Witch Queen's War

Forgotten Ghosts

The Book of the Ghost

The Book of the Claw

The Book of the Sea

The Book of the Staff

The Book of the Rune

The Book of the Sails

The Book of the Wing
The Book of the Blade
The Book of the Fang
The Book of the Reaper
Dreams of the Forgotten Dead
Garden Gnome Graves

The Vesik Series Box Sets

Box Set One (Books 1-3)
Box Set Two (Books 4-6)
Box Set Three (Books 7-8)
Box Set Four: The Books of the Dead Part 1
Box Set Five: The Books of the Dead Part 2

Mason Dixon: Monster Hunter

Episode One
Episode Two
Episode Three
Episode Four

Want to receive an email when one of Eric's books releases?
Visit ericrasher.com to get started.

STEAMBORN

THE STEAMBORN SERIES, BOOK ONE

By

ERIC R. ASHER

Edited by Indie Solutions by Murphy Rae
Cover typography by Indie Solutions by Murphy Rae
Cover artwork by Enggar Adirasa

The forgotten will never be.

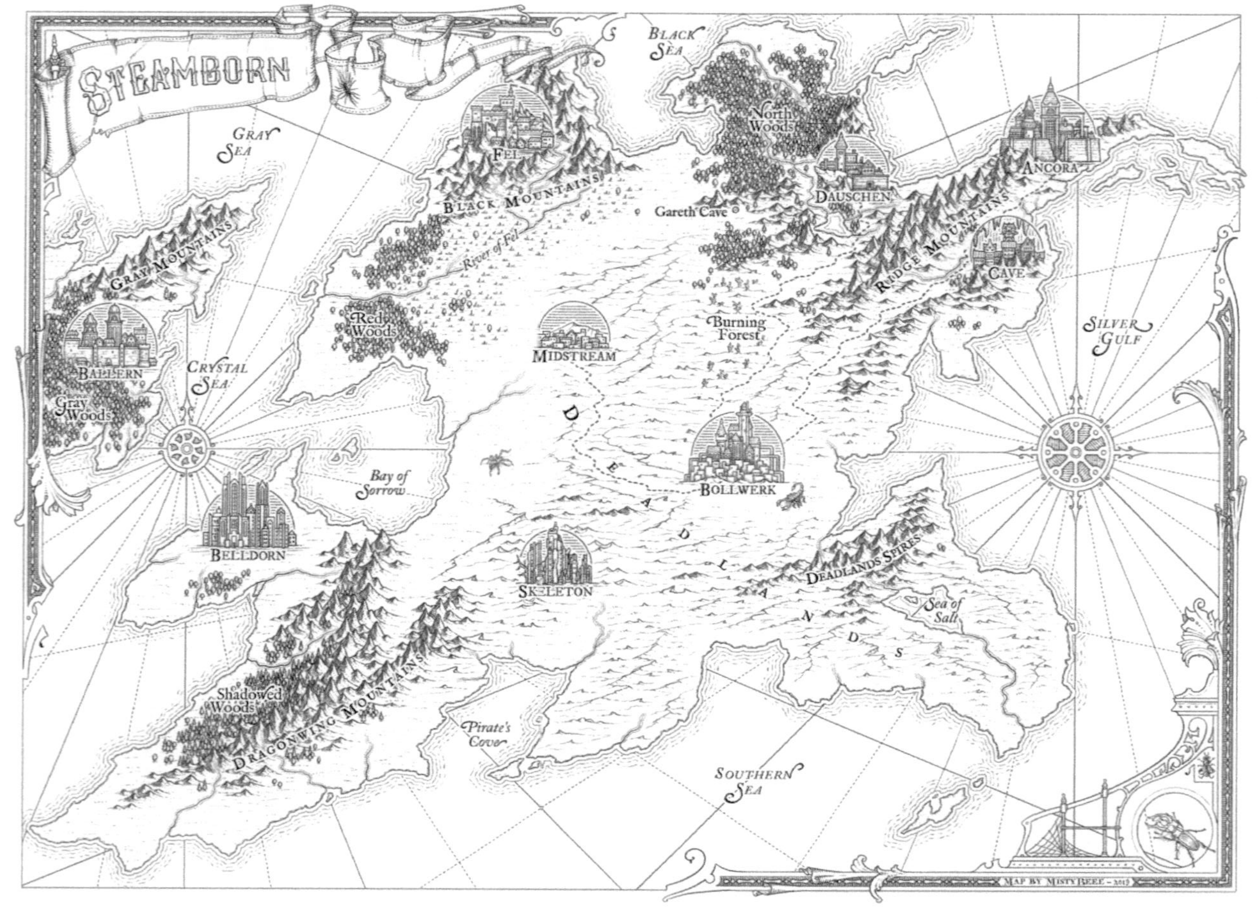

STEAMBORN
GRAY SEA
BLACK SEA
North Woods
Fel
Black Mountains
Gareth Cave
Dauschen
Ancora
Ridge Mountains
Cave
Silver Gulf
Gray Mountains
River of Fel
Red Woods
Burning Forest
Midstream
Ballern
Crystal Sea
Gray Woods
Bollwerk
D E A D L A N D S
Bay of Sorrow
Belldorn
Skeleton
Deadlands Spires
Sea of Salt
Shadowed Woods
Dragonwing Mountains
Pirate's Cove
Southern Sea
Map by Misty Beee – 2013

CHAPTER ONE

JACOB RAN. HE HEARD THE shouts of the market guards as they chased him through the muddy cobblestone streets of Ancora. Their armor gave away their position as the metal plates clanged together and their boots fell heavy on the stones.

"There!" a guard said.

Jacob dove under a peddler's table, scattering rugs and crates as the woman hissed at him to run faster. Jacob grinned when he realized the peddler was rooting for *him* and not the guards. The armored guards would never be able to dip under the thick stone tables that rested across the ancient troughs. They'd have to go around, or over, and Jacob knew their armor was too heavy for that.

"Get back here, you Lowland maggot!"

Jacob glanced back. The enraged armored forms were momentarily frozen in front of the brightly colored tents and tables before Jacob vanished down an alley. They could still catch him on the next street if he wasn't careful, or if he wasn't fast enough.

Something sizzled in a large metal pot near the last stall he sprinted past, and for a moment, Jacob wished it were food in his pocket instead of the loot he'd been lucky to take. He slid around the corner of an old brick house with a tiled roof and slipped into a narrow alley most people never would have noticed. The Highborn guards, used to the wide streets behind the city wall, didn't have a chance of tracking Jacob through the maze of dim back alleys.

He eased farther into the shadowed space as the shouts and curses of the guards grew louder and then faded as they passed him by. He caught a glimpse of polished silver armor as two of the men rushed onward. None of them glanced at the small alley. Jacob smiled and felt his pockets. Still there, his fingers met the reassuring bumps of his prize. He forgot the smell of food as he imagined finishing the pistons he'd built with Charles for the new boiler. With a good cushion, they could run for hours, or more. They'd just have to—

"Jacob Arthur Anders," a voice said from behind him, deeper in the alley.

Jacob spun, knocking his elbow on an uneven brick in the wall and cursing as he stumbled back a step. "Alice! What are you doing here?"

Alice leaned forward, her gray wool dress barely clearing the wet ground. Her red hair hung in curls, brushing her shoulder as she looked down at Jacob's hand and frowned. She raised her eyes to meet his, and he could still tell they were blue, even in the dim light of the alley. "What did you steal now?"

"What are you talking about?"

"You have your hand over your pocket." The amount of accusation in her voice startled him. Alice pointed at his hand. "You only do that when you're hiding something."

"None of your business," he said, squaring his shoulders and standing up as straight as he could. It left him a fraction of an inch taller than Alice.

"Oh, I think it *is* my business," she said. "Festival is coming up, and we're supposed to dance. You're my partner."

Jacob rolled his eyes.

"Stop that. You're my partner, and if you get caught, they won't let you dance, and I'll be stuck alone."

"It's just a stupid dance."

Alice snapped. "*Just* a *stupid* dance?" She glared at Jacob. "Once per year we have Festival to celebrate the end of the Deadlands War, that's it.

Festival is the biggest fair of the year, and *this* is the only year we get to dance, Jacob, the year we turn sixteen. I'm not missing this because you can't keep your priorities straight." Alice wrinkled her nose—Jacob thought she was rather cute when her nostrils flared—before she turned around and stomped off. At the alley's end, her foot came down in a mud puddle, sending a small arc of filth up onto her gray dress. She paused and stared at her mud-caked boots, shot a look at Jacob that he thought might literally cut him, and then disappeared around the corner.

Jacob followed Alice to the end of the alley. She continued on, vanishing down another narrow street before he carefully studied the sparse crowd, making sure none of the guards were around. The afternoon sun cut a clear path past the few clouds in the western sky, a fact he hadn't much noticed while he'd had his mind on his thievery. The Highlands stood to the north. A fine layer of clouds obscured the highest towers, but he could still make out the city walls.

He hadn't been to the city since he was a young child, and in his own eyes, that was many years past. Some part of him wanted to see the Highborn men and women, to see how other children lived when they didn't have to fear what might come over the walls.

Jacob casually stepped out of the alley and merged into a slow-moving group of townspeople as they continued downhill. They were all dressed in muted grays and browns, with an occasional burst of color from something purchased at the market.

He followed the crowd as they moved to the south. A few carried fresh, steaming bits of chicken and some dried beef from the Highlands. Jacob hadn't tasted beef since the last Festival, and he eyed another boy's snack with jealousy.

A shout from across the street startled Jacob. His eyes landed on one of the guards, and he was relieved to find the man occupied with a fight between two older teenagers. Jacob drifted over to the other side of the group, just to be safe. He slipped down an old winding street as soon as they were clear of the guards.

It was quiet there. Most of the retired folk lived in the higher parts of the Lowlands. A few people waved and smiled at Jacob as he walked by. Most of them knew he was a pickpocket, but they didn't mind so long as it wasn't their own pocket being picked.

The street came to an abrupt end at the edge of a cliffside. Jacob leaned on the fence and looked down. The lift was all the way at the bottom. He frowned and studied the cable. Even with the gears that Charles, the old tinker, had installed, it would take forever to get it back to the top.

Jacob unlatched the gate, even though he knew he wasn't supposed to do that unless the lift was topside. He pulled a pair of gloves from his back pocket and slipped them on. After making sure his loot was secured, he reached out for the nearest pole supporting the lift.

"Jacob! Don't you dare!"

He turned his gaze over his shoulder and saw his schoolteacher, Miss Penny, scowling at him from her parents' yard.

"Bye, Miss Penny!"

"Jacob, you get back here right—"

He didn't hear anything else she said. The wind screamed past his ears and pulled on his jacket as he wrapped himself around the pole and dropped. The cliffside was a blur beside him, but the sweeping mountain range across the canyon was clearly in focus. Jacob grinned as he tightened his legs and hands on the pole to begin slowing himself down.

He could see details in the lift now. The huge flywheel on top of it sat idle beside the grate on the lift's roof. Once he was slow enough and close enough, Jacob let go. His boots slammed into the top of the lift, causing the grate to clatter in its frame. No one waited at the bottom when he jumped to the ground, so he didn't have to worry about explaining himself. That made him quite happy as he hurried down the hill and into the deepest parts of the Lowlands.

The homes weren't as nice here, not even as nice as the north side of the Lowlands, but it would always be home to Jacob. The roofs didn't match, showing an array of tile and slate where they'd been repaired. A few homes couldn't afford even that, and instead they layered thatch for insulation and to stop leaks.

Jacob slowed as he started up out of the poorest part of town. The outer wall was partially collapsed here, and Parliament's men were still cleaning up the last of the invaders from the latest breach. They'd have a temporary wall built by the end of the night, but it could be a while before the brickwork was restored. The sky had darkened since Jacob started his trek, and a few sparse raindrops littered the street around him. He watched a group of men in dark blue uniforms push the great mottled brown carcass of a Walker—it was up to Jacob's waist when he stood beside it—back through the hole in the wall.

The monster had large jaws and what seemed to Jacob to be a hundred orange legs. A portion of the thing slid down the mountainside before the men moved on to the next segment, sawing through it and pushing it outside the wall in turn. It had only been a day, but most of the invaders had already been harvested or at least pushed back outside.

The thin bricks and wood of the wall here was nothing like the mighty stone fortress around the Highlands. The invaders grew bolder every year, reaching higher and breaching the Lowlands as often as they could.

Something had burrowed through the wall here, exposing the people to this Walker and two other invaders. They'd been fortunate to have a Spider Knight on patrol when it happened. No one had been hurt this time, but they weren't always so lucky. A giant beetle had managed to smash through the home nearest the wall, but the family had been at a neighbor's house.

Miss Penny used to tell stories about a time when the invaders almost never came through the walls looking for food. The mountains kept the

Lowlands safe, the elevation too great for the creatures to thrive in the thin air. When the invaders grew larger and climbed higher, Parliament raised the walls around the Lowlands. The thick stone walls rose up around the Highlands soon after, leaving the Lowlands wall to slowly decay into disrepair.

Jacob turned back to the road and shivered. He didn't want to look at the monsters outside the wall. He daydreamed about leaving and fighting off the invaders, keeping his people safe. Alice had the smarter idea, he knew. She planned to use her studies to get a job in the Highlands behind the city wall, where she'd be safe from the constant threats of the Lowlands. When Jacob saw the havoc the creatures could wreak, sometimes he'd rather pretend they weren't there. Jacob ground his teeth and increased his pace, happy to get away from the carnage. The excitement to show Charles what he'd stolen returned as he put more distance between himself and the breach.

CHAPTER TWO

THE OLD OBSERVATORY SAT ON the largest hill in the Lowlands. It stretched high into the air, a huge cone that came to a fine point. Jacob smiled as the wind picked up and sent the long grass around the observatory swaying. The door was closed, but he could see the yellow glow of the old man's lanterns through the small windows.

Jacob reached out for the etched steel handle on the old wooden door. It didn't so much as rattle in its frame. Charles had it locked, which probably meant the tinker was doing something interesting.

Jacob turned to the left and walked away from the door. The first sounds of the spring crickets could be heard. They were quiet small creatures that time of year, but soon they'd be a nuisance, wailing louder than the neighborhood cats.

He followed the curve of the giant metal plates at the base of the observatory until he found what he was looking for. A gap he'd covered with a small wedge of wood waited, just wide enough for him to slip through undetected. The metal pulled at his jacket as he wiggled past. The small crawlspace led him to the back of one of the many shelves the old man had filled with treasures and parts and junk. Complex knots of rope supported the scaffolding above him.

A small Jumper stared at him for a moment and then scampered up the wood to a higher part of the tower. A low whine replaced the chirp of the crickets. Jacob shifted a box of metal fasteners, as quietly as possible, so he could see the old man's workbench.

Charles looked up, lifting his spectacles and resting them on his graying head. Rhythmic puffs of steam from a small, dirty engine joined the low whine. The candles cast a flickering orange glow around the room, and it was only then that Jacob realized Charles had extinguished the lanterns.

Jacob's eyes followed Charles's gaze and he almost shouted. Jacob noticed the dancing reflections on the glass globe only in passing. It was the rising glow within the glass that kept him riveted. The timbre of the whine grew higher. Charles adjusted the knob on a small valve, and the tiny black ball beside the globe spun faster and faster, the glow growing brighter and brighter until the candles seemed dim.

Charles laughed and clapped his hands together. Even when the spinning mechanism seized and cracked and the glow died, the old man didn't stop smiling. He released the valve with a gloved hand, and the steam engine slowed immediately.

Jacob gasped as the candles once more became the only light source in the room.

"I know you're there, son," Charles said. "Come on out."

Jacob sighed. He knew better than to make noise. That was almost always how Charles caught him poking around. Jacob set his back against one of the scaffolding supports and pushed a wooden crate full of piping forward about six inches. The grating, squealing crate left just enough room for him to squeeze through. He crawled out from beneath the chaos and ran a hand through his dingy light brown hair.

"You have a Jumper on your shoulder."

Jacob frowned and glanced at his shoulder. He couldn't be sure it was the same spider—there were a lot of three-inch Jumpers in the old observatory—but he liked to think it was. It rotated its furry body back and forth, looking at the young man with all eight of its eyes. He held out his hand and the Jumper skittered onto his palm. He studied it for a moment longer before raising his arm and letting the spider hurl itself up into the scaffolding.

"Jumpers aren't pets."

"They're not poisonous," Jacob said, unable to keep the exasperation from his voice. If he was smart enough to know they weren't poisonous, the old man certainly was too.

"A knife isn't poisonous either, but it will cut you just the same. I don't want to explain it to your mother."

"Uh huh," Jacob said, only half listening at that point. His eyes were all for the cracked glass globe, which had lit the room like a small sun before it had broken. Well, maybe not quite as bright as a sun, but it *had* been bright. "What was that?"

Charles bent his head down to look at Jacob over the rim of his glasses. He pushed the glasses farther up his nose and said, "It was called a lightbulb a long time ago. Before the war."

"Which war?" Jacob asked, half curious and half wanting to annoy Charles because the old man only ever talked about one war.

Charles sighed and turned his attention back to a binder full of yellowed papers. "It's the same principle as the lights in City Square, but on a much smaller scale. They used to be in every home, Jacob. Can you imagine that? No lanterns, no candles, just light whenever you needed it." Charles lifted the glasses from his nose. They weren't really glasses, but even after three years of apprenticeship, Jacob couldn't remember the name for them. There were extra lenses attached to a brass frame. The old man used them to look at little things.

Jacob smiled and fished around in his pocket, eventually pulling out three small black orbs. He set them in a green bowl on the workbench. "I got these at Festival. Will they work for the new pistons?"

Charles picked up one of the balls and looked at Jacob over the rim of his glasses. Charles sighed and ran his hand over his wide white beard. "Yes, but how did you get these? This looks like the work of the city smith, and if I can't afford his goods, I'm quite sure you can't either."

"I found them."

The old man's lips tightened, and he frowned. "You're going to have to return them, Jacob."

Jacob's jaw opened slightly as he scrambled to think of a better alternative. "I can't."

"And why is that?"

"Alice would … Alice would never let me forget," Jacob said in a very small voice.

Charles laughed and flipped the ball up into the air. It thumped against the workbench and bounced nearly as high as where it had started. Charles caught it and eyed the dark piece of rubber. "I wouldn't want to miss seeing you at the dance with Alice either."

Jacob blew out a breath and glared at Charles.

"I'll pay the city smith for these," he said. "You just worry about getting those steps down."

"I hate dancing," Jacob grumbled.

"I appreciate the thought, Jacob," Charles said as he gestured at the rubber orbs. "I believe you have Cotillion tonight, yes? You better run along. Miss Penny won't be happy if you miss another rehearsal."

Jacob groaned. "I forgot about Cotillion. What am I possibly going to do there that's better than getting the new boiler up and running?"

"You'll be out and living," Charles said. "You need to do that while you're young if you want to be a proper hermit when you get to be an old man. Be sure to tell Miss Penny hello for me."

Jacob turned away from Charles and grumbled.

Charles smiled and pointed to the door. "I do enjoy your company, but I don't enjoy Miss Penny's stern talking-tos. Now get yourself down to the Hall."

Jacob looked at the windows. It was getting dark. It was time for Cotillion, and Miss Penny was going to tear him up one side and down the other.

Charles laughed and quickly shooed Jacob with his hand. "Run along.

You won't be much of an assistant if Miss Penny throws you off a cliff."

Jacob hesitated and thought about arguing, but when the logical side of his brain decided the old tinker was probably right, he nodded repeatedly and ran through the door.

CHAPTER THREE

J ACOB PASSED THE LANTERN MEN as he ran back through the Lowlands. They'd already lit most of the street between the observatory and the Hall. Yellowish-orange light revealed the worst of the holes in the sidewalk, and he only stumbled twice in the darker parts of town.

The Hall was in the middle of the Lowlands, as any proper Hall should be. Jacob glanced up at the enormous cut stones that piled one atop the other until they met in a sharp peak to form the roof. The Hall was the nicest stone building in the Lowlands, filled with stained-glass windows and ornate carvings. It was once the center of the entire city.

The old man had said that had been almost a century ago, before the invaders came through the walls. Then, the Highborns wanted to build higher, too high for the bugs to climb. Jacob didn't think any place was too high for the bugs to climb, but the wall around the Highlands could keep out just about anything.

Jacob leaned back to pull open the old oak door and made his way into the Hall.

He looked up at the ceiling, as he always did. How could anyone not marvel at that height? A cough brought his attention back to the crowd of people in the center of the Hall. There were a few bored-looking parents on carved wooden chairs on either side of the room. The other kids were lined up on the sides of the floor, boys on the left, girls on the right.

Alice glared at him.

Miss Penny cleared her throat, and Jacob smiled sheepishly as he made his way over to the boys' side.

"Now," Miss Penny said, "if there won't be any more interruptions?"

Some of the girls laughed and pointed at Jacob. The boys looked jealous of his late arrival. There were only one or two boys in the entire village that enjoyed Cotillion. Frankly, Jacob thought they were crazy.

"Good," Miss Penny said, lifting the hem of her skirt slightly and moving her feet in a three-count rhythm.

It could only mean the waltz. Jacob wasn't too fond of the dance, as he always felt bad for stepping on Alice's toes.

"Girls, request a dance of your partner. Use proper language." Miss Penny turned away and started talking to two seated women.

"I'm ready for the toe crusher," Alice said.

Jacob turned to her and narrowed his eyes. "That's not funny. I can sit this one out if you'd prefer."

"Hey, they're not your toes," she said, completely disregarding his second comment. "I can make jokes about my crushed toes if I want to." She had a point, but he'd never tell her that.

Jacob glanced back at the seated women, and his dread of dancing died off. Miss Penny had brought in two actual musicians for rehearsal. It made all the toe crushing jokes worth it, just to hear them play.

One of them held a guitar, and the other had an instrument Jacob had never seen before.

"What is that?" he asked as Alice took his hand.

She put her arms out and began to flow toward the musicians. "It's a cello," Alice said. He'd heard of them, but he couldn't recall ever seeing one played. The strings came to life in the woman's hands. A bow made of hair moved gracefully across the instrument, filling the Hall with a layered sound that brought everything else to silence.

Alice spun on the third beat, and Jacob moved his hand to the small of her back. Miss Penny had drilled the waltz pattern into their heads for almost two months now. Not surprising, since their big performance at

Festival was coming up soon, after all.

Jacob took two small steps and swooped forward with Alice for a big step as they slowly turned with the rest of the dance floor. He kept his eyes on the musicians when he could—that is, when Alice's hair didn't get in the way. The guitar was subtle, letting the cello breathe without struggling.

Alice giggled as Jacob spun her around again. He even found himself smiling at Alice while her skirt twirled and the music slowly died away. All the kids applauded. It wasn't often they received a treat like live music. It was usually the old hand-cranked music box with the big discs that weighed as much as he did.

"Didn't step on my toes once," Alice said.

Jacob looked down at her feet, and then met her bright green eyes. "Not once?"

"Nope. Apparently we just need music for you not to be a complete klutz."

The musicians bowed and began packing away their instruments.

Miss Penny clapped her hands together and beamed at the room. "Not perfect. A little sloppy in the form, yes, but good job, all of you. Now, if you can do that at Festival tomorrow, I won't need to throw any of you off the cliff."

Jacob blinked and stared at Miss Penny. Sometimes she could be a little crazy. Miss Penny crooked her finger at him and he walked toward her, shoulders slumped. He wasn't sure why Alice followed him over.

"Are you hurt?" Miss Penny asked.

Jacob furrowed his brow and looked up at her.

"From earlier? You scared me when you slid down that pole."

"I … I thought you were mad."

Miss Penny shook her head. "No, I don't want you to get hurt."

"Yeah," Alice said, "then I wouldn't have anyone to dance with."

Miss Penny laughed and nodded at Alice. "Are your hands okay? It's a long way down those poles."

Jacob fished around in his larger pockets, which ran from his thigh to his knee. He pulled out the gloves Charles had given him. The little metal scales woven into the palms and fingers clinked as he turned them over to show Miss Penny.

"Oh my," she said. "I see." She brushed one of the coppery scales with her fingers.

Jacob placed his gloves in his pockets once more when it became obvious Miss Penny wasn't going to do anything else with them.

"Be careful, Jacob. I don't want to have to tell your mother something terrible has happened to you."

"I'll have my white shoes on tomorrow," Alice said, "so try not to step on them. Or something terrible *will* happen to you."

Miss Penny smiled at Alice.

"Well," Jacob said, "we'll have real musicians there too, so maybe I won't."

Alice pushed his shoulder and he swayed backward. She smiled as she picked up a small wool satchel and left the Hall.

"Bye, Miss Penny," Jacob said as he ran after Alice.

CHAPTER FOUR

"DID YOU SEE THE BUGS that broke through the wall?" Jacob asked.

"Yes," Alice said, her voice trailing off. "One of them was a Walker, but they said it tried to attack everything it got close to. Walkers don't do that. They're not hostile."

"Watch out," Jacob said. He pointed to a hole in the sidewalk. One of the cobblestones had gone missing.

Alice stepped around it, and they continued through the yellow warmth of the streetlights. Jacob always walked Alice home from Cotillion. She didn't like to be alone on the streets at night. It's not that they weren't safe, but sometimes things did come over the walls.

"Not all Walkers are friendly," Jacob said, remembering a driver who got a nasty bite from the two-foot scythe-like mandibles of a Walker. He looked up at the broken-down wall as they neared it.

"It's gone," Alice said. "I guess they finished cleaning it up."

"Jacob, Alice." Jacob jumped in surprise and Alice gasped when a slightly deep voice called their names from above.

A Spider Knight was perched on one of the stone roofs. The streetlights glinted on the obsidian-black eyes of the spider and the gleaming, coppery armor of the man riding it.

"Samuel?" Jacob asked.

The knight nodded, his armor squeaking briefly with the movement. The knights who patrolled the city wore flawless golden armor that never made a sound, nothing like Samuel's. Samuel told Jacob the golden armor wouldn't stop a sword, or even most bugs, so he didn't have a use for it. His mount was a rare giant Jumper. Most Spider Knights rode on beasts that preferred to stay on the ground. Jumpers were fast, but incredibly dangerous to ride.

"What are you two doing here?" Samuel asked. He tapped his foot near one of the spider's legs, and the beast hopped down from the roof, barely making a sound when it landed in front of Alice.

"He's walking me home," Alice said as she reached out and touched the furry bristles of the spider.

"Careful now," Samuel said. "Old Bessie's been a bit grumpy."

Alice smiled and fumbled her satchel open. She pulled out a fairly large, and very dead, fly. The spider began to pump its legs up and down as it stared at the treat.

"Alice," Samuel said, putting a bit more strength behind his words. "I wouldn't—"

The spider lunged forward and snapped the fly out of Alice's outstretched hands. Jacob frowned and scrunched his face up as the spider's jaws began moving side to side, grinding up its unexpected treat, while its smaller limbs—what did the old man call them, pedipalps?—kept the fly in chewing distance.

"That could have been your hand," Samuel said.

Alice laughed and patted the beast between its two largest eyes. "No way, Bessie knows who gets her the best Sweet-Flies."

Samuel looked as though he was about to offer an argument and then thought better of it. "Okay, get moving you two. There are more of us watching the wall tonight than usual, but those boards won't be able to keep anything large out." He gestured at the makeshift structure blocking the hole. The rest of the wall had long, narrow-angled spikes that most invaders couldn't grasp. Sometimes the bugs would get smart, though, or lucky, and that's when people got hurt.

Jacob nodded as his gaze moved back to Samuel.

Samuel unlatched a leather pocket on the front edge of Bessie's saddle. He pulled something out that glistened in the dim light and tossed it to Jacob. "There's a lot of activity on the mountainside. You two hear anything inside the wall, blow on that."

Jacob looked down at the shining silver whistle and could barely contain his excitement. It was a wall whistle—one of the Spider Knights' whistles! It was big, a bit oval-like, with twelve holes and covered in rich etchings, a Widow Maker carved into the center. They were terrifying creatures, Jacob knew, but they were also the emblem of the Spider Knights.

"You know the song already, yes?" Samuel asked.

Jacob inclined his head.

"And if he forgets," Alice said, "I know it too."

Samuel nodded at Alice. "Keep him out of trouble, will you?" He tapped one of the spider's rear legs, and Bessie spun around before leaping back to the rooftops.

"Let's get home," Alice said.

Jacob looked up from the whistle and grinned.

"Yes," Alice said. "It's cool. Now let's go home."

Jacob undid the buckle on the leather pouch at his side and carefully slid the metal whistle in. He had a couple of Charles's Bangers left over from the last time the old man had let him have some fun, and he didn't want to set them off accidentally. They were small, but Jacob did *not* want a Banger blowing a hole in his clothes. He shuddered at the thought of his mom's face the last time that had happened.

"Okay," Jacob said, "let's go."

They'd barely walked past Piers Place, one of the nicer streets in the Lowlands, when Alice reached out and put her hand on Jacob's arm.

"Did you hear that?"

"Hear what?" Jacob asked, but then he heard it for himself. He moved his head to pinpoint the faint sound of someone crying and the vicious laughter of another.

Alice took off at a run, and Jacob struggled to keep up. She'd always been fast, but lately she seemed even more so. She pulled up short in an alley. Jacob walked up behind her and anger stirred inside him.

"It's mine now," a skinny black-haired boy said as he held up a small stuffed Pill-Bug.

The boy on the ground wiped his eyes and stared up at his attacker. "It's my sister's. Please, she's sick."

The taller boy gave him a swift kick in the ribs and started laughing again. Alice ran at the black-haired boy.

"You leave them alone!" In one quick motion, she placed her foot behind the taller boy's ankle and shoved with all her weight.

He looked surprised as he started falling, and the crack of his shoulder on the cobblestones was nothing less than he deserved. Jacob ran up beside Alice and snatched up the stuffed toy.

"Bradley," Jacob said with disgust. "Always picking on people." Jacob pulled his arm back, intent on punching Bradley as hard as he could, before Alice grabbed his arm.

"No, you don't want his family coming after yours. They'll use their influence to make things even worse for your dad."

Jacob glanced at her. Alice's lips were pulled into a tight frown. She didn't approve of Bradley or his family, and on some level, he knew she was right for stopping him. He jerked his arm away from her and turned his attention to the other boy on the ground.

"You leave now, Bradley Piers," Alice said. "I don't care if this street *is* named after your family, Miss Penny will still give you a lashing for it."

Jacob heard Bradley grumble a curse before the boy stood up and ran. Jacob watched him go before holding his hand out to the fallen boy and helping pull him to his feet.

"Thank you," the boy said, but something didn't sound right in his voice.

Jacob jerked in surprise as the realization hit him. "You're a girl!"

"Of course she is," Alice said as she leaned closer to the girl. "You'll have to forgive him, Betty. He can be kind of dense."

Jacob didn't feel like he was being dense; he felt like someone had lit a fire in his chest. That kid deserved to have his face cracked against the cobblestones. Jacob wanted to hurt Bradley Piers, and he wanted to hurt him badly.

✧ ✧ ✧

THEY ARRIVED AT ALICE'S HOUSE first, and Jacob undid the latch on the little fence. A small cluster of miniature Pill-Bugs were milling around the yard. They'd become popular pets over the last two years in the city. Whenever they grew too big, they were usually sent off to live in the Lowlands or down the mountain to live on the plains of the Deadlands, especially when the food stores were abundant. Jacob figured the plains were a death sentence anyway. He reached over the fence and let one of the more curious bugs check him with its antennae. It rolled up into a ball a moment later.

Alice laughed and rolled the bug out of the way. In a ball, it was up to her knee. The front door of the two-story home cracked open. A plump woman was only a silhouette in the evening light, the lanterns behind her leaving the rest of her body in shadow.

"Hi, Mom," Alice said.

"Come in, Alice," her mom said. "I was getting worried."

"Sorry, ma'am," Jacob said. "We had a little trouble and had to take Betty home first."

"Was it that Bradley boy again?" Alice's mom asked.

"Yes," Alice said as she rolled another Pill-Bug away from the stairs.

"Someone needs to teach that boy a lesson."

Jacob planned to do just that the next time he saw Bradley.

"Get yourself home safely, Jacob."

"Goodnight," Alice said.

"Night," Jacob said. He waved goodbye.

His own home wasn't far from Alice's at all. He cut through an alley and made his way down the cobblestones to Dragon's Ridge. He was quite sure his street had the best name in the Lowlands.

The homes here were all two stories, built from old gray mason stones. Most of the bricks were leftovers from the construction of the massive city wall. Jacob's grandfather had always told him it was the most generous gift he'd ever seen from the government. That was well before Jacob had been born. Jacob was pretty sure it was even before his dad had been born.

He watched a large owl perched on top of his neighbor's green tile roof. Most of Dragon's Ridge had the same tile, and Jacob's home was no different. He liked to see the owls around. They tended to eat some of the more irritating bugs. The tiles beneath the owl's claws were roughly shaped like scales, and Jacob figured that's how the street had gotten its name in the first place.

Orange light and shadows flickered in the front windows. Smoke rose from the old stone chimney, and Jacob took both as a sign his parents had guests. He reached the edge of the walkway that led to the front door, and stopped.

Jacob could hear the coughing from the street. His heart sank a little as he made his way up the short, winding stone path to the porch. Another series of tight, coarse coughs echoed from behind the door. He took a deep breath and walked into his home.

"Hi, Dad!" he said. He always tried to stay upbeat around his father.

"Jacob." A smile raised his dad's pale lips. He started to struggle up off his rocking chair, but Jacob held out his hand to stop him.

"You don't have to get up. I'm just going to bed anyway."

"How was Cotillion?" his dad asked as he adjusted the brightly colored afghan around his shoulders. "Miss Penny give you much trouble about Festival?"

Jacob shook his head. "No, not at all. She thinks we're ready, Alice and me. Oh, and you know what else? She had actual musicians at the Hall tonight. Have you ever heard a cello played? I love how it sounds."

Jacob's dad sank back into the rocking chair and smiled. Jacob didn't know why his dad was always so interested in everything he did, but he had fun telling him about his day almost every evening.

His dad silenced another coughing fit before taking a drink out of an amber bottle of medicine on the little end table. There was a small black bag beside the hearth.

"Is the doctor here?" Jacob asked.

His dad nodded. "He's in with your mother, in the kitchen."

Jacob started to go, and then hesitated.

"Go on, go on."

Jacob took a couple steps and gave his dad a hug. He cringed as the mass of whiskers scratched at his face before he started to disentangle himself. His dad's beard was the same salt-and-pepper color as his hair. Jacob almost ran into the kitchen.

"—so you see, it's not nearly as bad as we feared." The man speaking was short and looked through half-moon spectacles as he adjusted his shirt.

"Jacob," his mom said, gesturing for him to come closer. She wrapped her arm around his shoulders, and he had to fight off the mass of curly hair that caught him in the face. He'd never admit it, but it was always nice to come home to his mother. "Dr. Edwards has good news."

The doctor nodded. "It *is* pneumonia, son, but so long as he keeps up his medicine, I think he'll pull through."

Jacob felt his mom tense up at the mention of medicine. He knew why. They weren't as poor as some of the other Lowland families, really, but medicine was terribly expensive.

"That bottle should last a week or more," the doctor said. "I'll have the apothecary bring more by afterward."

"Thank you, Doctor," Jacob's mom said.

The doctor shook both their hands before taking his leave. Jacob heard him say something to his father before the front door closed and the house was left in silence once more.

"It's not the black lung." Jacob's mom teared up as she hugged him closer. She released him and ushered him away. "Get some rest. Your big show is tomorrow. We want you to be ready for it."

Jacob knew she was getting him out of the room to talk to his dad about money. His mom thought Jacob's thievery got worse the more he knew about the struggle to pay for his dad's medicine. She was right. He wanted to help. Jacob blew the candle out when he got to his room before sliding a blanket up against the bottom of the door. Jacob didn't want to waste the candles or the lanterns—not when he had perfectly good glowworms.

He slid a jar out from under his bed. A dim greenish-yellow glow rose up from the two fat white worms inside. They still had plenty of leaves to eat, so Jacob just gave the jar a little shake. The dim glow turned into a bright light to rival the lanterns.

The new book from Charles was small. Jacob liked reading small books. He could get through them fairly quickly, and that felt like he'd accomplished something. He knew adults who didn't even read a book in a month. Jacob tried to read one every week.

This one was about the war. *The* war, Jacob thought as he picked up where he'd left off. There were amazing stories there, about giant mechanical suits that fought in the Deadlands, to a time when people didn't have to live in the mountains.

Eventually his mind drifted back to his parents as the glowworms dimmed in their jar.

Jacob's parents may not have approved of his pickpocketing, but there were three things he knew for fact: His dad needed medicine. Medicine cost money. He knew how to get money.

CHAPTER FIVE

T HE NEXT MORNING SAW JACOB off with a stomach full of flatcakes, and he cherished every bite. Jacob kept an eye on his dad throughout breakfast. He didn't seem to be getting any worse, but he didn't seem much better, either.

After breakfast, Jacob left, heading toward the observatory. He wanted to see Charles before Festival started, and he figured he had plenty of time to do just that. It was a beautiful day for Festival. The mountain winds were mild, helping to keep the Lowlands at a wonderful, cool temperature. Jacob enjoyed the breeze as he walked up the street, smiling as it tousled his hair. In the distance he could hear the winds howling through the mountain passes, but here the wind didn't have the strength to make him stumble.

Jacob turned the handle on the observatory door, expecting it to swing inward, but instead he smacked his face on the window and cursed. He hunched his shoulders and looked around. Thankfully no one had heard him, because his mother would *not* have been happy.

He heard a slide and a click. Jacob tried the door again. This time it opened as expected. Charles settled himself back at his bench. "Sorry about that. I've been working on the new boiler and a new hammer, of sorts."

Charles leaned in and peered at something on his workbench. He raised his arm, leaned back a bit, and punched it. When his fist connected, it made a terrible sound, like a small boiler failing and metal rending. Jacob ran over to Charles and then he saw the gauntlet.

"What *is* that?" Jacob asked as he stared at the brass contraption lining Charles's hand. A webbed glove fit over his fingers and a wide metal box sat across his knuckles.

"It's a nail punch," Charles said, as if that were the most obvious thing in the world. "Not sure I like the name yet, but it fits."

"Is it steam powered?" Jacob asked. "I don't see a boiler."

Charles shook his head. "It's all springs and levers. I'm working on a bigger one—one you can use on metal sheets—that will be steam powered. Well, I thought it would be, but it may not need it."

Jacob was silent for a moment.

"I hear you had a little run-in last night."

"What?"

"I heard you helped get someone's bug back," Charles said as he tightened the screws on the edge of the nail punch and flexed his hand.

"Right, her," Jacob said. "It was Alice, really."

"Not just Alice," Charles said. "Rumor is you frightened that Piers boy something fierce."

"I wish I could beat him up. I should have beaten him up."

"Bah," Charles said. "You did what needed to be done, as did Alice. There's no need to be cruel."

"Cruel?" Jacob asked. "What he did was wrong."

"I'm not arguing that, Jacob, but you don't fix what's wrong by doing something wrong." Charles closed a jar full of screws and set it on the workbench. "Cruelty is an earmark of murderers and politicians. I have no use for cruelty. Now, hand me that wrench."

Bradley was the cruel one, pushing kids around and stealing from them and threatening families with his own family's influence. Jacob stole too, but he'd never steal from other kids, so it was different. He'd never steal from a family he knew to be poorer than his own, so it was better, wasn't it? The front door to the observatory opened, distracting Jacob from the old man's request.

"Charles!" said a short man with sparse black hair. He had a deep tan, and Jacob figured it was from working outside. "Is it done?"

"Just wrapped it up, Ambrose," Charles said with a smile. "Should feed the belts through without an issue now."

"Best thing you ever invented, tinker. If you ask me, at least."

Charles smiled and eyed the man over the golden rim of his glasses.

"What's the fee? I know you said it could be more if you had to replace parts."

Charles shook his head. "Have your wife bake me one of those amazing cobblers. We'll call it even."

Ambrose smiled. "You let us know if you ever get the punch made for metal plating. The city will buy fifty of them, and I'm not exaggerating."

Charles shook the man's hand. Jacob and the old man were alone again after that.

"Charles, I want to see the city."

"You've been there before," the old man said as he spun the tool in his hand around in circles. Every quarter turn, it clicked.

"That's what Mom said, but I don't remember." He watched Charles some more until he could figure out what the tool was. "Is that a small ratchet?"

"It is indeed, a gift from one of the wall repairmen." Charles glanced up at Jacob over his half-moon spectacles. "At least, that's what he tells everyone." Charles grinned. "He lost it in a bad game of poker. So tell me, why do you want to see the city?"

"They have puffing demons!" Jacob said, and he couldn't contain his excitement. "Can you believe it?"

The old man laughed without humor as he inspected the bolts he'd been working on. He nodded and began wiping the grease off his hands. "I designed the engines, boy. Of course I believe it."

"You did?" Jacob asked. He couldn't keep the small edge of skepticism out of his voice. Sometimes the old man liked to tell stories.

"They work on the same principles as the steambike, just on a larger scale." Charles gestured to the tarp covering the bike in the corner.

"Okay, but that doesn't work."

Charles smiled at Jacob. "It will. Just wait."

"You've been working on it forever."

"I've been working on it a couple months," Charles said as he picked up his other glasses. He leaned in close to the small disc he was working on and flipped a couple different lenses down in front of his right eye.

"Like I said, forever."

Charles smiled and swapped his glasses out again. He started bolting the disc onto some sort of metal construction.

"What is *that?*" Jacob asked. He stepped up closer to Charles before leaning down to look at the long metal brace. A brass gauntlet adorned the end, connecting three curved bars of metal. A series of interlocking gears joined the first set of bars to a second set of bars, and as Jacob picked up the contraption, he realized it was all connected to a backpack. "Is this a suit? Like they wear in the Deadlands?"

Charles wiped his hands off on an oily rag before he took the gauntlet, and everything attached to it, out of Jacob's hands. He set it gently back on the far corner of the workbench and patted the disc he'd attached over the gears.

"You mean Biomechs?" Charles asked as he frowned slightly and shook his head. "This is ideal. It's not an implant. It's a lightweight exoskeleton."

"Like a bug?" Jacob asked, moving the fingers of the gauntlet.

"Somewhat, yes. This is mainly to help men lift things. The mines are dangerous work, and this will at least help them keep up their stamina."

Jacob stared at the piston-like gears and shifted the arm back and forth. "You could put an engine on this."

"Jacob …" Charles said. When Jacob looked up, Charles was wearing a small, patient frown.

"It's the perfect size," Jacob said. "You already have the piston built in, right here." He pointed to the bars joining the two halves of the arm. One bar on each arm was a piston, and Jacob already knew why Charles had added it. It would help absorb the impact.

Jacob's eyes lit up. "You could put the balls from the city smith in here!"

Charles paused and stared at Jacob for a moment. "That's … that's not a bad idea, my boy. If we added a small engine here …" He pointed toward the end of the piston, near the gearbox. "We could mount it at the elbow. It would be too hot to have a boiler, but we may be able to use a Burner, for short bursts of extra power. Why, they would be able to move boulders if it worked."

"Let me try," Jacob said.

Charles glanced at the ancient clock above his workbench. "It's almost time for Festival. You'll need to get down to the Square."

"I have a couple hours still."

Charles gestured to the pile of metal and leather. "Have at it, then. Have at it."

The old man trimmed off a small piece of the city smith's rubber pellets while Jacob took the screws out of the shiny brass piston. "Careful, that one has liquid in it." He kept an eye on Jacob while the boy worked. Jacob's tongue was half out of his mouth, clenched between his teeth. It was a sure sign of concentration.

"Got it."

Charles leaned over and slid the slivers of rubber into the base of the piston. The boy was right, he knew. The strange rubber from the smith was the greatest shock absorber he'd ever seen, heat resistant and incredibly durable.

Jacob reassembled the housing and clamped a bracket onto one of the larger exposed gears in the elbow. Charles was impressed. The boy knew enough to keep it away from the hard stops—the thick metal squares that protected the operator from overextending their joints—and leave enough room for air when the Burner ignited.

Jacob threaded a trigger into the gauntlet. The user would be able to fire the mechanism with one hand. Charles nodded in approval. Jacob grunted and tried to push the other end of Charles's actuator into the clamp. Charles leaned over to help, dragging the mechanical arm a bit closer before pushing on the actuator until it clicked home.

"There you go," Charles said.

"Does it look right?" Jacob asked.

Charles nodded. Jacob was a natural with machines. He had a very mechanical mind, as Charles liked to say.

Jacob nodded to himself and fished around the dozens of drawers beneath the workbench. He finally found what he was looking for: the smallest Burners Charles ever made. Each was a black metal sphere with a series of holes all around it and a single cylinder sticking up in the middle. Jacob knew, when he pressed the cylinder in, the igniter would hit the fuel and the Burner would live up to its name.

He dropped the Burner into the edge of the actuator and fastened a metal latch to hold it in place.

"Ready?" Jacob asked.

"Let's see what your arm can do," Charles said. He didn't really expect such an early test to do much, but he did like to humor the boy.

Jacob didn't need any more prompting than that. He pushed the trigger on the Burner and jumped back. Small flames burst out of the little orb, and the mechanism in the actuator began to shake.

"I think it's going to work," Charles said. "Now, be careful when you initialize the—"

Without either of them touching it, the actuator engaged, metal screamed, and the arm snapped out perfectly straight. Charles shouted as the gauntlet punched through the back of the workbench and put a hole in the observatory wall.

The old man smacked his lips together while they both stared at the device now stuck in his wall. "Well, it works."

Jacob started to laugh, and then he bit his tongue. "I'm sorry, I didn't think it would do that."

Charles laughed and patted Jacob's head. "If I'd thought it would do that, I wouldn't have let you touch it. We're both fine, and this old place can always use a little ventilation. I've certainly had experiments end worse than that."

The Burner was still going, so Charles began pumping his old fire extinguisher. He'd geared the old tank so it only took a few pumps and a few squeals of the rusty gears to build up quite a bit of pressure. He aimed the air nozzle at the Burner and twisted the release valve on the extinguisher. A blast of air extinguished the fire.

Charles glanced at the clock again. "You better get going. I'm not going to be the one to deal with Miss Penny if you're late for Festival."

Jacob glanced up at the clock. "I still have to change!" Jacob could hear Charles laughing, even after he'd run through the door and started down the hill.

CHAPTER SIX

JACOB SMILED AS THE WIND tugged at his shirt. Even as he ran, something told him it was time for Festival: the colors. Colors of every shade imaginable lined the streets. Even the Lowlanders, dressed in their grays and browns, wore explosions of color in scarves and parasols and gloves. It seemed there were more people in the streets leading back to the Hall than could possibly live in all the lands combined.

Carriages carried Highlanders along the cobblestones. Guides pointed out some of the old buildings, shouting and gesturing so everyone could see where royalty had once lived. Some of the structures had been converted into an orphanage, another into an old museum.

A particularly large beetle pulled one carriage. It had an enormous horn, nearly as long as its body. A girl sat on top of the white carriage behind the black behemoth. She waved at Jacob, flashing a white lace glove, and he smiled back at her. She leaned over and whispered to the older woman beside her as he ran by them and into the courtyard around the Hall.

"Jacob!"

Jacob slowed his jog as he looked around, trying to find the source of his name. He found her across the street, near the entrance to the Hall. Alice wore a bright yellow gown with a string of blue flowers hung around her shoulders. Her spotless white shoes caught his eye and he said a silent prayer that he wouldn't be the one to ruin them.

Jacob stopped beside her. "You look pretty today."

"You look sweaty and like you need to change," Alice said, shaking the curls of her red hair with one hand.

"You seem awfully calm about that." Jacob eyed her, knowing full well how angry Alice could get with him. Her anger was usually justified, but he'd never admit that.

Alice smiled and watched a carriage go by. It was the Highlanders again, riding behind their beetle. Alice lowered her gaze back to Jacob, her eyes bright blue in the midday sun.

"I'm calm about it," Alice said, "because the dance got pushed back an hour. Someone spilled wine all over the speaker's jacket. We have some time. Just get into the Hall in about thirty minutes, okay? Miss Penny will kill us if you're late."

"You mean me."

"I mean *us*. I promised her I'd make sure you got here on time."

"Okay, okay. I'll be back in thirty minutes."

Alice gave him a little nod as he took off for the cluster of vendors set up all around the courtyard in front of the Hall. Extra time meant more exploring. There, deeper in the Lowlands, were the less expensive vendors. Most of the Highland vendors would stay closer to the Square. It wasn't very far away from the Hall, but Jacob didn't think he could make it there and back before their dance.

Jacob deftly dodged two running children. He didn't recognize them, but considering how nice their clothes were, he was pretty sure they didn't live nearby. The next person was a somewhat plump man with a bald head, and rosy cheeks that told Jacob the man had probably been in the drink. Jacob intentionally bumped into him and apologized profusely.

"It's quite alright. Just be more careful next time." The man went to tip his hat to Jacob, then looked surprised when it wasn't there. "I seem to have left my hat at the saloon. Have a good day."

Jacob smirked when the man turned around. He glanced down at the pocket watch he'd swiped. It was gold and intricately etched. Jacob flipped it over and saw the engraving.

> Our daughter lies eternal now
>
> Lost to us, but not to time
>
> Maddie
>
> Only five years

Jacob's heart lurched. He'd stolen someone's grieving gift. He looked up, and the man was only a few dozen steps away. Jacob took off at a run, trying to think of a good story. He thought about telling the man he'd seen him drop it, but there weren't any scratches. He thought about scratching it so his story would fit better, but that was a terrible thing to do to such a nice watch. In the end, he just ran into the man again, sliding the watch into a jacket pocket as easily as he'd stolen it.

"Child, I think you may need to lay off the rum," the man said as he laughed and patted Jacob on the back. "Lord knows I do." He smiled at Jacob and then turned to walk down another street.

Jacob fell back, relieved to have returned the watch without getting caught. He'd just have to find something else to help pay for his father's medicine. Jacob made his way back to the courtyard around the Hall.

Men and women selling every imaginable kind of trinket and toy were lined up in crooked rows all across the yard. A few vendors were spaced farther apart, leaving room for games and tests of skill that no mortal could win. Meaning, of course, they were rigged. Jacob laughed as another boy cursed at a vendor in a top hat, claiming the large ball he was given to toss couldn't possibly fit into any of the jugs.

"Hey, kid!"

Jacob looked up and stopped dead when he almost walked into another vendor, dressed all in black except for a fine silver chain that led from his belt to his pocket. Jacob hesitated to call him a vendor. The man looked more like a huckster, the kind that only came out to pilfer money when people were celebrating. Not a bad strategy, Jacob knew. Some of his best pickpocketing had been during last year's Festival. Jacob also knew that chain didn't belong to a watch. There would be something deadly on the other end.

"You play?" the man asked. Jacob looked behind the man. He was organizing a game of Cork. The vendor leaned down and caught Jacob's eye. "Try your luck, boy! We only need one more player. Winner gets an *entire* bushel of strawberries." The man in the black clothes held up more strawberries than Jacob had seen in his entire life.

"I have no money, sir."

A lady in a fine gown stopped and looked between Jacob and the man. She rested a parasol on her shoulder while she pulled a purse out and handed the man a coin. Jacob could see it was gold, and likely worth more than his family made in a month. "For any boy who wants to play and can't afford it," she said with a smile. She winked at Jacob before she disappeared into the crowd. A moment later, Jacob realized she'd been the lady on the carriage who'd waved at him. He wanted to say thank you, but she was already deep into the crowd.

The huckster stared after her. A broad grin split his face when he looked back to Jacob. "It's your lucky day! Take your side."

Ten upright rings shifted in the breeze at eye level, five per side with a slightly taller center ring on the opposing ends of the field. Each stand that held up a ring stood three feet from the next. Three boys waited across the small playing field—which, at twenty-four feet, was rather large, considering Festival was under way—and Jacob joined a pair of boys on the closest side. There wasn't much question that the other team worked for the huckster. They were older, and the stains on their hands said they probably worked in the mines like his father. He figured they'd throw hard but probably didn't know a thing about strategy.

"First to ten!" the huckster said as he placed three small corkballs on the line at the center of the field. They were spaced far enough apart no one could grab two at a time.

"Who's faster?" Jacob asked as he turned to his teammates.

The taller boy with dark brown hair hooked his thumb and said, "Reggie, my brother."

"I'm Jacob."

Both boys nodded. "I'm Bobby." Bobby was quite a bit shorter the Reggie, closer to Jacob's height, with the same hair as his brother.

"Alright, you guys play much?"

"No," the brothers chorused before sharing a sly grin.

Jacob glanced up at the goals. They weren't like the rusted-out buckets he was used to playing with. These goals had mesh across them, and he could see bells that would ring when one of the corkballs scored.

"Let's go!" an older boy shouted.

Jacob hid his own smile. "Alright, Reggie, stay back by me. Leave the center goal unattended. They'll all aim for it. Bobby, get a cork. Just one. Wait until the other two start throwing, and then go for the clearest goal behind either of them."

"You sure?" Bobby asked.

"Yes, this is more about his strategy," Jacob said with a nod toward the huckster, "than theirs. After the first goal, just catch the corks and aim for the outer goals."

"Enough talk!" the huckster said. "Begin!" He smacked a small hanging gong.

The other team sprinted into motion before Bobby started running, but he still made it to the line first, grabbing one of the corks and taking a step back.

Jacob positioned himself between the first and second goal, while Reggie mirrored him. The corks came in fast, but they were both ready. Jacob reached out, and the first smacked into his left hand with a pop. He didn't even have to look to know Reggie had caught his.

Reggie stepped forward and launched the cork at the same time Bobby shot. Bobby's hit first, and Jacob heard the bell before he'd even let his cork fly. One of the boys got a fingertip on Bobby's cork as he tried to dive for it. Another goal sounded as the boy flopped onto the stones and cursed.

Jacob's cork sailed into the goal right behind him.

The other team just blinked at each other. Then they started shouting as they picked up the corks and started throwing them randomly. Jacob knew they would. These boys were only concerned about one thing, and that was making sure they kept the huckster happy. That made them sloppy.

By the time the score was seven to two, a crowd had formed around the field. Jacob clapped his hands and laughed. Bobby was grinning.

"Strawberries," Reggie said. "I want the strawberries." He pulled back and fired another cork. It left his own nets exposed, but Jacob slid in behind Reggie to catch another cork as it came back toward Reggie's goal.

Jacob spun without stopping, whipping the cork forward in a sidearm motion. It slid beneath the arm of the largest boy and slammed into the side of the goal, pulling the net tight and setting another bell to ringing.

The crowd cheered, and Jacob couldn't stop smiling. Highlanders and Lowlanders alike circled them, and they'd already chosen their favorite team.

"Two more," Jacob said as he started to stalk around Bobby and Reggie in a large circle.

Bobby swatted a cork to the side before he said, "One more."

"No!" the huckster shouted when another bell sounded. "What am I paying you fools for? You can't beat a handful of riffraff?"

"Now!" one of the older boys said, and all three of them threw their corks at once.

Jacob heard the bells sound as two of the corks scored. The other smacked into the palm of his hand. He stepped forward and brought his arm around a smooth, overhand arc. His left foot slid over the rough cobblestone as he twisted his body, putting everything he had into the throw. Everyone watched as the little beige cork streaked through the air. The other boys had their nets guarded well, but Jacob's aim was uncanny.

Jacob could almost hear the blood rushing in his ears in that moment of silence, where nothing but the wind and the crowds in the distance made a sound. The bell rang out.

Bobby and Reggie made incoherent sounds of joy as they realized they'd won. A brief applause rose from the crowd with a round of cheers. Jacob reveled in the people congratulating his team before the audience began dispersing.

The huckster cursed and turned back to his wagon. When he turned around again, he had an enormous crate of strawberries. "Well, no one can call me a liar. I said you'd win a bushel, and here it is." The wooden crate made a distinct thump as it hit the cobblestones.

"How are we going to carry those?" Reggie asked, laughing. "There're so many."

"It's a nesting crate," Jacob said as he pulled the top of the crate off and turned it over. "Here, look," he said as he tugged on the corners of the cloth resting beneath the top layer of the strawberries. "Grab that side."

Bobby and Reggie both grabbed a corner and the three boys lifted the top half of the strawberries up and set them gently into the top of the crate.

"Good call," Bobby said. He paused and looked at Jacob. "Do you live around here? I don't think I've ever seen you before."

Jacob nodded. "I'm down in the Lowlands."

"Well, you're a hell of a Cork player," Reggie said. "You should come up and see us sometime. We play on Saturdays up by the city wall."

"We live just outside the wall," Bobby said, as if he felt a need to let Jacob know they weren't really Highlanders either.

"I will!" Jacob said. "That sounds like fun." Jacob stumbled when someone slapped him on the back. He turned around, slightly annoyed until he saw who it was. "Charles!"

"Nicely played, boys. Nicely played." Charles adjusted his leather vest. It seemed to have an infinite number of pockets and flaps.

"Reggie," Jacob said. "Bobby, wait a minute."

The boys paused before lifting their strawberries.

"Take some more of mine. I couldn't eat all these if I tried."

"Are you sure?" Bobby asked. "I mean, you could sell them if you weren't going to eat them."

That gave Jacob pause, but then he shook his head. Sometimes it was just nice to share things with friends.

"Thank you," Reggie said, helping Jacob unload some of his strawberries into their crate. Reggie and Bobby said thanks several more times as they lifted their half of the crate, one brother on either side, and made their way to the north.

Charles snatched up one of Jacob's strawberries and started chewing on it. "That was awful nice of you, boy. And you left this in the shop." Charles held out the Spider Knight whistle.

Jacob didn't even remember taking it with him, much less leaving it there. "Thank you!" Jacob slid the whistle into the deepest pocket on his right thigh.

"Why don't you leave those with me?" Charles said, gesturing at the strawberries. "I'll get them back to your folks for you on my way to the observatory."

"That would be great," Jacob said. "I need to change, or Alice is going to kill me. And then Miss Penny will kill me again. And then my mom will kill me."

Charles raised his eyebrows and nodded. "Well then, you best be off. I've no use for an apprentice three times dead."

"Don't eat all of them!" Jacob said as he laughed and plunged into the crowd once more.

CHAPTER SEVEN

J ACOB HEAVED A SIGH OF relief as the door to the Hall closed. Two of
the ice fans near the entrance were running, and they were blissful
after a game of Cork. Charles had helped build them, right down to the
quiet little engines affixed to the base of each one. The dull brass blades
hummed, pulling air over the blocks of ice just behind them.

Jacob watched the mechanism for a moment, remembering what
Charles had told him about the melting water cooling one metal plate
while a small flame heated the other. It caused the bellows to pump up
and down, spinning the blades and keeping the system running.

"Jacob!"

He looked up and saw one of the other boys adjusting a rounded hat
with a thin brim on his head.

"You're going to be late!"

Jacob left the fan behind and nodded at the other boy as he took off
at a jog. Miss Penny had a makeshift changing room set up where they'd
been rehearsing the night before. He pulled the gray cloth to the side and
stepped through the fabric doorway. Inside were several smaller rooms,
draped on all four sides with fabric. There was only one jacket and hat
left, and that's when it really hit him that he *was* cutting it close.

He slid the navy-blue jacket over the darkest brown pants he owned.
Miss Penny had been very specific about everyone wearing the darkest
brown they had. He knew a few kids wouldn't have any browns, because
even though it was cheap, it still cost money to dye their clothes.

Jacob didn't wait to finish fastening the brass buttons. He started running back out of the Hall. He threw open the door and squinted as the sun almost blinded him. He kept working the buttons together as he jogged through the crowd, dodging kids and grandparents alike.

There wasn't a game at the Cork field, so he sprinted across it and cut into an alley on the other side of the crowd. It was a thin pathway, enough so that most adults avoided it. There weren't any kids there either, and he saw only a Jumper skittering from one shadow to the next.

He exited the other end of the alley, having cut quite a distance off his run, but the rest was uphill. The farther Jacob made it up the steep cobblestone streets, the more carriages he saw. As much as he'd thought the white carriage with the girl had been fancy, that had been run-down compared to the gilded works he ran past closer to the Square.

Jacob rounded the corner by the Lowlands' only bank. Its pillars stuck a little too far out into the street, interrupting the flow of traffic. Jacob dashed in behind those stone columns, where almost no one was standing, and when he cleared the other side, he was at the far edge of the Square.

He couldn't help but laugh and smile when he saw the mob of people and creatures and colors exploding across the entirety of the Square. Oh, he'd seen the carriages, yes, but here they were a constant, churning line, two rows deep. They came in from the side streets, dropping folks off in the Square. Some walked up into the elevated seating areas, and others mingled in the crowd around the fountain.

Jacob stopped beside a strange-looking mount. Its head was almost like a triangle, bright green with huge eyes. It cocked its head to one side and began to sway. Jacob noticed a series of metal bands around what he could only describe as arms—enormous arms that were folded together.

A flash of light caught his eye, and he followed it back to the mirrors around the stage. They were already prepping for the dance, which meant he was out of time. Jacob didn't pay much mind to the enormous fountain as he jumped onto the rim and ran around it. The sculpture at the center bore a group of men hoisting a great cornucopia of food and weapons above their head. His dad had once told him what it meant, but Jacob couldn't remember.

He leapt off the rim of the fountain and jogged over to the stage.

"Unbelievable," a frazzled-looking Miss Penny said. "You're on time."

Jacob smiled. "It was all Alice."

"Well, whoever it was, I'm glad you're all here. Now, up on the stage with you. We're just getting ready."

Jacob didn't bother walking over to the stairs. He adjusted his hat, took a step backward, and vaulted up onto the stage.

Everyone from Cotillion was already there. They were loosely arranged across the stage, not having taken their spots yet. The boys wore their rounded hats, and the girls all had bright red bows at the backs of their heads.

Jacob stared at one of those bows when the girl turned around and caught his eye.

Alice rolled her eyes and pointed at the back of her head. "It clashes terribly, doesn't it? Red hair was *not* meant to have a red bow in it."

Alice wore a rich brown dress with subtle bits of brighter color woven into it along the seams. She followed Jacob's gaze down to the hem of her dress. "Do you like it? Gram added it in this week. She thought it would be pretty for Festival."

He looked up and met Alice's eyes. "It's very pretty."

"And you see the shoes?"

He looked down again.

"They're white," she said. "Let's see if we can keep them white."

Jacob sighed. "I'll try."

Something hammered a brief staccato. Jacob and Alice both looked around for the noise.

"It's the conductor!" Jacob said. He placed his hand on Alice's shoulder and turned her toward the orchestra pit. "It's almost time."

There was a roiling motion in the pit as the musicians took their seats. Every kind of instrument Jacob could imagine was right at the edge of the stage, along with the guitarist and the cellist from the night before. They stood surrounded by more musicians with violins and huge upright basses. A row of percussionists with large copper drums tapped on the stretched heads of their instruments and adjusted a series of levers.

Miss Penny began to usher the kids into rows. Jacob and Alice squared off. Jacob faced the balconies on the buildings behind the stage while Alice looked over his shoulder, off into the crowds.

A man in a tall top hat and white jacket stepped up to the podium near the fountain. He leaned down to a snarl of brass mouthpieces. They were all pointed in different directions, and their ends were made up of coppery plates riveted together. They expanded into enormous cones, and Jacob thought they looked like metal flowers.

"Welcome," the man said, and his voice burst from the horns, magnified as though he could speak louder than the entire crowd.

The Square fell silent outside of a few whispers and the wail of a crying baby.

The man stood up a little straighter, and Jacob could almost feel the excitement as he said, "Welcome to Festival!"

Cheers exploded around the Square. Little pockets of confetti shot into the sky—propelled by thundering air cannons—only to drift slowly back down into the crowd.

The man waited for the noise to fade into a low chatter before he spoke again. "This is the fiftieth year we've held Festival in the Square. Fifty years since the Deadlands War ended and we found our peace behind the walls. In that peace, we built our rails, planned our trade routes, and bolstered our city so that war would never threaten us again."

Applause rose as the man went on, raising his voice to talk over the noise of the crowd. It was the same speech every year. The only thing that changed was how many years it had been since the war.

"Now, in our city of Ancora, as we come together as one, there are no Lowlands. There are no Highlands. There are only Ancorans. Ancora is one."

The crowd echoed the man's last words and then the musicians started playing. It was a brief tune, a march. It played at the end of the speech every year. This year, though, it would be followed by a waltz, as chosen by the Cotillion's graduating class.

Jacob shivered slightly, surprised when he realized he was a bit nervous. The Festival dance was a rite of passage in Ancora, a sign they were reaching adulthood, and it only ever happened once.

The music started.

Alice stepped up close to Jacob and whispered, "Toe crusher."

Jacob couldn't stop his smile. Alice grinned at him and they stepped into the rhythm of the waltz. There was practically a wall of musicians playing at the foot of the stage, and Jacob stole a glance at them each time Alice spun.

Near the middle of the song, Jacob shifted his hand to the small of her back once more.

"They're amazing," Alice said, her eyes trailing over the musicians.

Jacob nodded and moved his feet close to Alice's. "It's the city's symphony and the best Lowland musicians."

Miss Penny mimicked the conductor as she moved at the front of the stage. Everyone kept time, better than they ever had in rehearsal. Alice laughed as Jacob took two small steps and they both swooped forward, slowly turning with the rest of the dancers.

Alice twirled her skirt as the musicians slowly ended the waltz. There was a brief moment of silence, and Jacob didn't think he'd never forget the cheers of the crowd that broke the calm. He'd been in that crowd before, waving his own pennants and flags and throwing sparkling bits of confetti, but being on the stage was entirely different.

Miss Penny bowed to the Square. She gestured for the dancers to do the same.

Jacob thought it should be the symphony that was bowing, but he didn't mind too much.

CHAPTER EIGHT

T HE DANCERS ALL GATHERED BEHIND the stage. There was a small dressing area set up there, and Jacob was happy to be getting out of his jacket and hat. It wasn't particularly hot outside, but it sure felt like it with the extra layers.

"Hats on the racks and jackets on the hangers, please," Miss Penny said. "I'll get them back to the tailor for you."

Jacob heard "Good job" and "Well done" and "I wish we could do it again next year" from a dozen different kids. He agreed. It had been fun. It was nice now that they were older. They were still kids, technically, at fifteen, but now they had a lot more freedom. Jacob slid the jacket off and hung it up carefully, the wooden hanger clinking against the metal bar.

"It was so much fun, Miss Penny," Alice said.

Jacob glanced at Alice over his shoulder as he hung up his hat.

"And your shoes are still white," Miss Penny said.

"You don't have to sound *that* surprised," Jacob said, turning to face them both.

Miss Penny smiled, and it was one of the largest smiles Jacob had ever seen on her. "You both did very well. I couldn't be more proud." She stood up and motioned for the kids to gather closer.

"Now, I promised you all a treat if this performance went well, and a treat you'll have." She pulled a little leather satchel off her belt, and Jacob could already hear the coins.

"Are you giving us coppers for candy?" one of the younger girls asked, barely containing her excitement.

Miss Penny smiled as she pulled the strings of the purse open. "The mayor was feeling a bit more generous than that, my dear."

The kids all gasped as Miss Penny poured a handful of silvers out. "Now, take one as you leave, and have fun today."

There were shouts of riotous joy and unbridled laughter as the boys and girls scooped their prizes out of Miss Penny's hands and ran into the crowds on the Square. Jacob and Alice were the last to see their teacher.

"Thank you so much," Alice said as she took the coin. She stepped past Miss Penny and waited by the flap that led back into the Square. It still swayed a bit from the last kid to run through it.

"Jacob," Miss Penny said, "thank you for being on time today. I know your father is not well, so please take this extra coin to him." She pressed two silvers into Jacob's palm, and he closed his hand around them.

"Thank you." He started to walk away. He hesitated before throwing his arms around Miss Penny, hugging her briefly, and running out the door after Alice.

The sun was blinding now, but Alice was still easy to follow. Her hair was a beacon, no matter how crowded the Square was. He watched her pat a giant Pill-Bug between its antennae. It was harnessed to a nice black carriage and draped in black silks.

"Are you getting hot out here?" she asked the bug.

One of its antennae smacked her in the face in response.

"He's quite fine, miss," the driver said, leaning forward from the top of the carriage. "He's a bit old, so we like to keep him in wraps."

"He's friendly," Alice said.

"Or he's just a bit too lazy to be mean." The driver gave her a crooked smile and Alice continued on, giving the driver a small wave.

"Can you imagine what the nighttime Festival must be like inside the city walls?" Alice asked, looking out over the Square.

"No, but I'd love to see it."

"I've heard this is still the biggest celebration," Alice shouted over her shoulder as she wove through the crowd. "I bet the Highlands have a grander one behind the city wall."

"Seems like something they'd do," Jacob said. "Keep the Lowlanders as far away as possible." He didn't really care right then, surrounded by Festival and food, and tailing Alice through all the chaos.

There were even more carriages around the edges of the Square now. Jacob marveled at the array of creatures pulling the carts this way and that. Some were borne by giant Pill-Bugs like the old one Alice had stopped by, while others slowly rolled along behind brilliantly colored beetles. Several had stopped, their carriages unfolding to reveal a wild array of food and treats. Alice headed straight for a bright blue carriage. The rear hatch had been opened and a painted sign hung down, declaring its contents "The Best Cocoa Crunch in Ancora."

Jacob's mouth started watering. He slid the two coins together in his pocket but left them both where they were.

They waited in line for a bit, and it wasn't long before Alice bounced up and down on her heels.

"They aren't free, little miss," an old woman said from the back of the carriage.

"Four, please." Alice handed a silver coin to the woman.

"Oh, you must have been in the dance. You all did a wonderful job," she said as she began carefully wrapping up the chunks of cocoa and candy into neat squares.

Alice dropped two of the squares into her satchel, along with the coppers and a token she received as change. She handed one of the little bundles to Jacob as they walked away from the cart.

"For me?" he asked, taking the little green square out of her hand.

She nodded and started unwrapping her own. "I know you're saving those silvers for your dad."

Jacob looked at the small square of candy in his hands. He wanted to argue, say his family didn't need the money, but he knew Alice understood. She never really judged him for being a pickpocket, or for stealing food. She knew what it was like to be poor.

"Thank you," Jacob said. He started unwrapping his own candy.

Alice took a nibble, gasped, and then took a huge bite of the Cocoa Crunch. "It's so good!"

"Don't fall down in the gutter, now," Jacob said. He hopped up past the stone curb and took a bite of candy. It was soft, almost like fudge, and something crunched in the middle. It was rich, with a nutty flavor, and when it mixed with the chocolate … "It's so good!"

"Right?" Alice said with a laugh.

"It's like toffee, and fudge, and …" Jacob stopped trying to think of words to say. He opted for grunting as they devoured the rest of the candy and weaved through the Square.

They watched the festivities for a while. There were jugglers and dancers and illusionists, but Jacob's favorite was always the gadgets. One man—he looked a little younger than Charles—had an incredible array of wind-ups laid out across his table.

"Can I?" Jacob asked. He pointed to one of the clockwork creatures.

"Yes, of course!" the man said. His hair was graying, and he wore a mustache that seemed to defy gravity, sweeping out and almost curling back far enough to touch his nose.

Jacob studied the intricate lines and perfect seams all around the toy. Carved into the base, beside the keyhole, were the flowing letters *NVB*. Jacob turned the little key and set the sphere back down. Three notes played, and it reminded him of the Spider Knight's whistle. As he thought of that old song, the little sphere popped open. Eight legs sprang out from inside it and skittered forward. A small figure with a sword rode on the back of the miniature copper spider. As the spider stepped forward, its legs clicked and the gears inside it moved, and the knight swung his sword back and forth.

"That's amazing," Alice said. She leaned in to get a closer look.

When the spider found the edge of the table, one of its front legs went over the edge. Jacob reached for it, but the vendor stopped him.

"No, watch."

The first leg missed the table, and then the second. Once both legs went below the surface of the table, something clicked inside the spider, and it spun away from the edge. It started walking back toward the vendor.

"What?" Jacob asked. "How!"

The vendor smiled at him. "I'm selling them today for one silver. It's quite a bargain with all those moving parts."

"I … I don't have the money for that," Jacob said. He was somewhat disappointed, as he'd have liked to show Charles, but he needed that money for his dad. "Is it all running on springs?"

The vendor rubbed his eyebrows and smiled at Jacob. "It is."

"No steam?"

"Not in this one, but I do have some larger ones with their very own boilers."

Jacob picked up the little spider as it slowed down and began curling into a ball once more. He watched as the legs folded and the knight lay down before the shell closed over the mechanism once more.

"You could put a steam engine in this one too," Jacob said.

"It's too small," the vendor said.

"Charles could do it. He could put a little boiler under the spider's abdomen and use a tiny Burner for it."

"Ah," the vendor said with a smile. "You know Charles?"

"He's Charles's apprentice," Alice said.

"I was Charles's apprentice once too," the vendor said. "That was before I worked with the city smith of course. Eventually I decided I liked springs and clockwork more than steam and weapons."

"Weapons?" Jacob asked.

"Oh, that's an old story for old men," the vendor said with a smile.

"Would you sell one for five coppers?" Alice asked as she fished around in her purse.

"I can't afford that," Jacob said before he sighed. He'd thought about coming back later to see if he could steal one of the little contraptions, but now that he knew the vendor was a friend of Charles's, he couldn't do it.

"For a fellow apprentice?" the vendor said. "I would indeed."

Alice handed him five coppers, and he took them with a nod before picking up the little sphere and placing it in a roughly woven beige sack.

"My name is James," the vendor said. "Charles always liked to call me Jimmy, but do tell him I said hello, won't you?" He held the bag out to Jacob.

Jacob looked over at Alice.

"It's yours," Alice said. "I don't need that much more candy, and I've still got a few coppers left."

Jacob took the sack and stared at it. "Thank you," he said, not entirely familiar with people doing nice things for him. "Thank you."

Alice patted his shoulder. "What are friends for?" She reached out and flipped the bronze switch on the side of a small rectangular box. It looked like a modest jewelry case, silver and adorned with intricate etchings. A run of high-pitched notes played, bright and happy.

"A music box?" Jacob asked, somewhat unimpressed, even if it did have a beautiful melody.

The lid popped open and a strange white bird waited inside. It spun to one side and then the other as it flapped its wings.

"Oh, wow," Jacob said.

They all cringed when a horrible sound blared from the music box before the bird's wings folded in and the lid snapped closed.

"Ouch," Alice said. "Is it broken?"

James shook his head. "It's a cock-a-doodle-doo. That bird went extinct a long time ago. It couldn't fly very well."

"It's … great?" Alice said.

"The mechanics are pretty amazing," Jacob said, "but that was an awful sound."

Alice shrugged. "If I could fly like a bird, I wouldn't much care what I sounded like."

James laughed and wound up the old music box again. "Go on now, you two. Enjoy Festival!"

"We will!" Alice said as she grabbed Jacob's arm and pulled him down the street.

They walked for a while before Alice said "Look" as she pointed at the courtyard outside the Hall. "There are more games. It looks like someone set up more Cork fields."

"You want to play?" Jacob asked.

"I want to win," Alice said, laughing and dragging him toward the nearest game.

CHAPTER NINE

J ACOB WASN'T SURE HOW LONG they'd been playing games, but they'd won almost every one. He groaned and put his hand over his stomach when he and Alice flopped onto a wooden bench.

"Too much candy?" Alice asked.

Jacob looked up at the sky. "Too much … everything." It was starting to get dark now, and the brighter stars were already plain to see. It wouldn't be long before the only other light came from the streetlamps. He couldn't remember how many matches of Cork they'd won. Alice had a great arm, and her strategies could be even crazier than his at times. Their victories had led to food and candy and more food.

"I think I'm going to explode."

Alice unwrapped a hard candy, a butterscotch, and Jacob looked away in revulsion.

"You couldn't pay me to eat another bite," he said.

"Oh, I'm pretty sure I could," Alice said.

Jacob watched her for a moment. "You're a fantastic Cork player."

Alice flashed him a smile and said, "Thank you." She finished her candy and leaned into the back of the bench. "Did you ever think about trying out for the city league?"

Jacob shook his head. "No, but you should. That one shot you had? Where you looked at one goal, but aimed for a different one?"

"My granddad taught me that before he died. He was one of the best players around." She crumpled up a candy wrapper and stuffed it into her purse. "I could never play for the city league."

"Why?" Jacob asked. He immediately felt like an idiot. "Right, you're a girl. Well, they're dumb. You'd be a great player." He paused. "You *are* a great player."

"Thanks, Jacob. Maybe one day I'll be able to play."

"It's just a stupid league. You know some folks in the Highlands don't even call it Cork? That's what my dad says. Some of them just call it league."

Alice nodded. "They use those rubber balls. They don't use cork. Have you ever played a game of Cork with one of those?"

Jacob shook his head.

"I have to say, they're better than corkballs. You can bounce them off the ground to score. I mean, you can do that with cork too, but it's a lot harder to do. I think—"

Someone screamed in the distance. An explosion of sound shook the stones beneath their feet. Jacob's heart leapt and he froze.

"What was that?" Alice asked, her voice rising to a very high pitch.

Jacob stood up. He could see some dust in the distance, but no more.

"Oh, gods," Alice said as she stood up beside Jacob. Her hands flashed up to cover her mouth, and there was a choked scream behind them. Another cloud of debris went up in the distance. Something moved on the top of the wall.

Jacob saw a pair of knights pointing to the shadow. It vanished and then reappeared. Whatever it was, it was fast.

It was close.

Too close.

A whistle sounded, and more knights gathered in the courtyard. More whistles blew.

"No," Jacob said. The shadow shifted at the top of the wall again. Jacob watched with a rising sense of horror as the top edge of the stone began to buckle. "No!" Some of the knights started to run. They all shouted.

"To the city! The wall has fallen! Run, you fools!"

Disbelief caused him to hesitate for only a moment before he grabbed Alice by both her arms and stared into her eyes. "Run, Alice. Follow the knights. Run!" He pushed her toward the knights and turned to start in the opposite direction.

She nodded as tears and terror rolled over her face. "Where are you going!"

"Charles doesn't know! I have to warn him and find my parents! They stayed home because Dad's sick!"

"They'll sound the bells," Alice said. "I'm not leaving you here!"

Something huge reared up over the collapsing wall. It looked like a Walker, giant and segmented with countless legs, but it was a brilliant blue. Its faceted eyes sparkled as the rest of its body surged up and over the wall. One thing Jacob had learned a long time ago: the most colorful bugs were the deadliest.

"Go!" Jacob shouted, and it sounded far more cruel than he'd meant it to. "I'll find you!"

Alice turned and ran, following the rush of the crowd.

Jacob watched her for a moment and then dove into a crowd of screaming festivalgoers. Charles and his parents would both be in danger. Jacob grunted as someone bumped him, tripping him and knocking him to the ground. Dirt and grit ground into his palms as he scrambled up off the cobblestones. Something like a chittering screech echoed down the street. It was the cry of the invader, Jacob knew, but he didn't know what it meant. Another cry sounded in the distance. There were more.

Jacob stayed close to the houses as he ran, and gradually the crowd thinned. Everyone had taken shelter in their homes, or run toward the city walls, while the knights defended the citizens' retreat.

Something crashed behind him, but he didn't look back. He pulled his gloves on as he approached the lift. Jacob's feet pounded the cobblestones, and his heart beat like it was trying to get him to run faster than he was already moving.

Don't look back.

Don't look back.

Jacob didn't pause as he reached the edge of the cliff. He dove for the pole that led deeper into the Lowlands. His hands clamped around it, and he managed to half-hook one of his legs around it in his wild grab. The inertia spun him slightly as he started his controlled fall down the pole.

He glimpsed a black shadow with thin legs and what looked like giant fangs. Then it was gone. Jacob looked to the left as he fell, and he almost broke into tears. The cliff face near the Square writhed with movement. He couldn't make out what was moving, only that there were a great many things laying siege to the walls.

He barely noticed the lift before he smacked into it. Jacob tightened his legs and slowed his descent as much as he could, but the impact was still brutal. His ankle throbbed as he bounced off the grate and fell to the ground.

Jacob ran as hard as he could, and the pain in his ankle vanished in his panic. He passed the broken wall from the night before. Then he heard it again. A glance backward showed him shattered roofing tiles strewn across the cobblestones. He raised his eyes and choked back a scream.

Long, spindly obsidian-black legs propelled a Widow Maker along the rooftops. It moved effortlessly, calmly stalking Jacob as he pushed himself even harder. Somewhere in his mind, he knew he couldn't get away. There was no way to survive an attack by a Widow Maker. He ran, and tried to think, and then—

He remembered the whistle.

Jacob stumbled as he pulled the silver whistle out of his pocket. He wanted to shout with joy when he saw it hadn't been destroyed in his fall. He clamped his hand over all twelve holes. He lifted the middle finger of his left hand as he exhaled, followed by his ring finger. He covered all the holes of the whistle again and blew into it as hard as he could.

It cost him more breath than he had. His pace slowed. Something clicked above him, but Jacob couldn't bring himself to look back. He ran as best he could, but it seemed like he'd been running forever. His breath grew ragged, and roofing tiles still cracked onto the cobblestones behind him. The observatory may have been closer than before, but still too distant for shelter. Maybe the Widow Maker wouldn't realize he could hide in a building. Charles could help, if he could just—

"Jacob!"

He glanced back toward the voice. The Widow Maker was close. So very close. Its fangs were raised, along with its front legs. The spider readied itself to strike.

Samuel's lance cut through two of the Widow Maker's legs, and the beast fell from the roof. Its carapace crunched as it hit the cobblestones, and Jacob watched in awe as the Spider Knight leapt from Bessie's back and ran his sword through the Widow Maker's head. Blue blood ran into the gutter as Samuel jerked his sword free.

"You have to get to the city!" Samuel said.

"No, Charles and my parents!"

"That old man can take care of himself."

"No!"

"Dammit, boy." Samuel looked at Bessie. She tentatively touched the dead spider with her front legs. "Get on."

Excitement warred with sheer terror as Jacob swung up behind the Spider Knight. He wrapped his arms around Samuel's waist, and the knight urged Bessie forward at a bone-jarring pace.

"Your parents are already headed into the city. They were the first block we evacuated to the lift."

Jacob didn't say anything. Something unknotted itself in his gut. They still needed to find Charles.

The streets grew more vacant the farther the trio sprinted into the

Lowlands. The observatory loomed into view, and Bessie shot up the hill. When they were close to the door, Jacob leapt off the saddle.

He stumbled as he hit the ground, ramming his shoulder into the front door. "Charles!" he shouted as he pushed on the handle and threw open the door. Jacob stopped immediately.

A strange round cylinder was pointed at his face.

"Jacob," the old man said, raising the cylinder away from Jacob's head. "Not safe to come barging in at a time like this." He flipped a switch on the side of the—thing. It looked like wood and copper with some kind of lighted tube and a thick sliding gear running down the side. The cylinder was darker than the rest of it.

"Is that an air cannon?" Jacob asked. The realization of what had just been pointed at his face made his knees wobble a bit.

Samuel pushed in behind Jacob. "Charles, we have to go. They want everyone inside the city walls. This isn't a normal attack. There are multiple breaches near Festival."

"Idiots," Charles said. "I've told them for years the thinner walls in the Lowlands wouldn't hold up." He started picking things up from his workbench and stuffing them into leather pouches on his vest. "You don't need Jacob riding on that damn spider, slowing you down. I'll get him to the city."

Samuel followed Charles deeper into the observatory. "With what? We don't have time for—"

No one spoke after Charles threw the tarp off the steambike. Charles didn't say a word as he leaned down to light the fires. He grabbed a miniature Burner, another of the metal balls that could give off a blast of heat, depressed the igniter, and tossed it beneath the boiler. Jacob stared at the dingy steel gears mixed in with the newly forged bronze that formed the chassis of the bike. The wheels had rubber around them now, and that was new since the last time he'd seen it. He'd always wanted to ride it, but Charles said it wasn't safe.

"You're crazy, old man," Samuel said, but there was something like admiration in his words.

Charles nodded as he holstered the air gun across his back. He handed a leather backpack to Jacob, and Jacob put it on without any questions. It was heavy, but not too much for him. Charles buckled two huge saddlebags closed on either side of the bike before he mounted it. He started pushing it toward the door with his legs. "Get the door behind us, Jacob."

Jacob closed the heavier of the two doors and pushed a button on the outside. He heard the clockwork come to life, locking the door in a dozen places with bolts of metal.

"Climb on," Charles said.

Jacob struggled over the tall seat and the wide saddlebags. He was careful not to catch his pants on the flames near the boiler before he wrapped his arms around Charles. Charles was a bit thicker than Samuel, but he could still reach.

"I'll see you at the city," Samuel said. "Be safe."

Charles nodded, but what he said was, "No one's safe outside the Highlands anymore."

CHAPTER TEN

T HE BIKE SURGED FORWARD IN near silence. The tires on the cobblestones made more of a racket than the engine did, but Jacob wished the bike would roar and scream and drown out the terrible sounds all around them.

He could hear the cries of the Lowlanders as more and more invaders tore through the city. People had been left behind, and the walls were falling. Jacob squeezed Charles tighter as the bike bounded off a large stone.

"Hang on!" Charles twisted the throttle on the steambike, and they lurched forward at a terrifying pace. Jacob's teeth slammed together as they bounced across the street. "Watch our flank and don't focus on the dead!"

Charles's warning came too late, and Jacob screamed. He couldn't see the houses off to the west anymore. The walls were gone, and in their place came a surging tide of invaders. The faster creatures had almost made it to the street they were riding down, but it wasn't just the creatures that made Jacob scream. People were there, in that sea of invaders. At the edge ran Bradley Piers. A bright blue spear exploded from the boy's gut, and he screamed as the Walker dragged him to the ground. He vanished into darkness.

Jacob buried his face in Charles's back. He should be glad Bradley wouldn't be hurting anyone else, but Jacob felt sick. He saw only the blood now, and heard the screams. How many of them were his family? His friends?

"Charles!" The shout came from the rooftop beside them. Jacob didn't have to look to know it was Samuel. "Cut east and circle around the Hall. Take the long way up the ridge to the Square. Everything else is blocked."

"Or buried," Charles snarled as he jerked the bike to the side. Jacob felt a blast of heat as his leg got too close to the boiler.

Jacob gathered up the courage to peek at where they were. He saw the bank at the corner of the Square pass them in a blur of shadows. Jacob was clamped firmly onto Charles's back, but he still saw the old man's head turn to look over his shoulder when a calamity sounded behind them. Jacob could tell another part of the wall had fallen without seeing it with his own eyes and then came a rapid staccato like ten thousand men marching out of sync.

Charles cursed.

Jacob didn't think the vision could be any worse than what he'd already seen, so he turned his head. A wall of horrible black carapaces chased them. Red wings hummed and buzzed, and their eyes glowed like empty eye sockets. The wings didn't lift the creatures more than a few feet off the ground, but the churning, roiling chaos was terrifying. Bugs slammed through the corners of stone houses and fell through the tiled ceilings. Mandibles gnashed together as the beetles—known as the Red Death—bore down on them.

"Get the Bangers out of the bag on your right," Charles shouted over the scream of the wind and roar of the invaders. "The big ones! We need to blow these bastards to kingdom come."

Jacob's hands were shaking, but he still made quick work of the buckles. There were two brass cases near the top of the bags. He pulled a lever on one side and the edge of the case popped up, exposing a Banger twice the size of a corkball. Jacob pulled the lever on the smaller case and snatched a Burner out of it. The Banger opened at the press of a button. Jacob pressed the metal nub to activate the Burner before dropping it into the larger sphere. He pressed the button on the Banger. He had no more than fifteen seconds.

"Ready!"

Charles righted the bike and turned slightly, giving Jacob a clear shot at the horde. He didn't need it. At the speed they were going, Jacob knew where the bugs would be when the Banger blew. Jacob let the metal sphere fall to the ground as it began to smoke.

"Go!" Jacob screamed at Charles as he wrapped his arms around the old man as tightly as he could, pressing his face against the gun across the old man's back. "Go, go, go!"

Charles didn't need to be told twice. He leaned forward as he twisted the throttle as far as it would go. They shot up the ridge, heading toward the city walls.

The Banger detonated, and he could *feel* the shockwave. Jacob turned and watched the fireball send pieces of bugs so far into the sky they cleared the opposite wall, falling down the east side of the mountain.

Charles glanced back and laughed like a madman. "Well done." He leaned the bike into another sharp turn, and they could see the path leading up to the city gates.

"Don't stop!"

Jacob looked up to see Bessie leaping along the rooftops above them. Samuel's eyes were all for the courtyard, and Jacob followed his gaze.

"Pull the gun out," Charles said.

Jacob squeezed his knees as tightly as he could and unholstered the gun on Charles's back. He'd used smaller air guns, so he had an idea of how it worked. Jacob started sliding the long wooden pump beneath the barrel. The gears offered little resistance at first, but three pumps in, Jacob could barely budge the slide.

"It won't move anymore," Jacob said.

"Three pumps," Charles said. "That's all you need, the way it's tuned. It's already loaded. Don't fire unless you have to."

The courtyard outside the gates looked like something out of the old stories. The stories Jacob's father used to tell them around the fireplace—stories meant to scare him, but stories that only lived in old books about forgotten times.

Bugs and men and fires roared in the overrun courtyard. Hot ash fell all around them, and Jacob tried to ignore the tiny embers that smoked when they hit his arms. Smashed carriages lay strewn about the small fountain. Knights were on the ground, unmoving in pools of dark red liquid. Jacob's stomach fluttered as he realized the men were lying in their own blood.

"Behind you!" Samuel leapt across the courtyard in front of them. He jumped off Bessie's back and dove into a knot of Walkers. Bessie followed him in. Countless legs rose and fell as the beasts reared up and struck at the city's defenders.

Jacob turned, bringing the barrel of the gun around with him. He almost screamed when he saw the huge glinting eyes of a Red Death a few steps away. Something gray and metallic was stuck in the top of its head, but Jacob didn't have time to care. He raised the gunstock to his shoulder and his fingers squeezed the trigger. The gun sounded like a cannon as it slammed him up against Charles.

Charles shouted and the bike wobbled for a moment, but relief flooded Jacob as he watched the Red Death stumble and collapse.

"Hold on tight!" Charles said.

Jacob put one arm around the old man and kept a death grip on the gun. Charles swerved past bulk of an invader, and something crunched under the steambike.

As soon as the bike straightened out, Jacob primed the air gun again. "Where's the ammo!"

"I told you, it's loaded. Self-feeding, you won't need to reload before we're inside."

Jacob watched as a Widow Maker surged over the enraged Walkers

Samuel fought. It raised its front legs and reared back. Jacob knew it was about to strike at one of the Spider Knights. Jacob aimed high. He didn't want to risk hitting a knight. "Firing!"

Jacob felt Charles tense a moment before he pulled the trigger. The gun boomed, slamming against Jacob's shoulder as a Widow Maker's legs spun away in a fountain of blue blood. It caught the attention of one knight. He ran the spider through with two quick jabs from his spear.

The gates started closing. The knights were falling back, ever closer to them. Charles didn't slow down. He blazed through the gates, nearly crushing the feet of the gatemen on either side.

Jacob didn't look back to see how many knights came through the gate behind them. He only prayed that Samuel had made it out. Samuel, he'd jumped into that knot of Walkers with no hesitation. The scene played over in Jacob's mind. Without Samuel, at least one of the knights facing the Walkers would have died, maybe more. He shivered, and his knuckles turned white where his hands clenched around the gun.

"Are you okay?"

Jacob didn't really hear the man speaking, or realize who it was, until Samuel grabbed Jacob's face and tilted it up.

"Are you okay?" Samuel asked again.

Jacob nodded. He wanted to ask where his family was, where Alice was. Jacob wanted to tell Samuel how happy he was to see him, ask him what had caused the huge dent in his chest plate. Every time Jacob opened his mouth to speak, no words would come.

"Dammit, Charles," Samuel said. "The kid's shaking like it's winter."

"It's shock," Charles said, adjusting a saddlebag and pulling out a metal wedge. "It will pass. He's a tough kid." Charles stood up, resting the bike against the angled metal piece. He carefully pried Jacob's hands off the gun, holstering the weapon across his back once he'd gotten it free.

Samuel turned back to Jacob. "I told your parents to go to my uncle's.

We'll find them there, okay? I'm sure they're fine."

A high-pitched scream rang out closer to the gates. There was a man being wheeled away from the gatehouse on the back of a cart. A huge green scythe stuck out from his chest. It took Jacob a moment to realize it wasn't a scythe, but the foreleg of a mantis, like one of those he'd seen earlier, pulling a carriage. A woman ran beside the cart. Her dress was emerald green where it wasn't doused in blood. She looked like royalty. The man reached out and touched her hand before he went limp.

Jacob didn't think the man could possibly survive. There was so much blood, and then, as the cart moved a little farther, Jacob could see the mass of wounded knights laid out before the gatehouse. Some of them moved, some were tended by doctors or friends, but the rest were covered in stained white sheets.

"Alice," Jacob said, turning away from that awful scene. "Did Alice make it?" He swallowed, trying to get the tremor out of his voice. "I left her … I told her to run."

"You told her right," Samuel said.

Something outside the walls screeched, and everyone around Jacob cringed.

"You told her right."

CHAPTER ELEVEN

Jacob and Charles waited by the steambike while Samuel reported in to his commander. Their escape had been a very near thing. Jacob leaned against a polished stone wall once the tremors from adrenaline finally stopped. The building was small for the city, only two and a half stories, but shops didn't need to be large near the gates. They received more traffic than they could handle on most days, and today saw the stores swollen with wide-eyed citizens, unsure of what to do with themselves.

Children screamed, dragged into alleys and makeshift hospitals by wounded parents. Some people only stood, staring at nothing, as though they could see right through the crowds around them. Several Lowlanders gathered in clusters around the courtyard with nothing on their backs but the Festival clothes they'd worn, slowly getting ushered away by knights and the Highland police force.

Amid all the chaos, a Highlander stopped to ask Charles about the steambike.

"And it stays upright?" he asked. "With only two wheels?"

Charles nodded and ran a hand over his beard. "Same principle as a kid's bicycle, only bigger, and faster."

"Amazing," the man said, leaning down to look at the brass and copper piping around the boiler. He studied it for another minute or so in silence before extending his hand to Charles. "I do appreciate the distraction, my friend. You do good works."

Charles smiled and bowed his head slightly. "Appreciate it."

The man wandered away. Jacob's gaze followed him until his eyes caught the glint of Samuel's dented breastplate in the city streetlamps. The lights here were more like magic than fire. Not entirely unlike the small lightbulb Charles had been working on, but much larger and much brighter.

"They're impressive," Charles said while Jacob glanced between Samuel and the nearest light. "They're a terrible waste, though."

"What do you mean?"

"The power it takes to light one of those lamps for a night?" Charles said as he pointed at the soft golden glow. "You could power the water pumps in the Lowlands for an entire month."

Jacob raised an eyebrow and looked at Charles.

"Don't believe me?"

"Well …" Jacob started to say he didn't, but then he remembered some of the stories he'd heard. "My dad always said it was different here, in the Highlands. I haven't been since I was a little kid, but I've always wanted to come back. He used to tell me how life inside the walls is a different world from the Lowlands."

"He's not wrong," Charles said. "You'll find softer people here, and more cunning people." He kept his focus on the street. "Here's Samuel."

"I'm to stay armored," Samuel said, stepping up beside them as he adjusted the sheath belted at his waist, "but I can escort you to my uncle's."

"What about Bessie?" Jacob asked.

"She's staying at the stables tonight in case the watch needs her, and she's getting patched up. One of the Walkers managed to crack the armor under Bessie's saddle."

"You mean, where you sit?" Jacob asked.

Samuel nodded as they began walking down the street, Charles pushing the steambike.

"Thankfully, I wasn't sitting there at the time. Hard to believe I was better off going toe to toe with one of those Walkers than staying in Bessie's saddle."

"Bessie's okay?"

"Oh, she'll be fine," Samuel said. "She was bleeding a bit, but we got the dressing on her pretty quick. She'll heal up after a little rest and some water."

"That's good," Jacob said as they turned a corner and followed the road up a long, gentle hill. The cobblestones here were even, making the footing easy. "The roads are so flat here."

Charles huffed as he pushed the steambike. "Good thing too, or I wouldn't make it."

"You want a hand with that, Charles?" Samuel asked. "I'd be happy to get it up the hill for you."

Charles shook his head. "Fine, I'm fine." He took a few deep breaths and leaned into the bike. "Besides, anything comes over that wall, you'll need to be swinging that sword, not pushing this damned bike."

Samuel smiled and pointed at the next intersection. "Take a left here, and my uncle's place is on the next corner."

"Wow," Jacob said. The storefront burst with colors and a modest pyramid of fudge in the front window.

Samuel glanced over at the building with the blue awnings and nodded. "Best sweets shop in town." He lowered his voice and said, "If you ask the owner."

Jacob smiled slightly as they walked by. He watched a small girl pull an enormous cone-shaped candy out of a display made up like a rainbow-colored tree. Each branch of the little tree had different colors, shapes, and sizes of candy. More stayed behind a petite glass display on the dark wood counter. She handed the candy to a small boy whose head was wrapped in a bandage. Jacob frowned.

"You can take Alice there later," Samuel said.

Jacob turned away from the shop at the mention of her name.

A minute later, Samuel helped Charles slide two wide doors into the walls on either side of his uncle's home, revealing a dark room beyond.

Jacob stared up at the brick face of the building. "How many floors is that?"

Samuel grunted. "Five."

Jacob's gaze trailed down from the distant roof, past the smooth stone of the balconies and decorative mosaic of a giant Jumper, to the doorway they'd just opened. He almost jogged into the workshop behind Charles and Samuel once he saw what was inside. It wasn't as grand as Charles's lab in the old observatory, but someone had filled it with enough tools and gadgets to keep Jacob occupied for hours.

"This is fantastic," Charles said, setting the metal wedge beneath the steambike.

"I know it's small …" Samuel said. "This used to be my uncle's stables."

Charles shook his head. "It's plenty big for what I need. Thank you. Truly." Charles reached out and grasped Samuel's hand.

"Come on inside. I'll introduce you to my uncle and we can see who else is staying with us." Samuel tugged the outer doors closed and hooked two simple metal latches on the interior.

Jacob followed Samuel and Charles through an arched doorway. The door would have looked just as good in the Hall in the Lowlands, all ancient oak and iron bars.

"Jacob!"

Jacob just had time to smile before his mother crossed the room and threatened to suffocate him in a bear hug. He heard Charles and Samuel talking to someone, their voices muffled by his mother's. Jacob barely made out that Charles was going upstairs to get some rest. He tried to say goodnight, but his face was fully smothered by the ruffles on his mother's green dress. For a moment, he remembered the Highlander at the city gates, her dress splashed in gore, and he shivered.

"Thank the gods you're okay," his mother said. She put a hand on either side of his face.

"Is Dad here? Is he okay?"

"Yes, honey, yes. We're both fine. Samuel—bless him—Samuel helped us evacuate the street."

"Good thing he did," a tall, broad-shouldered man said. He stroked a salt-and-pepper beard before narrowing his eyes and extending his hand. "You must be Jacob."

Jacob shook his hand, and it felt like half his arm disappeared into the man's palm. The man was *huge*.

"This is my uncle, Bartholomew," Samuel said, settling onto the floor and leaning against the wall.

"Call me Bat," Samuel's uncle said. "Full name's got too many letters to do anyone much good." He grinned, and it lifted the edges of his beard.

Bat turned around and led the way into a parlor. The room was so large it made Bat look normal, and everyone else look small. A low, round table sat in the center of the room. Crushed velvet peeked out from between three women and a small stack of photographs. Jacob guessed the photos used to be displayed across the table, but they'd been stacked up to make room.

Bat introduced everyone as Jacob took a seat beside his father on a long, wood-framed couch. A large chandelier hung from the ceiling. It looked like iron with candles as thick as Jacob's arm. He followed the chain up to the ceiling and turned his head so he could trace it to the far wall and down to a brass crank. The chain seemed like a much better idea than what they used in the Lowlands. Rope, no matter how well treated, could still catch fire.

He turned his attention back to the people in the room while Bat continued talking. It surprised Jacob how few of those people were members of Samuel's family. It seemed Bat was taking in anyone who needed shelter. There were three other families from the Lowlands. They were all older than his parents and seated on ornate, paisley-patterned chairs and another wood-framed couch on the far wall. A few of the younger folks in the group sat on the ground, leaning against walls or family members.

Jacob couldn't remember half the names by the time Bat was done. It all turned to mush. He was just happy to be with his parents again.

His dad coughed, and Jacob was glad to hear it didn't sound as bad as it had the night before. He still looked pale, but the doctor had said it could take a while for that to change.

A sudden snore betrayed Samuel's exhaustion.

Bat looked down at his nephew and smiled. "It's been a long day for everyone. Let me show you to your rooms. Some of you will need to share, but we have plenty of space." He started taking people away in groups. Some climbed the stairway that spiraled up in the northwestern corner of the room, while others trailed to the back of the house behind it.

"Did you see Alice?" Jacob asked, turning to his mother. The room had quieted down, and the loudest sound left was Samuel's snoring. Bat escorted another group away.

"We didn't," his mom said.

"Don't worry," Jacob's dad said. "You know Alice can take care of herself." He took two deep breaths.

"I left her in the Square," Jacob said. "I never should have left her."

"You did the best thing anyone could have done," Samuel said, his voice groggy. He slowly climbed to his feet, the plates of his armor slithering together and clinking as he adjusted the mail shirt beneath. "I already told you that, kid. You know she made it."

"We saw so many people," Jacob said. He looked toward the shadowed corner of the far hall. "So many didn't make it."

Samuel took a few steps and put a gauntleted hand on Jacob's shoulder. "You just wait. You'll see her again."

Bat came down the stairs and paused. He watched Samuel for a moment before coming closer. "Samuel, why don't you take my room."

"Because it's on the fifth floor?" Samuel said.

Bat smiled at him. "Go on. You could use the tub. You're looking a little rough."

Samuel nodded. "Goodnight. Let me know if the gatehouse comes calling."

Bat patted Samuel's shoulder as the Spider Knight walked by and started up the spiral staircase. Jacob watched him until Samuel vanished into the floor above.

"You can explore tomorrow if you like," Bat said. "Find your friends and go anywhere you want. Nothing's off limits."

"Don't tell him that," Jacob's dad said with a small smile.

"Would you all mind spending the night here?" Bat asked. "I know there's not much privacy, but we have a lot of guests this evening."

"It's no problem at all," Jacob's mom said. "Please, don't concern yourself. We're perfectly comfortable here." She patted the couch cushion.

Bat nodded.

"Are you going to put the candles out?" Jacob asked, looking up at the chandelier.

"Ah," Bat said. "Samuel told me you were one for gears and gadgets. Come here, boy. I'd like to show you something."

"You're going to lower it?" Jacob asked. He walked over to join Bat by the wheel and lever that would lower the chandelier.

Bat shook his head. "You see this lever?" he asked, placing his hand on a lever beside the chain supporting the chandelier. Jacob hadn't noticed the other chain. It was thin, so fine it almost disappeared beside the thicker chain. "Pull it."

Jacob wrapped his hand around the cool metal and pulled. Something in the wall whirred and clicked.

Bat pointed to a chandelier. "Watch."

Half spheres of metal arced slowly up across each candle, sealing it off and putting the room into a darkness broken only by a small lantern on an end table.

"You have automatic snuffers?" Jacob asked, squinting at the chandelier. "Where do you wind them up? What's the ratio like on the gearbox?" He fired off three more questions before Bat held up his hands in surrender.

"I couldn't tell you," Bat said with a small laugh, "but you and Charles are welcome to poke around tomorrow."

CHAPTER TWELVE

"No!"

Jacob bolted upright from the nest of blankets he'd made on the floor by the couch. He stared at his shaking hands, remembering the screams and the tears and the blood. Jacob closed his eyes and took a few deep breaths, clenching his hands into fists.

He opened his eyes and looked at the window across the room. Daylight was just breaking through the darkness, etching a thin line of gold around the shuttered glass.

He lay back down and pulled a blanket up to his neck. "It was only a dream," he whispered to himself. "Dad's okay, Alice is okay, Bradley … it was only a dream." He squeezed his eyes shut, but it only brought the horrible vision back to life. He'd told her to run. She'd trusted him. The mantis had been so fast when it stabbed Alice. His dad tried to help and then they both …

Jacob's eyes snapped open. He hoped the vision of his father and Alice tumbling off the cliff with the mantis would go away. It didn't. At the bottom, their bodies fell beside Bradley. Jacob stared at the high ceiling for a time, remembering the screams and how quickly Bradley had disappeared into the horde. Exhaustion finally won out, and Jacob stole another hour of restless sleep.

✧ ✧ ✧

BAT SERVED A FANTASTIC BREAKFAST of fruit and flatcakes. Jacob was pretty sure some of the people staying with Samuel's uncle hadn't had food that good in a very long time. They were all so grateful, but Bat would hear nothing of it. It made Jacob smile, knowing that Samuel's uncle could do something so nice for people without expecting to be repaid.

He'd explained to his parents that he planned to ask after Alice at the hospitals. They didn't complain when he told them he wanted to go, as long as he promised to be back for dinner.

Jacob found himself waiting outside the candy shop a bit later. He leaned up against the wall and sighed, watching the people mill around the stone street. No one in the tents near the gate remembered seeing a redheaded girl. A piercing cry caught Jacob's attention. He couldn't see who was screaming, but he ran down the block, dodging Highlanders and Lowlanders alike. The scream grew louder, and when he turned toward the sound, he saw a little boy, not more than six, being wheeled into a small stone building.

The boy's arm was bandaged, and blood seeped through the gauze. The boy screamed again and raised his wounded arm. Jacob walked closer to see what was happening when he noticed the arm looked shorter than it should. He clenched his jaw when he realized the boy's hand was missing.

He heard more cries from inside the building as he neared it. A few more steps took him to the doorway, and he could hear the moans of men and women mixed with the cries of a dozen children. Doctors worked frantically over the wounded, applying tourniquets and balms where they could. Bloody sheets and rags were strewn around the room. A young nurse with red eyes gathered them up as fast as she could, placing them inside a hamper.

"Give me another belt!" one of the doctors shouted when the boy was wheeled up beside him. "He's bleeding out. Get me a goddamned belt!"

Jacob met the eyes of another boy, his head wrapped in a bandage that covered one of his eyes. The boy nodded slightly, and Jacob started to wave until he recognized the face. He backed away as fast as he could until he bumped into someone.

"Careful where you're walking, son."

Jacob glanced up at the old woman. It wasn't the same nurse he'd seen earlier. Her hair was long and gray and pulled up into a tight bun, except for a single braid. She wore a plain white apron covered in pockets and adorned with a red cross. She shuffled toward the building.

"Have you seen a red-haired girl named Alice?"

She shook her head. "Red hair, you say? I would have remembered that I think."

"What happened to them?" Jacob asked, glancing at the patients inside.

"They just came in from the Lowlands," the woman said. "Lucky they're alive. Most of them, anyhow."

He wanted to go back in and say hi to the injured boy he recognized. He knew it was Bobby, but there was so much blood. Jacob's stomach soured and he put his hand over his mouth. He could be strong. He could be like Samuel. Jacob took a few deep breaths and walked up the street a little ways. He paused and looked around when he realized he was back by the shop where he and Charles had waited for Samuel.

Jacob pulled a silver piece out of his pocket. He knew he needed it for his dad's medicine, but he had to do *something*. He hurried back up the hill and headed for the sweets shop. He didn't hesitate as he set the coin on the counter and waited for the girl in the red-and-white-striped hat. She started over to him when she finished helping an older woman and her kids.

"Hi there," she said. "What can I help you with?"

Jacob pushed the silver coin closer to the clerk. "What can I get for this?"

She laughed and said, "More than you can eat."

"It's not for me."

"Really?" the girl asked.

"It's for …" Jacob turned his head, almost like he was trying to see down the hill, through the walls. "It's not …"

The girl followed his gaze and frowned. "Are you … are you buying these for the kids at the hospital? The ones who were hurt?"

Jacob nodded. He refused to cry, but Bobby's face and that boy's screams flashed through his mind. He was afraid if he tried to speak, he'd just embarrass himself by crying in front of a stranger.

The girl wasn't nearly so reserved. "That's so nice," she said as she hung her head. "I should have thought of it." She took a deep breath and had a broad smile for Jacob when she looked up, even with the tears in her eyes. "Wait here, will you? And put that silver back in your pocket."

"But I need to—" Jacob stopped talking when he remembered Bobby again. Bobby had been fast, and a good Cork player, and now he was laid up with gods only knew what kind of injuries.

The girl shook her head. "In your pocket." She disappeared into the back room.

Jacob stared at the Cocoa Crunch piled up in the counter display. It looked better than what he and Alice had shared. He hoped so much that she was okay. She had to be okay. His thoughts returned to his nightmare and he shivered.

The girl came back into the front with two enormous paper bags in either hand. "Here, you take this to the kids."

"I can't pay for this," Jacob said, his voice quiet.

The girl leaned over the counter until her brown eyes were level with his. "I won't let you pay for this." She stood up and pushed the bags toward Jacob.

"Thank you," Jacob said, pocketing his silver. "Thank you so much." He gathered the bags up in his arms. He could scarcely comprehend the girl's generosity. People could be kind in the Lowlands, but no one could afford to be *that* generous. He kept both arms wrapped tightly around the bags as he made his way back to the hospital.

Someone screamed again as Jacob paused in the entryway, and he felt foolish for thinking candy would help anyone. The kids, though ... it might help them a little. He stood up straighter and walked through the open front doors. The bloody sheets were no longer strewn across the ground, but small wet stains betrayed where they'd been.

Jacob walked up to a small wooden table and set the bags down. He opened the first and could barely contain his surprise. He knew the bags had been heavy, but inside was enough Cocoa Crunch to feed fifty people. He unrolled the other bag and found an enormous pile of Bitter Bears. Jacob frowned. Kids didn't like Bitter Bears—if they had any sense, at least—but adults loved the awful things. The candy store clerk had been thinking even more than he had.

"What's that?" a nurse asked, stepping up beside Jacob.

"It's, uh, I brought it for the kids."

She peeked into the bags and then looked at Jacob. "You brought this? Just for ..." She looked around the room slowly. There was an old man slumped over in the corner beside a bed with a young girl. Bobby was along the other wall, and there wasn't an empty bed to be seen in the place. "That's very nice of you."

"It's stupid," Jacob said. "They're all hurt, and I just brought candy." He felt even more stupid as he eyed Bobby's bandaged head again. "Stupid."

There was a pressure on his shoulder, and he looked up at the nurse. "This was not stupid." Jacob didn't know why it appeared the nurse was going to cry again. He hadn't seen anyone new come into the hospital.

The nurse grabbed Jacob and hugged him. "Thank you, thank you. This was not stupid."

Jacob wasn't sure how to react, so he kept his arms stiff at his sides and studied the room awkwardly until the nurse finally let go.

"Go take some to your friend," the nurse said. "Bobby said he knows you. I'll pass out the rest. I'll check with the doctor. I know some candies are bad with pain medicine, but I'll take care of that."

Jacob watched her shuffle around the room for a moment, handing out little round Bitter Bears to the adults. A kid took some too, and Jacob figured he must have been hit in the head pretty hard to be eating the things. Jacob took a deep breath and walked over to Bobby's bed.

"Hey, Bobby," he said.

Bobby slowly turned his head so his uncovered eye was looking at Jacob. "You made it."

Jacob inclined his head. "What about …" Jacob started to say, but he had to gather himself to ask. "What about Reggie?"

Bobby nodded. "He made it. Not a scratch on him, either." Bobby pointed at the bandage covering his right eye and the side of his head. There was a faint red patch bleeding through. "I wasn't so lucky."

"You got a scratch?" Jacob asked, trying to lighten Bobby's mood.

Bobby smiled a little. "Yeah, you could say that. Doc stitched my ear back together, but it's never going to look right. My eye's okay too. When I got hit, I couldn't see. Doc says it was just all the blood."

Jacob nodded, trying not to remember the blood, and glanced at the little boy sleeping in the corner. He had fresh bandages where his hand used to be. Someone, maybe his mother, stared at him from her seat beside the bed. Her shoulders were slumped, her hair matted and messy.

"I know," Bobby said, drawing Jacob's attention away from the boy. "It could have been a lot worse."

"It's not much," Jacob said as he handed Bobby a small square wrapped in twine, "but there's some for everyone."

"Crunch?" Bobby asked as something approaching a real smile appeared on his face. "From a city shop?"

Jacob nodded. "Right down on the corner. They gave me more than I could pay for and then didn't let me pay for anything."

"My dad used to tell us no one in the city cared about anyone but themselves," Bobby said before he took a bite of the Cocoa Crunch.

The rich smell of chocolate and toffee hit Jacob, and he realized he was hungry. Jacob watched the nurse disappear into one of the back rooms. The loudest scream quieted down before the nurse reappeared.

She smiled at Jacob and held up a bag of candy. He was glad to see it was doing some good, however small.

"There are good people here," Bobby said, watching the nurse enter another room. "Dad was wrong."

"Charles says there are good people everywhere," Jacob said. He paused before continuing. "And bad people. People will always be people. So, where's Reggie?"

"Out with Alice, looking for you," Bobby said as he stuffed another bite of Cocoa Crunch into his mouth. "I tried to tell you, but you ran off." He stared at Jacob as he chewed, just waiting.

"Alice?" Jacob asked when his mind finally processed Bobby's words. "Alice is okay? Why didn't you tell me that first!"

"I thought it would be funnier if I waited until she was standing right behind you." Bobby smiled and finished his candy.

Jacob spun around. Alice was close enough to touch. Her gaze lingered on the boy who had lost his hand. There were tears in her eyes as she looked at the room full of wounded kids, until she saw Jacob. Jacob only hesitated a moment before wrapping Alice up in a bear hug, blinking away his own tears.

"You're here," she said, squeezing him until he thought his ribs might crack.

"I am," Jacob said, hugging her tight before letting her go. He didn't like seeing the tears in her bright blue eyes.

Alice stared at Jacob. "We were looking for you. I didn't know if you made it. You ran off after Charles, and then the walls fell. They weren't just breached, Jacob. They *fell!*"

"Samuel helped me," Jacob said, keeping his eyes on floor. "I came back on the steambike with Charles."

"I'm so glad you're alive," Alice said before she briefly hugged Jacob again.

"Where's my hug?" Reggie asked through a mouthful of Cocoa Crunch.

Jacob smiled at the taller of the two brothers. "I'm glad you guys made it. I'd hate to see the team broken up so soon."

"We're a team now?" Bobby asked. "Not sure how good my aim will be with this bandage on."

"Just heal up," Jacob said. "We'll have plenty of time for Cork once you're up and about. Where are you staying?"

"We'll be here for a few days at least," Reggie said. "Doc says Bobby has to stay off his feet until they're sure he didn't get any venom exposure."

"I'm over at the Midnight Inn with my parents," Alice said.

"Right off City Square?" Bobby asked.

Alice nodded. "We can't afford it, if that's what that look is for. My father's cousin owns it."

"We're staying with Samuel's uncle," Jacob said. "It's on the other side of the sweets shop. You can't miss it."

Bobby grimaced and held his hand up to his head. "Sorry, I think I need to lie down."

"Of course, of course," Alice said. "We'll leave you alone."

"We'll be here if you need us," Reggie said.

Jacob looked up at him. "I'm glad you made it."

"Me too," Reggie said with a small smile.

"I have to tell my folks I found you," Jacob said. Then he lowered his voice. "And I have an idea for that boy who lost his hand." He walked back toward the front door with Alice.

She nodded. "I think I'll stay here a while."

"You're okay?" he asked.

She reached out to hug him again and nodded into his shoulder. "I am, but these kids …"

"I know." Jacob almost asked if she wanted to come back with him, but he knew she'd want to stay and help in the hospital if she could. "Come and find me later?"

"I will," she said. She slowly released Jacob and they parted ways.

CHAPTER THIRTEEN

J ACOB HEARD ONE OF THE doors slide open behind him, but he didn't turn his attention away from the metal spring he had stretched out between his hands. The brass cylinder that encased the spring reminded him of a small piston. It was hard to get a grip on it without the right gloves, but his fingernails held on well enough.

The metal loop at the end of the spring-loaded cylinder slid over the threads of a screw. Jacob sighed as he released the tension. He grabbed a threaded nut from the same jar he'd taken the screw from and hand-tightened the whole assembly into place. With the fifth pairing in place, the contraption finally took shape.

"What are you working on there, Jacob?"

Jacob didn't have to turn around to know it was Charles. He leaned back and stared at the webwork of brackets and springs and screws. "I saw a kid in the hospital that lost his hand."

Charles leaned over while Jacob topped all the screws with a brass cap and began tightening them with a wrench. "So you're making him a new one?"

Jacob slammed the tool against the bench and clenched his hands together. "I can't make him a new one; he *lost* his *hand*. I just … I just want to help."

"Let me take a look," Charles said as he picked up the pile of black webbing and brass fittings. He pulled at the base of each cylinder and nodded until he got to the thumb. "This one's a bit too easy to move. He'll drop whatever he's trying to pick up if it's heavy."

Charles set the hand back onto the workbench and started digging through one of the saddlebags on his bike. "Ah, here we are. Change that thumb spring out for this."

Jacob took the thicker cylinder from Charles's hand and looked it over. He tried to pull the spring out with his fingernail, but it wouldn't budge. "Too tight."

Charles shook his head. "Nonsense. Take that other spring off."

Jacob did while he half watched Charles pull a flat tool out from under the bench. He slid it into the vise mounted beside Jacob, tightened it, gave it a shake, and then nodded.

"Now," Charles said, "you be careful when you use one of these. That spring has a lot of power. You keep your eyes away from it when stretch the tensioner." Charles picked up the hand after Jacob removed the smaller spring with a sharp snap.

Charles fastened a clamp on one end of the hand, and adjusted the length of the tensioner with a wheel on the side before setting a second screw into an isolated clamp. "Push that bar down."

Jacob leaned slightly on the wooden handle sticking out of the tensioner. The lone screw slid forward and stopped when it was even with the thumb bracket. "Perfect, pull that handle in and let's see that spring."

Jacob put the handle back in place and then slid one of the metal loops onto either screw.

Charles bent down and squinted before nodding. "You see how it's set between the threads? That's how you want it." Charles pulled the handle, and the spring whined as it stretched out the length of the hand. "If you miss the threads, it's more likely to come right off the screw without catching."

Jacob slid the thumb bracket over the tensioned screw at the end of the cylinder, and Charles began tightening the whole assembly.

"That should do it." Charles lifted the mechanical hand as Jacob released the tensioner. The hand curled into a fist as it slid off the tool.

Charles stared at the hand and slowly raised his eyes to Jacob. "It's a magnificent design. Simple but effective. Did you sketch it out?"

Jacob shook his head.

"All in your mind?"

"It just made sense. It works like a real hand. Mostly."

"How do you open it?" Charles asked.

Jacob was pretty sure Charles could tell and was just humoring him. "Turn the big knob."

Charles lowered a lens on his glasses and turned the hand over. He twisted the brass knob on the back of the wrist, and Jacob watched the line of gears mesh and twist, easily opening the hand. "Magnificent."

Jacob sat up a little straighter, unable to stop himself from smiling.

"If you put a glove over this, one would scarcely know it was mechanical."

It sounded like Charles was talking about hiding the hand. Jacob wasn't sure why at first, but then he asked, "Do you think people will make fun of him for it?"

Charles nodded. "Not for this hand, mind you, but just for being different. It's the way of the world."

Jacob thought back to all the horrible things his classmates had said to him when his dad first got sick and couldn't join them for Cork on family day. His dad had just started having trouble breathing. People could be mean, and some of the kids he knew were the worst. Jacob's hand clenched into a fist until he remembered something else Charles had said.

I have no use for cruelty.

He watched Charles for a moment while the old man poked and prodded at the bindings on the glove and checked each gear in the mechanism. Charles eventually nodded and looked up.

"Couldn't have done it better myself."

"Really?" Jacob asked.

"Well, except for the thumb spring, but you already fixed that."

Jacob smiled and took the hand from Charles. "You don't think it's silly?"

Charles shook his head. "No, my boy, I think it's a gift. Now, I'll tell you, when you first give it to the injured child, he may not know how to react. Don't think that's a judgment on you or your work. It's going to take time for him to understand his injury. It always does."

"You've known people like him?"

"Yes, I knew many soldiers in the war. A lot of them died, but some survived without legs to carry them or arms to hug their families."

"Did you ever build them new arms?"

Charles nodded. "In some ways, yes. I never thought to make such a simple design though, Jacob. I built powered limbs with Burners and actuators. They were far more complex, and a great deal of work to maintain. I suppose I felt a need to show off when I was younger."

"Now you just build steambikes," Jacob said.

Charles narrowed his eyes and laughed before he slapped Jacob on the shoulder. "That I do. That I do." He dug through the other saddlebag and pulled out a black glove. "Here, see if this will fit over that hand."

Jacob held the arm up while Charles pulled the fingers down snugly over the mechanism. Jacob set the hand on the workbench and they both stood back. Jacob couldn't help but smile. It looked like a real gloved hand, aside from the knob that stuck out to adjust the tension.

Charles put his hand on Jacob's shoulder. "You've done a good thing here. Pack it up and take it down to the hospital. Those people need some good news."

✧   ✧   ✧

JACOB TRIPPED AND CURSED BEFORE Charles caught his arm. "Careful now. We don't want to be in need of the hospital's services by the time we get there."

Jacob glanced back at the metal plate in the street he'd tripped on. A simple square seemed an odd shape for a sewer cover.

"You know what those holes in the street are for?" Charles asked.

"The sewers, you mean?" Jacob said. "Everybody knows that."

"No," Charles said. "I mean the holes covered with squares of steel." He pointed out another of the hinged doors in the street as they walked by it. "Like the one you tripped on."

It looked rusty, and Jacob had serious doubts that anyone could open it. "What are they?"

"There's a train track under the streets."

"What?" Jacob asked, and he couldn't keep the laugh out of his voice. "That's ridiculous."

"Before the war, it served the trade routes. Once the fighting began in earnest, we used it to smuggle goods beneath the walls. Not everyone in Dauschen was against us, even if they were allied with the desert cities. That's when the bridge was built across the mountain pass."

"Really?" Jacob asked, the laughter gone from his voice. He knew Dauschen had been a powerful enemy in the Deadlands War, but they'd slowly helped build up a trade alliance in the decades after the war. Jacob had seen that track more times than he could count, but he always assumed it wound around the mountain and went somewhere else. If what Charles said was actually true, that meant the tracks didn't go around the mountain, they ran straight into the cliff face and under the city. "The tracks are still there?"

Charles nodded. "Through doors like those, and down into the catacombs."

Jacob adjusted the backpack he was carrying that held the mechanical arm. "Can we go down one? After we finish at the hospital?"

"Do you have a key?" Charles asked.

"No," Jacob said. "You need a key?"

"Yes, most of the catacombs have been locked for the better part of a decade."

"There has to be some way down," Jacob said. He stepped around a woman in a fine cream gown, pushing a baby stroller. She spun a lace parasol in her hand and nodded to Jacob. He smiled before Charles grabbed him by the collar. "What?" he asked as he looked up.

"Food," Charles said, handing a street vendor two coppers. "Two plain."

"Here you are," the vendor said. He passed Charles two long, thin pieces of bread.

"What is that?" Jacob asked.

"Saltbread." Charles stuffed the end of one piece into his mouth and handed Jacob the other.

Jacob hesitated, and then took a bite. He *was* hungry, after all. The bread was slightly chewy with a thin crust all around it, and the salt crunched on the outside. "This is great!" He promptly stuffed half the saltbread into his cheek.

"Can't get it in the Lowlands," Charles said. "It's an old recipe they keep guarded."

They passed a man in a finely cut suit, perfectly cleaned. He raised the edge of his lip and exhaled in disgust. "Lowland filth. They should have left them outside the wall."

"What the hell?" Jacob said as he slowed his pace. The man kept walking as though nothing out of the ordinary had been said.

Charles grabbed Jacob's arm and ushered him along. "Ignore them. You'll find many Highborns who don't sympathize with the plight of the Lowlands. For all we know, that man may own one of the inns that are sheltering so many of the Lowlanders, commanded by Parliament to do so. Many people here have influence and power, and sometimes it's best not to antagonize them."

It didn't feel right to Jacob, and the man's snide words gnawed at him. He finished the saltbread, and once that distraction was no more, he realized he was actually nervous. "Is this a good idea? It just doesn't seem like enough."

"Do not doubt yourself," Charles said.

Jacob took a deep breath as he walked through the front door of the hospital. It was still light outside, but most of the people in the front seemed to be asleep.

"They've had a long couple days," Charles said.

Jacob nodded and led Charles past the thin linen divider. He smiled when he saw Reggie against the left wall beside Bobby's bed, both snoring. Jacob looked to his right and the boy stared back. His mother slouched at his side, and the heavy bags under her eyes told Jacob how exhausted she was.

"Hi," Jacob said, sliding off his backpack and setting it on the foot of the bed. "I saw your hand."

The boy slowly moved his injured arm under the blanket.

"How could you?" his mother said. She started to stand up.

"No, no, no," Jacob said as he hurried to open his backpack. Charles made a placating gesture to the mother, and Jacob was relieved as she eased herself back into the chair. "Here, look."

He held up the gloved mechanical arm. The black leather looked slick in the bright lanterns of the hospital.

"What is it?" the boy asked. His arm slipped out of the blanket as he grew more interested in what Jacob was holding up.

"It's, umm … it's to help you." Jacob peeled the edge of the glove back to reveal the brace.

"How far down is your arm cut, son?" Charles asked.

The boy held up his injured arm and pointed to a spot about two inches below his wrist.

Charles eyed the ties of the brace and nodded. "It should be safe to try it on, but I wouldn't wear it too much until you heal up a bit more."

Jacob held the brace up. "Want to?"

The boy nodded.

"Slide your arm in and I'll tie it up."

The boy winced as he bumped his wrist against the brace. Jacob heard the mother inhale sharply, but she didn't stop them. Once the boy had his arm all the way in, Jacob pulled the ties and buckled the strap farthest from the injury, close to the boy's elbow.

"Okay, once you're healed, there are two more straps you can tighten. It'll make it more stable. Now turn that knob."

The boy reached over with his left hand and began twisting it. He smiled when the hand began to open.

Jacob looked around and found a glass on the bedside table. "Here," he said, holding it out. "Put your hand up next to it and pull that second lever."

The boy did, and the fingers slowly closed around the glass. Jacob let go.

The glass stayed in the hand.

"Oh my goodness," the mother said.

Jacob glanced at her to find her hand over her mouth and tears in her eyes. It surprised him.

"It's amazing," the boy said. He tugged the glove down to cover everything but the knob. He smiled and took a drink from the glass. "You can't even tell I don't have a hand."

"You don't have to hide it," Jacob said.

The boy twisted the knob and gently set the glass on his bedside table. "What's the other lever do?"

Jacob didn't press him any more about hiding his hand. "It releases all the tension and makes a fist. Go ahead and … Wait, don't do that. It may give your arm a jolt."

"It's so amazing." He looked up and smiled. "Thank you. What's your name?"

"I'm Jacob. The old guy is Charles."

Charles harrumphed and the boy's mother laughed.

"My name's Peter."

"That's my dad's name too," Jacob said.

"You have any problems with that," Charles said with a nod to Peter's arm, "bring it over to the house next door to the sweets shop. We'll fix you right up. Come on, Jacob. Let's go."

Peter's mom stood up and hugged them both. "Thank you."

Charles nodded and Jacob gave her an awkward smile while she hugged him again.

They walked out the door and back into the busy street.

Charles looked at Jacob for a moment before he said, "Hold your head up high, kid. You did a good thing in there."

Jacob thought he might never stop smiling.

CHAPTER FOURTEEN

A WEEK PASSED BEFORE THE terror of the invasion had subsided enough for boredom to set in. Jacob couldn't get the thought of the old catacombs out of his head. He watched Charles tinkering with an old watch on the makeshift workbench. The old man still had his goggles. Jacob tried not to laugh when one of the lenses got stuck and Charles had both his hands over his head, trying to loosen the hinge.

Charles raised an eyebrow. "You could give an old man a hand instead of laughing at him."

"How long are you going to work on that watch?" Jacob asked. He untied a leather roll, spread it out, and slid a tiny screwdriver from one of its slots.

"It's almost done," Charles said, putting his arms down.

Jacob leaned in and started fiddling with the hinge on Charles's lenses. "Looks like there's something stuck in here." He used the blade of the screwdriver to pick at a small metal object. It finally started rattling around a bit. "Try taking them off and shaking them. I think it's loose."

Charles did, and dumped a tiny screw into his hand. "Hmm, that's odd. I guess it worked its way out." Charles set the lens to the side. "I'll put it back together later. Now, as I was saying, the watch is almost done. Then we can get back to making another arm."

Jacob grinned. Charles obviously knew exactly what he'd been thinking.

Word of Jacob's mechanical hand had spread. Three tinkers had come by to see the boy who had built the hand. A few people had come asking to buy a hand of their own. One man hoped to have a leg made for his son so he wouldn't be stuck with a peg leg.

"Are we going to try building that leg tonight?" Jacob asked.

"Oh yes," Charles said. "I think we'll get some dinner first, though."

"Fine," Jacob said, not wanting to stop for something as trivial as food, but also not wanting to listen to his mom if he skipped dinner. Jacob leaned over the plans Charles had sketched out on the back of an old yellow parchment. He still didn't understand all the markings and symbols, but he figured he could ask Charles about them while they ate. "Fine, let's have some dinner."

Charles smiled and screwed the watchcase back together.

✧　✧　✧

BAT SERVED UP ANOTHER FEAST, and Jacob couldn't remember ever having eaten so much food.

"Seconds?" Bat asked, holding a bowl of buttered mashed potatoes out to Jacob.

Jacob groaned and shook his head.

"He means 'No, thank you,'" Jacob's father said. His pale complexion hadn't changed in the past week.

Jacob's mom started clearing the dishes. "So, what are the inventors up to tonight?"

"Don't worry about those, Mags," Bat said. "I'll get the dishes."

"We're uninvited guests. It's the least we can do."

Jacob recognized the tone of his mother's voice. She was having none of it. It looked like Bat recognized it too, because he eased himself back into his chair and stayed quiet.

"Well?" Jacob's mom said.

Charles finished chewing his last bite of braised pork and leaned back. "I'm planning to throw your son off one of the towers if the city guard will let us up there."

"Really?" Jacob said, unable to hide his excitement.

Jacob's mom rolled her eyes as she picked up Charles's plate.

"You finished the harness?" Samuel asked. "For the backpack glider?"

Charles nodded as he wiped his glasses on the edge of a tan cloth.

"You're serious?" Jacob's mom said, her voice rising in pitch. "I'll not have you throwing my boy off a tower. Don't be ridiculous."

"Come on, Mom. Charles has thrown the glider off the observatory like a hundred times."

Samuel handed his plate to Jacob's mom and smiled. "It's true. I've seen it. Nothing but sacks of grain to weigh it down, either. No pilot, and it still landed softly."

Charles leaned forward. "The wind pressure changes with altitude. I added some switches that compensate for any sudden changes. I wouldn't say it's self-guiding, but it does a good job of not crashing." Charles smiled and crossed his legs after scooting his chair back a bit.

Jacob could tell the old man was proud of his invention, and he had a right to be. Jacob looked up at his mom, and she scowled at Charles.

"What do you think, Dad?" Jacob tried not to look like he was pleading for his father to support him, but everyone knew that was exactly what was happening.

His father glanced at his mother. He sighed and adjusted the blanket around his shoulders before looking to Charles. "Is it safe?"

Charles hesitated, giving the question a great deal of thought. "It is one of my safest inventions. I would think it more dangerous for Jacob to be in the mines than piloting the glider."

Jacob's dad nodded slowly. "I think that's fine." He looked to Jacob's mom. "Let the boys have their fun. For the sake of your mother, though, why don't you try it here first? Maybe from the second floor?"

Charles raised his eyebrows slightly and pursed his lips. "Not a bad idea."

"Oh, fine," Jacob's mother said. "It's not that I don't trust you,

Charles. It's just …"

"I know," Charles said. "We'll be careful."

"Just, think of him as if he were your own son, will you?"

"Yes, ma'am." Charles nodded and slapped Jacob's back. "Come now, let's get you suited up so we can show your mom how this works."

✦　✦　✦

Samuel followed Charles and Jacob into the small lab. "I didn't realize you'd finished it."

"I did," Charles said. "The main problem was getting the switches to be sensitive without being overly sensitive. You don't want the glider pulling too much in any one direction."

"How much weight can it hold?" Samuel asked.

"I've tested up to two hundred pounds." Charles tapped his chin and ran his fingers over the backpack's shoulder straps. "I'd guess it could handle double that if it had to."

"Four *hundred*?"

"Mind you, I wouldn't want to be the one with a payload like that. If those wings collapsed, well …"

"You wouldn't have to worry about it for long."

"Can we not talk about wings collapsing when I'm about to jump off a house?" Jacob said under his breath.

Samuel laughed and squeezed Jacob's shoulder. "Don't worry, kid. It's only two stories up. You could survive that without a glider."

"Yeah, well, I don't want to end up next to Bobby in the hospital. He snores too much."

Charles leaned in and checked the last switch. Jacob watched the silvery metal shift beneath the glass when the old man moved it. Charles folded the metal bracket in and tucked the leathery wings into the pack before he picked it up and held the straps up.

Jacob fed his arms through the biggest straps with the most padding.

"How is it?" Samuel asked.

"Not bad," Jacob said, adjusting his shoulders. The backpack definitely had some weight, but not enough to complain about. "I think I could walk around with it most of the day if I had to."

Charles blew out a breath as he pulled a leather strap tight across Jacob's chest and fed two lengths of leather between the boy's legs. "If you have that kind of stamina," Charles said as he fastened all the leather straps to a starburst-like buckle on Jacob's chest, "you should join the Spider Knights with Samuel."

Samuel leaned against the door by the workbench. "Sure, he could double as a Walker."

"Ha. Ha. Ha," Jacob said.

Charles gave each strap a firm tug and nodded. "We're ready."

✧   ✧   ✧

Jacob stood on the second-floor balcony. Bat's house wasn't structured like homes in the Lowlands, so the second-floor balcony was actually on the third floor, and *that* was a bit higher than Jacob expected.

He could see the edge of the courtyard from there, lined with tents near the gates. It reminded him how lucky he was to have a shelter with Bat, and his family. Many Highborn families refused to take in Lowlanders, paying massive fines levied by Parliament instead of welcoming survivors into their homes. The wealthy paid a fine, and the common people had to live in the streets.

Jacob shook his head and glanced down at the cobblestone street below. His parents stood on the opposite side of the road with Samuel, Charles, and almost everyone else staying in Bat's home.

Jacob looked toward the city gates again and the wind caught his hair.

"Now, you remember," Charles shouted over the low noise of talking, bustling pedestrians, "pull the lever as soon as you jump. You're not all that high up, and we want to give the wind plenty of time to catch."

"Got it!" Jacob released the leather loop around the lever near his right shoulder. He climbed onto a chair that Bat had on the balcony and then placed one foot on the gray stone railing.

Charles glanced either way. Jacob knew he was waiting for a fairly wide break in traffic on the street. Part of their plan had been trying not to crash into people.

"Now!"

Jacob didn't hesitate. He could have sworn he heard his mother gasp and his father cheer as he launched himself into the air and pulled the lever in one swift motion. The mechanism in the backpack clicked and whirred, and the leathery wings exploded from Jacob's back. He felt the wind catch him and lift him slightly. The quiet click of the switches whispered behind the rush of air as his flight path leveled out.

"Yes!" Charles shouted. "Yes!"

Jacob smiled, and he didn't think he'd ever smiled so wide. He glided through the air for only a few seconds before he gently descended to the street. Jacob ran forward a few steps, pulled along by the breeze, before he threw the lever on his left shoulder. The wings collapsed, evading the wind well enough to let him walk normally. He turned and walked as fast as he could back to the cheering mass of family and friends.

"That was incredible!" Samuel said.

"Oh, Jacob," his mom said. "It was beautiful. You were flying."

"Well, gliding," Jacob said with a laugh, "but yeah. What did you think?" he asked as he turned to his dad.

"I think I'd like to know when it's my turn."

Charles slapped Jacob's dad on the back. "As soon as you're well. How's that for incentive to heal up?"

"It's very good. Very good."

"Now then ..." Charles rubbed his hands together. "Are you ready for the *real* test?"

CHAPTER FIFTEEN

JACOB TOOK A DEEP BREATH and shifted the straps of the backpack on his shoulder.

"Still feel like you could carry it all day?" Samuel asked as they climbed the gradual hill that led to the second tower on the wall.

"It's not bad."

"You may just be able to join the Spider Knights one day."

Jacob smiled at Samuel. Charles stepped out in front of them. The etched iron door to the tower stood a few paces away, guarded by two knights. Jacob studied the intricate detail carved into the door. One quadrant of the door showed the rise of the railways he'd learned about in school. The tracks led up to the peak of the arched door, and he was pretty sure the other panel showed the start of the war.

Charles had told him it wasn't long after the new trade route was established along the railways that Dauschen had attacked Ancora. Jacob hadn't been paying much attention to the conversation between Charles, Samuel, and the guards, but Charles's grunt caught his attention.

Charles fished around in an interior pocket of his leather jerkin and pulled out a dull gray medallion on a chain.

One of the guards leaned forward to inspect it, and then snapped to attention. "Sir, I am honored. If you wish to proceed, by all means, it is your right."

Charles nodded. The second guard opened the door and kept his head bowed. The old man gestured for Jacob to follow.

"What was that?" Jacob asked.

"It's just an old medal from the war, Jacob. It earns some respect from the guards here."

Jacob walked into the shadows behind Charles and stared at the spiral of stairs. He stepped farther in and looked up. The stairs vanished and reappeared above him, lit by torches in various spots and stone windows near the top. He could hear the wind whistling through the tower above.

"There's no lift," Jacob said, unable to keep a groan from his voice.

Samuel laughed. "How's that pack feeling?"

Charles chuckled and started up the stairs, but Jacob didn't think it was very funny at all. "Come on, boy. If these old bones can get me to the top of the tower, I'm sure you can make it."

"These are narrow," Samuel said. "Why did they build them so narrow?"

"Defense," Charles said. Their bootsteps thudded and echoed against the stone staircase. "It's a lot easier to keep men from breaching the tower if they can't come up in force."

"I wouldn't think that would be a big concern since we're inside the walls," Samuel said.

"I didn't say it was only to keep men from coming *up* the tower. Slows an army's descent as well."

Jacob looked up again. It seemed like they had a mile of climbing left to go. "No one could scale the outer wall. Who would be climbing down one of these things?"

"Kid's got a point," Samuel said. "Bessie couldn't scale the city wall with the way the masons keep the stone smoothed. Captain says no bug larger than an apple can get a grip on that surface."

Charles glanced over his shoulder. "I'll show you how to scale a wall sometime. I didn't realize they'd let the Spider Knights get so soft."

"Funny, old man. Funny."

Charles smiled and turned his focus back to the stairs. "See the iron there, Jacob?" he asked, pointing to a thick beam cutting across above them.

Jacob glanced at the stretch of metal. "Yeah?"

"It's part of the iron frame for the entire wall. Most of the wall is hollow, you know. It would have been too heavy to support itself if the masons hadn't built it like that. They used the iron to build it higher."

"Wouldn't that weaken it?" Samuel asked. "All the empty space between the walls?"

Charles shook his head. "The reinforcement's as good as any stone. I'd rather have the height anyhow." He took a deep breath between steps. "Keep the bugs out."

Charles started to sound winded, and Jacob knew exactly how he felt. Their pace had slowed a bit, but the light grew brighter overhead. It wasn't long before they came off the staircase and stepped into a wide stone room. The whistling sounds were louder here.

Plain, rounded walls surrounded the group. A doorway stood to either side, and the wind barreled through to greet them.

"Let's head out a bit," Charles said, leading them through the southern doorway.

There were heavy iron doors inside the pale stone watchtower, locked in an open position. Jacob noticed the weight of the ornate hinges on each door, and it seemed obvious they weren't strictly for decoration. Those doors were built to keep someone, or something, out.

Jacob squinted as he joined Charles out on the wall-walk. Ramparts stood to either side, but the stonework along the outer wall was much taller.

Charles turned to Jacob. "Now then. This is where you jump from." He made a sweeping gesture and Jacob's eyes followed.

Samuel stuck his head over the edge and whistled.

Jacob leaned out through a dip in the ramparts, glanced at the distant ground, and took two steps backward. "This is … umm, this is high." He took a deep breath and looked out toward the city gates. He could see a fairly clear path that led to the courtyard by the gatehouse that wasn't obscured by the tents.

"You ready for this?" Charles asked. "We can come back another time."

Jacob shook his head and pulled the leather straps between his legs so he could fasten everything to the buckle on his chest. "How's it look?"

Charles gave each strap a tug and then leaned in to inspect the buckle. "I think you're ready to go."

"Right then," Jacob said as he put his left foot on top of the rampart. He unbuckled the strap that held in the lever for the wings. The wind picked up, and he leaned to the side.

"Aim for the gatehouse," Charles shouted when a sudden gust howled through the stone ramparts. "You'll have the widest stretch of street for landing."

Samuel barked out a short laugh. "This is crazy."

"You going to catch me?" Jacob asked. He pulled a pair of wide goggles over his face.

Samuel eyed him for a moment. "Tell you what. I'll meet you by the gatehouse."

"You're not going to watch?"

"I'll watch from below." Without another word, Samuel ran back into the tower. Jacob could hear Samuel's rapid footsteps descending the watchtower. Jacob turned back to Charles.

They waited a minute in the wind and silence at the top of the wall. Another gust of wind caught the old man's beard, and the largest grin Jacob had ever seen on Charles's face lifted his beard even higher.

"Ready?"

Jacob nodded. He put one foot up on the rampart and then stepped backward, shaking his head. He took a deep breath.

"Go, go, go!" Charles said.

Jacob hopped up onto the ramparts and shouted, "Cock-a-doodle-doo!" He launched himself into the air before he could decide it might not be such a good idea. Jacob tilted forward slightly as the earth fell away beneath him. The cold, solid stone no longer held his weight, and he screamed in pure joy as his heart dropped into his stomach.

"Now!" he heard Charles shout from above him.

Jacob pulled the lever. He felt the backpack shift when the leathery wings snapped out and stretched to their full span. The brackets shook as they locked into place, and a gust of wind caused Jacob to tilt to the north when he meant to go south. He slid his arms up into the loops on the wings and carefully tilted them, changing his flight path over the streets below.

Jacob turned his arms, and the next gust of wind took him higher. He heard his name, only a distant shout. Far below him someone waved, and then the faces on the street all turned up to see what Samuel was yelling at. Jacob laughed and pulled the wings in, diving closer to the astonished crowd below. He spread his arms and twisted, soaring around the chimney of one of the highest roofs in the Highlands as he angled for the gatehouse.

"Come down farther!"

Jacob barely heard the words over the howl of the wind, but he saw Samuel running along the ground beneath him, diving and weaving through the crowds. The switches in Jacob's wings whirred and clicked as he dropped his altitude low enough that he could touch the roof of every home he soared past. Jacob streaked into the courtyard.

"Clear the way!" Samuel shouted.

Jacob twisted his arms, and his entire body swung forward when the wings caught the air. He came in at a sharp angle and ran with the inertia as it carried him forward. He pulled the lever on his left shoulder, relaxing the wings before he jumped into the air and shouted, looking around for Samuel.

The Spider Knight wasn't far behind, and he beat most of the roaring crowd to Jacob. "You did it, kid! That was just amazing."

The crowds closed in around them while Samuel helped tuck the wings back into the pack. "Let's get this closed up before anything gets broken," he said, snapping the pack closed.

"Sir Knight, what was that creation?" a man in a tall top hat asked. "I've never seen the like."

"It's a secret project," Samuel said, slightly exaggerating the truth. "One of the Lowlands tinker's works."

"The tinker who built that steambike everyone's been talking about?"

Samuel nodded. "The same."

"I heard the city smith was even asking after that steambike. The tinker who made that should live within our walls permanently."

"I'll give him the message," Samuel said as he ushered Jacob away from the crowds and onto a side street. "Mister …?"

"Ferryman. Robert Ferryman. Do give him my regards."

Samuel smiled and nodded, never taking his hand from Jacob's shoulders. Samuel fended off a dozen more Highlanders before they finally broke through the circle of people. "Quickly now, Jacob."

Jacob picked up his pace, and they gradually pulled away from the crowd. "I don't mind crowds, but that was crazy."

"Oh, I know why you don't mind crowds," Samuel said. "You better not have any extra money in your pocket. Charles won't be happy."

Jacob felt the blush crawling over his skin. "I didn't … I mean, I don't …"

"My family didn't always live inside the walls, kid. Don't worry about it."

Jacob glanced at the Spider Knight. Samuel smiled as they stepped off the side street and back onto the main road near the hospital. They passed two of the square metal covers in the street before Jacob thought to ask Samuel about the city's underground.

"Have you ever been into the catacombs?"

Samuel shook his head. "The catacombs aren't used anymore."

"Can we go in?"

Samuel chuckled. "You're really not supposed to, but I remember being your age."

"You aren't *that* much older than me …"

He shrugged. "I might know a place you can get in. The hinges won't be rusted shut either, like these," he said, nodding at a corroded plate of metal.

Jacob's face lit up.

Samuel pointed at him. "You have to make me a promise."

"Sure," Jacob said, without really considering what that might be. "What?"

"Don't go past the second level. Sometimes bugs get in there, and they're usually harmless, but the gates below the second level were destroyed in the war. The city never bothered to repair them since they abandoned the catacombs. The inner gates are enough to stop any would-be invaders. I need you to promise me that."

"Okay. I promise."

Samuel nodded, apparently satisfied with the word of a fellow pick-pocket, and that made Jacob happy. Samuel's eyes moved to the upper edge of the city wall.

"You see the fourth tower?" he asked. "It's two over from the one we climbed with Charles."

Jacob nodded as he counted them off and his eyes reached the fourth.

"Good. At the bottom of that tower is an old inn. The first innkeeper was a bit … well, most people would say crazy, but let's say overly cautious. Go through the cellar door and head to the far wall."

"Cellar door, far wall," Jacob repeated.

"The floor there is wooden, but it's also false. You'll find two heavy bolts. I'm sure you can figure out the rest."

"Charles!" Jacob said when the tinker appeared near Bat's house.

"You have to show me how to build one of these gliders!"

Charles caught up with them outside the workshop and patted Jacob's shoulder. "I will, and well done! You managed to avoid the roofs and lightning rods alike."

Jacob looked up toward the skyline. He hadn't really noticed the lightning rods. He flinched at the thought of what could have happened up there.

"What are you going to use that glider for?" Samuel asked.

The old tinker shrugged. "It could be handy if you're stranded on a mountain, or need to jump off one."

"Jump off a mountain?" Jacob said. "That's crazy."

"This is Charles we're talking about, kid."

Jacob grinned at Samuel and started unbuckling the harness while Charles opened the door to the workshop.

"There are more practical uses," Charles said. "Airships could use them in emergencies. The watchtowers could use them in case of a fire. We'll find a good home for these contraptions."

Jacob slid out of the backpack, and his focus returned to the catacombs. He was fairly certain he knew someone he could convince to go with him.

CHAPTER SIXTEEN

The next morning, Jacob had one thing on his mind. Catacombs.

He started packing before breakfast. Jacob was glad Charles was so excited about the glider. The old man didn't seem to get overly excited about very much, but he was thrilled with the glider's performance and the fact it hadn't let Jacob fall to his death. Jacob was pretty thrilled with that too.

He left soon after breakfast. The glider backpack had been swapped out for his normal pack, and he thought he had everything he'd need for his day's adventure. Jacob ran stories through his mind, trying to come up with some reason to get Alice to come with him. He really didn't want to go underground by himself. Small spaces didn't make him happy, and he figured something with a name like catacomb had to be small. Not that he was scared of them, like some of the other kids at school, but cramped spaces just weren't a comfortable place to be.

It didn't take long to reach the inn where Alice and her family were staying. It stood in one of the elaborate squares, almost impossible to miss with the huge carved dragon above its doors. A dozen doors faced the street on the front of the wide inn. Her family had been moving from room to room, depending on availability. After speaking with the innkeeper, he knew Alice was in the third from the end.

Jacob hesitated, his fist hovering above the knots and whorls of the oaken door while he set his story firmly in his mind. Alice might not want to go if she thought they were breaking a rule. He knocked a moment later. He expected to hear voices, since Alice's family was staying with a large group, but all he heard were footsteps.

The small panel in the door squeaked as it slid to the side and a pair of blue eyes appeared. The panel closed instantly, and two locks clicked open before the door swung in.

"What are you doing here?" Alice asked.

"I thought you might want to help me look for Samuel's cat. He thinks it snuck down under the streets." Jacob paused, trying to remember the rest of his story. "It's, uh, he thinks we can get … get to it under the inn by the wall."

Alice laughed and leaned up against the doorframe. "Samuel's cat? You're a terrible liar. Spider Knights can't keep pets in the barracks."

Jacob almost smacked himself in the forehead. "Fine, fine, okay. Charles told me there are train tracks *under* the streets, and I want to go see them."

Alice stood up a little straighter. "Under the city? You mean the old catacombs? You know how to get into them?"

Jacob blinked. "How did you know about that?"

"They used to bury people there," Alice said. "We learned about it in history class." She cocked her head to the side. "Probably one of the classes you were snoring in."

"Dead people?" Jacob asked.

"I would hope so. I'd hate to think they were burying people alive. I didn't know there were train tracks, though. I want to see them." She paused and looked back into the house. "Did you bring a lantern?"

Jacob slid his backpack off and pulled out a jar of enormous glow-worms. Their bodies pulsed as the worms gnawed on a tightly rolled pack of leaves.

"Wow," Alice said as she glanced toward Jacob. "Those are huge. Hold on a minute. Let me grab something, just in case."

She vanished from the doorway, and Jacob slid the jar back into his backpack.

"A Lowlander for sure. Keep your distance."

Jacob turned slightly to see who had been talking. There was a little old woman with curly gray hair glaring at him. She had her arm around a girl not much younger than Jacob. The girl looked bored and waved at Jacob when he met her eyes. Jacob waved back.

"Well, I never," the old woman said, hurrying the girl along.

Jacob frowned slightly before he turned back around.

"Ready!" Alice said, pulling the door closed. They started walking down the street.

"What did you get?" Jacob asked.

"A lantern and some snacks."

"We already have light."

"Well, if the glowworms decide not to glow, where will we be then?"

"In the dark."

"Exactly," Alice said with a satisfied grin.

They walked for a short while until they came to a man in a tattered suit, sitting on the street. The clothing had some bright colors on it, likely leftover from Festival. He played a guitar and smiled at the pair as he brought to life the most intricate melodies Jacob had ever heard. He wished he could understand music better than he did, but Jacob knew enough to know the man should be playing in a Hall, not on a street corner.

Alice bent down and dropped a copper into his cup. They listened for a minute and then continued on their way while the performer nodded his thanks without missing a note.

"So, where are we going?" Alice asked.

"The inn by the fourth watchtower."

"That's all the directions we have? What if there are five or six inns by the watchtower?"

Jacob glanced at Alice as he stepped around a pile of droppings in the road, wrinkling his nose at the pungent stench. "I'm pretty sure Samuel would have been more specific."

"Alright, we'll see."

It wasn't long before they found themselves outside an old inn. The dark stonework pillars outside the front door were worn down from thousands of hands brushing over them throughout the years. The place looked ancient.

Alice craned her neck back and stared up at the top of the inn. "How tall is that?"

"Tall," Jacob said. From their vantage point, it almost looked like the inn was as tall as the watchtower. "I think this might be the inn Samuel mentioned."

"Shut up," Alice said, smacking his arm. She turned away, but not before Jacob saw the smile on her face.

"Let's find the cellar door," Jacob said. He walked past the few people milling around outside the inn, keeping his eyes near the ground. Nothing looked remotely like a cellar entrance, so he led Alice around the building, into the mouth of a narrow alley between the inn and the city wall.

Jacob glanced back toward the other side of the street. The wall there had plenty of space between it and the nearest building, enough to fit a carriage or two.

"Why'd they build the inn so close to the wall?" Jacob asked. He turned back around and started down the alley.

"It's probably older than the wall," Alice said. "Or at least *this* wall." She patted the enormous gray and white stone beside them. "You've heard Charles talk about the old wall. It didn't used to be that tall."

"It didn't have to be," Jacob said as he slowed down. "Here it is." He walked down two short steps and looked at the cellar doors.

"No lock?" Alice asked.

Jacob shook his head. He reached out and grabbed one of the iron rings. It didn't budge. "I think it's rusted shut."

"Let me help." Alice came down the steps to stand beside him.

They grabbed the ring and leaned backward together, slowly pulling the warped oak door open with a loud creak.

Jacob looked around, but no one at the either end of the alley seemed to be paying them any mind. "Let's go." He held the door open while Alice walked in and then he followed her down.

The light vanished when he let the cellar door close over their heads. A pale light filtered through the cracks in the door as his eyes adjusted. He slid his backpack off and pulled out the jar of glowworms. They grew brighter, bathing the room in a faint green light.

"See? I told you they'd be fine."

"Alright," Alice said. "Let's find the door."

"Samuel said the floor is all wood, but part of it's fake."

"What else did he say?"

Jacob walked toward the far wall, stepping quietly once he realized his boots were loud on the hardwood. "He said there are two bolts on the door."

"There's a lot of stuff down here," Alice said. The room narrowed the farther in they went. Shelves that stretched from floor to ceiling flanked them on either side.

Footsteps sounded overhead, and they both froze. Jacob could hear the blood rushing through his ears as he strained to listen. The footsteps faded, and he slowly relaxed.

"Doesn't look like they come down here much," Jacob said, running his finger through the dust on a stack of pale, wooden crates.

"We should still probably be quiet," Alice said. She rose up on her toes to check another shelf. "It's all dishes and linens over here. And dust." She looked back down at the floor and took a few steps forward. The quiet echo of her footsteps changed. She thumped the floor with her heel and looked up at Jacob.

"That has to be it," Jacob said. "We're almost at the wall."

Alice crouched down. "Look there!" She pointed to the edge of the floor where it met the wall. "It's a hinge."

"But where are the bolts?"

"I don't see them."

Jacob set the jar of glowworms down. He knocked on the floor, following the hollow echo back until it changed to a dull thump. "The hatch ends here. There has to be something." A small perfect square caught his eye. "It's a spring bolt!"

"Shh," Alice said.

"It's a spring bolt," Jacob whispered, feeling a little stupid. He pushed his thumb down on the square until it clicked and the bolt popped up.

"How's that work?" Alice said.

"Watch, you just fold it over at the joint …" Jacob bit his tongue as he worked at the bolt. "Then you twist." He moved his arm in a half circle and the locks in the door popped open.

Alice moved off the hatch, picking up the glowworms as she went. "Let's open it."

Jacob inclined his head in agreement and pulled the hatch up, revealing the pitch-black catacombs beneath.

"Who's glad we have a lantern now?"

Jacob stared into the darkness and nodded. He knew the glowworms wouldn't be bright enough to light much of that expanse. "It was a good idea."

Alice took her lantern out, unclipped the small safety clasp, and pushed the igniter. A bright yellow flame grew more intense when she attached a reflector to the back of the lantern. She angled it down the hole, and they both gasped.

CHAPTER SEVENTEEN

Below them, hidden in the shadows beneath the hatch, was what seemed to be another city beneath the city. A collapsed staircase stood as nothing more than a pile of dusty stones underneath them.

"We need to lower the lantern," Alice said. She pulled a thin rope out of her backpack.

"I didn't even think about bringing a rope," Jacob said.

"To go underground? You should probably think things through a bit more, Jacob."

"Now you sound like Miss Penny," he muttered.

She smiled and tied off the rope before slowly feeding the light into the darkness. "I just hope the rope can hold *us* as well as it can hold the lantern. I think I can get it on the flat part there." The lantern set down with a faint clink.

Jacob leaned in. "Alice … I've never seen anything like it."

"Well, get your head out of there and let's go," she said, pulling on his shoulder. "Look, someone sank handles into the wall."

Jacob followed where she was pointing and smiled. They were almost perfectly spaced, like one of the iron ladders that led to the sewers.

They gathered their backpacks up and stared at the hole for a moment.

"I'll go first," Alice said. "I think it will be easier for you to close the door behind us."

"You want to close it?"

"So we don't get caught, right?"

Jacob nodded and watched Alice tentatively place her foot on the first rung. She kicked it a few times.

"Looks good." She stretched down to the next rung and quickly made it to the bottom without a problem. "It's solid."

Jacob swung his legs over the hole as Alice picked up the lantern below and shined it up for him. He lowered himself down two rungs before reaching back up for the hatch. Jacob wrapped his fingers around the edge, careful not to slam them in the hatch. It swung closed without much effort, and he was relieved that the hinges were quiet. He left the spring bolt dangling from the door, unlocked.

Each step he took down the rungs caused his chest to tighten. Jacob was excited about exploring the catacombs, but quickly remembered how much he didn't enjoy the dark. A gap three feet high waited for him between the last rung and the floor. He let himself drop, his boots scraping the wall lightly before he hit bottom. A small cloud of dust billowed up from his boots, highlighted by the lantern light.

Jacob could tell the walls were a very pale stone, even though the lantern gave them a yellowish hue. The floors were likely the same, but covered in decades' worth of dust and dirt. Jacob brushed his hands off and turned to face Alice.

"Ready?" she asked.

He nodded and stepped around the collapsed stairs. "It's quiet."

"It's kind of creepy," Alice said. She forged ahead with the lantern, holding the light up to the wall on their left as they continued on.

"Hold up," Jacob said. He took three quick steps to stand beside Alice. "Is that a flier?"

"Poster," Alice said. She leaned in toward the yellowed paper tacked onto an old wooden bulletin board. "Oh wow, it's for an old Festival. 'Come join the third Festival and celebrate the treaty with Dauschen.'"

"Third?" Jacob said. "If that's from the third Festival, it's older than Charles."

"Not quite that old," Alice said. She reached out and touched the poster. The contact was enough to make the lower corner crumble away. Bits of paper floated to the ground, casting eerie shadows in the lantern light before settling by Alice's boots.

"It's completely rotted." Alice brushed over the crumbled bits of paper with her foot.

"Come on, let's go." Jacob watched the lantern light move away from the old poster, leaving it in darkness once more.

They hadn't walked much farther when Alice came to an abrupt stop. "Jacob." She raised the lantern and Jacob gasped.

The room seemed to expand all around them. A grand staircase swept down into a causeway, flanked by ornate sculptures and overpasses. Shop fronts, frozen in time, stood along either side of the old train tracks.

Jacob took a step down and then another. The stairs were solid and stone.

"These aren't catacombs," Alice said. "It's like they buried an entire *city* beneath the city."

"Look at it all," Jacob said as he hurried down the last few steps. An ancient carriage waited at the bottom. It sat folded up like the vendor carts at Festival. Jacob squinted at the sign in the edge of the lantern light, but he couldn't quite make it out. He brushed his hand across the plaque to remove decades of dust.

"What is that?" Alice asked. She leaned in beside him. "It looks like some kind of meat stuffed into a weird bun."

Jacob shook his head and stood up. "I have no idea." He walked toward the edge of the platform and stared at the tracks. They were easy to see once Alice came up behind him with the lantern.

"Why are they here?"

"I don't know," Jacob said. "Seems like it would have been easier to build a train station above ground."

"There are just as many shops across the way as there are over here," Alice said.

Jacob looked at the other line of shops. Two levels faced them, with the upper level recessed a bit, almost like it was built into the wall. He pointed to either end of the station. "There are stairs on both sides."

"There's another one in the middle too," Alice said. "Just like this side."

Jacob stepped toward one of the walkways that arched over the train tracks. He saw hints of marble swirls on the railings, where the dust and dirt hadn't settled so thick. He stepped up on the wide arch and hopped up and down. His boots echoed around the abandoned station, dust billowing out around him.

"Seems solid."

Alice followed Jacob up onto the walkway and stayed beside him until they stopped in the center. She shined the light down the tracks and let out a short, muffled scream.

Something giant caught the light. Chitinous plates and horns gleamed below them, and Jacob recoiled right along with Alice. A moment later, they realized the thing wasn't moving.

Jacob leaned forward, trying to get a better look at the thick metal gates and the creature that lay beyond. "It's dead, and it's been dead a long time. Look at the legs. They're hollow, whatever it was."

"It's huge."

Jacob stared at the jointed legs attached to the pale shell. Something like a giant horn curled off the thing's head and looked to be embedded in the stone wall. "Must be the second level Samuel was talking about."

"I don't know," Alice said. "Well, it does look like it descends."

Jacob turned, and Alice followed him with the light until they were looking down the other half of the tracks. The tunnel was clear in the opposite direction, but two smaller tunnels flanked either side.

"Look," Alice said as she pointed to the right tunnel. "That must lead to the catacombs."

A dark stone cross hung above the entryway to the arched tunnel. Jacob and Alice walked back down the bridge and started toward the darker tunnel. A circle carved from pale stone encased the top of the darker cross, intersecting each arm of the cross an equal distance from its center.

"It's not stone," Jacob said. "Look at it. That's metal."

"A metalsmith made that?" Alice asked, and Jacob could understand the awe in her voice. Even caked in dust, the intricate lines and knots were beautiful.

He was looking at the cross and not his feet. Jacob stubbed his foot on something heavy and low to the ground. He shouted, and Alice's hand snapped out to catch him before he fell.

A heavy iron gate lay flat against the stone floor. Chips stood out in the thick tiles where the gate had fallen.

"Watch your step," Alice said.

"That thing is huge." Jacob stepped around the fallen gate and into the darkened archway. A cool breeze lifted his hair. Something like a low whistle sounded in the blackness, and Alice raised the lantern higher.

"I think it's just the wind," she said. Jacob started to walk past her when she grabbed his shirt.

"Look!" She hopped over a broken-down carriage and dragged him to a storefront a few doors down. "Do you see them?" she asked as she bounced up and down on the balls of her feet.

"Is that ..." Jacob cocked his head to the side and looked at the sign above the heavy wood door. Gray dust filled in most of the crevices, but he could just make out the shape of an open book carved into the old sign.

"It's all books," Alice said. She glanced back toward the entrance of the catacombs and then back to Jacob. She pulled on the door to the little shop. The old iron frame rattled against its lock. She frowned and looked through the dusty windows after wiping some of the dirt away and brushing it on her pants. "There are so many. Should we break the window?" Alice covered her mouth with her free hand. "I can't believe I just said that."

"Give me a minute," Jacob said. "Think I can get through the door." He unbuttoned his leather vest and folded it over, feeling for the tiny gap in the stitching. With a little effort, he managed to slide two thin black metal bars into his hands. One unfolded at a hinge to form an L, and the other was straight until the end turned into small curvy squiggle of metal.

"Lockpicks?" Alice said. Jacob didn't have to look at her to know she was frowning.

"Hey, don't go judging me now. *You* wanted to smash the window." He glanced up when she didn't respond.

Alice's mouth fell into a tight line, and he was pretty sure she was blushing. He knelt down so the lantern light penetrated the thin keyhole.

Jacob inserted the flat wrench first, putting just a bit of tension on it. It was one of the things he'd learned from Charles. This probably wasn't what the old man had meant for him to do with it. "I think …" the lockpicks clinked and rattled in the keyhole. "I think there are only three tumblers. Wow, this should be—"

He didn't even get to say "easy" before the lock popped and the door began to drift open.

"You're bad," Alice said with a smile as she walked past Jacob and into the bookstore.

Jacob followed her in, wearing a smile of his own.

"There're so many!" Alice hopped up to one of the walls and leaned in to look closer. The worst of the dust had stayed outside the store. They could still read most of the titles, and the old books didn't seem to be in bad shape at first glance, even if most of them were in disarray.

"Are they rotted?" Jacob asked. "That old poster fell apart by the stairs."

Alice picked up one of the books and flipped through it. "They look okay. A little smelly, but they seem alright."

Jacob paused by a yellowed sign labeled "Current Affairs." A leather-bound book with a silver skull on it stared back at him. Five metal studs were riveted around the skull, two on the top, two to the sides, and one below. The spine bore metal hinges that looked like copper. Jacob read the title, *The Dead Scourge*, before flipping the cover open to read.

```
          Memoirs of my time in the Deadlands.
                   A cause for war.

                 By Archibald Jones

    The Forgotten did not die in the desert prison.
Their exile did not end in the death our government
deemed their just destiny. Those men and their families
adapted—some may say flourished—among the invaders we
thought to bring nothing but death.
    There, they have honed their skills. Machinations
one can scarcely imagine have been brought to life. Some
are powerful, helpful, and meant to improve the lives of
their people. Others are clearly meant for killing and
nothing more.
```

Goosebumps ran over Jacob's arms. He wanted to get the book back to Charles and ask him what else he knew about the Deadlands and the Forgotten. He'd never even heard the term before.

"Alice? Have you ever heard of the Forgotten?"

"The Forgotten what?" Her muffled voice came over the shelves behind him.

"Yeah, me neither." He walked down another aisle and eventually stopped by Alice.

"Look at this," she said, holding up a book titled *Breeding Your Round Herd.* "It's all about Pill-Bugs. We might be able to use it to raise our bugs again."

They didn't know for sure that the bugs at Alice's house were all gone, but it seemed likely. Widow Makers and Red Death didn't have much use for Pill-Bugs outside of food.

"Did you see the books closer to the windows are more brittle?"

Jacob shook his head. "I didn't. Are they ruined?"

"You can still read them, but they're really fragile. I wouldn't want to try to carry one home."

Jacob walked around Alice and picked up a thin green book that was sitting on the counter. "*An Alchemist's Guide to Everything,*" he said aloud. "Seems pretty small to be about everything." The first page he opened spoke of the right mixture of minerals to create explosions of varying sizes. "This one's going with us." He smiled as he turned around.

"I want to take them all," Alice said, hugging the huge book on Pill-Bug breeding.

Jacob laughed and slid his backpack off. He tucked the alchemy book and the Deadlands book into the pack. "I don't think we can carry them all."

"We have to come back. We'll use it like a library, but you can't tell anyone."

"Me?" Jacob asked. "Why would I tell anyone?" He adjusted his backpack and then paused. "Charles is going to wonder where I found an alchemy book. And the book about the Deadlands War."

Alice's eyes flicked to the side. "Okay, you can tell Charles, but *no one else.*" She waited, impatiently, for a moment before repeating herself. "Okay?"

"Alright, alright." He, in turn, waited for Alice to finish packing so many books into her backpack that she could barely button it. "Ready?"

She nodded and hefted the pack up before picking up her lantern. She stopped just outside the bookstore and pointed to the tables. "Let's stop here and eat."

Jacob looked around. "You want to stop? We can just eat and walk."

"No," Alice said, shaking her head. She carried her lantern to a nearby table and set it beside her backpack on the braided metal surface.

"Let's sit down for a bit. Get the glowworms out, would you? We can save some fuel."

"Are we getting low?" Jacob asked, following Alice and pulling the jar out of his pack.

"No, but I'd rather have too much than be stuck down here without the lantern."

Jacob wasn't going to argue with that. It was a *lot* darker than he'd expected.

Alice twisted a brass dial on the side of her lantern. A snuffer, not unlike those on Bat's chandelier, curled up and extinguished the flame. Alice twisted the dial again in the green glow of the worms and set the lantern on the floor. She wiped the table down with her backpack and unpacked two square parcels of butcher's paper wrapped in twine.

"Sandwiches?" Jacob asked, unable to keep a hint of excitement about them out of his voice. Alice's mom made the best sandwiches, not that he'd ever tell his own mom that.

"Chicken," she said, handing one to Jacob, "and some of that stinky cheese you like."

Jacob grinned and tore the twine off his sandwich before unwrapping it and immediately stuffing it in his face.

Alice smiled as he chewed a bit that had been far too large. "The bread's from the inn's baker." Her eyes trailed across the nearest line of shops.

Jacob followed her gaze. "Looks like it used to be an eatery down here," he said before he stuffed his mouth with the thick sandwich again. He looked back at Alice. "Wow."

"What?" Alice said around a mouthful of food.

"You're almost done!"

"It's a good sandwich."

Jacob brushed his hands off on his pants before he picked up his backpack again. He pulled one of Charles's vacuum flasks out and unscrewed the cap. Jacob looked at the little pressure gauge on the side of the copper cylinder. It was getting a little low. He'd need to pump it up again soon with the bellows. Jacob frowned when he realized the bellows were back at the observatory.

He shrugged and took a deep drink before leaning back into the metal chair. It didn't look like the chairs should be comfortable, as lumpy as they were, but Jacob was pleasantly surprised. "Well, you want to go a little farther before we go back?"

Alice nodded as she finished her sandwich. "Oh yes, you're not getting me out of here yet." She held her hand out and Jacob passed her the flask. "Does Charles know you're using his equipment to carry water around?"

Jacob reached for the flask when Alice finished. "Yeah, Charles does it too. You have to be careful about what he puts in there though. I accidentally drank his firewater once." Jacob shivered. "It certainly earned its name."

Alice laughed as Jacob closed the flask and put it away, along with the butcher's paper and twine. "I'll fire up the lantern if you want to pack up the glowworms," she said.

Jacob did, and they both hefted their backpacks and started toward the catacombs.

CHAPTER EIGHTEEN

J ACOB STOPPED IN THE ARCHWAY and looked at the top frame of the doorway. The old iron gate had clearly been broken out of the wall. His eyes traced the jagged line of rock that had been chiseled out to install the lift mechanism.

"Something tore it out of the wall," Jacob said. He pointed to the dangling chains and fractured stone. "That big chain would have run through the channel." He followed the shaft that connected to two large gears.

"Here's the lever," Alice said. She grabbed on to an old handle in the wall. She gave it a little tug. The only sound was a short click of metal on metal. "It's all rusted."

"I wonder how they opened it from the outside. I don't see another switch."

Alice shrugged. "Let's go deeper. I'm hoping we find something more interesting than a broken door."

"Well, it doesn't sound so exciting when you say it like that."

"Really?" Alice asked as she raised an eyebrow.

Jacob laughed and followed her as she started down the hall. They barely had room to walk side by side when they first started out, but it wasn't long before the hall widened and they slowed to a stop.

"What in the …" Alice stared at the archway that loomed above them in the darkness.

"How high is that?" Jacob asked. A pair of ornate pillars, carved deep into the stone, flanked the sides of a tall arch. "It looks old." He walked closer to get a better view.

"Look at the pillars," Alice said. "They all have the same patterns as the cross over the entryway."

Jacob looked up, and he could see the cross at the top of each pillar, and another at the peak of the archway. Some of the stone had broken away from the arch's curve. "How do you think it broke? It looks too thick to break for no reason."

"You think?" Alice asked as she ran her fingers over the petal-like stone at the base of a pillar. Each pillar seemed to be growing from a stone flower. "It could have been too heavy. You remember when that stone tavern collapsed by the Square last year?"

Jacob nodded. "Charles said it was too heavy to support itself."

Alice walked through the arch. "Maybe that happened here."

"Yeah, or one of those giant bugs came through here too."

"Not funny, Jacob. Not funny."

Something loud and low bellowed in the distance. The sound came from all directions, bouncing off the walls of the catacombs. Jacob shivered in the edge of the lantern light. He jumped when something grabbed his arm. It was only Alice.

"Jacob," she hissed. Her fingernails dug into his arm.

Jacob took a deep breath before he spoke. "Should we go?"

"No," Alice said. "You said Samuel told you to avoid the second level. We're still on the first level. We're fine."

Jacob nodded as she released his arm. "You're right, but don't you want to know what made that sound?"

"If it means getting *killed?*" she hissed. "Stop and think, Jacob." Alice walked through the archway, and he stayed close behind her. They'd only taken a few more steps when Alice stopped dead. She swept the lantern from one side of the catacombs to the other.

"There're so many." Jacob stared while the light played over the coffins on their left. They'd been carved from stone, each with a name and date above intricate murals and portraits.

Alice raised the light a little higher and almost shouted. She wrapped her arm around Jacob's and lowered the lantern. "It's a person," she said. "It's a whole person."

"Raise the light again."

Alice did, but she didn't look where she was pointing it. Jacob helped guide it so he could see the bodies set into the walls. "They're mummies. Miss Penny taught us about that, remember?" Jacob struggled to keep his voice calm. The mummies' faces were taut and dry. They made his skin crawl, but something urged him to get closer and study them.

"I remember," Alice said. She gently pulled on the lantern to move the light down and away.

They walked farther into the room. "Look at these," Alice said, crouching down. "The coffins are all getting smaller." She turned the lantern onto the wall farthest to their right.

Jacob stared at what had to be a thirty-foot-high burial wall. Shelves carved into the stone held more coffins than he could count. He watched Alice's light trace a path down the wall until it vanished around a corner.

Even the smaller coffins were carved with admirable skill, bearing family crests or flowers or dragons. Jacob trailed after Alice. She seemed to be less frightened by the wall of closed coffins than she was by the room with the mummies. Jacob could understand why.

The outer wall curved a bit, and narrowed, so the coffins grew ever closer. Something scampered through the shadows and Jacob shivered.

"What was that?" Alice whispered, pulling a cobweb off her shoulder. She started to rub it off on a nearby stone, but then stopped, probably remembering all the stones were coffins.

"I don't know," Jacob said. "How much farther in you want to go?"

"Let's just see how deep it goes."

They stayed on the path long enough that neither of them was sure how long, or how far, they'd walked, but the catacombs were clearly descending. The lower they got, the colder the air became, until the wall of stone coffins gave way to thick wooden coffins.

"Some of those look like they're falling apart," Alice said, leaning in close to one of the coffins. She read the name carved into the wood aloud. "Avery. You think it's one of the city founders?"

"In a wooden coffin?" Jacob asked. "I'd guess if any founders are buried here, they're by the mummies."

Alice shivered at the mere mention of the corpses, and he wasn't faring much better.

"You can't read most of these." Alice squinted at a few more of the coffins. "They're too rotted."

They continued down the path, following the slope until the coffins stopped. Another carved stone archway led them into a large circular chamber.

"What is this place?" Alice asked. The lantern revealed a glassy floor and a room filled with stalactites and stalagmites. The old stone had actually grown together in some areas, and it formed an eerie pattern, almost like the teeth of some ancient beast.

A drop of water fell and hit the floor. Ripples radiated out from the center of the drop.

"It's a lake," Jacob said.

"Kind of small to be a lake, but it's definitely a lot of water. I guess we should head back."

Jacob nodded in agreement. Something caught his eye in the darkness when Alice turned away. "Alice. Alice, wait. Look over there."

She leaned back to see what he was pointing at. Off in the distance, near the right edge of the water, something glowed. "What is it?"

"I don't know. Let's check it, and then we can go."

"We've been down here a long time, Jacob."

Jacob rubbed the straps of his backpack. "I know. We can make it quick."

"Alright," Alice said, stepping out in front of Jacob. She led the way around the water. A narrow stretch of rock created a walkway between the walls of the cave and the underground pool. They squeezed past a wide pillar of stone and then they could see the hallway.

Something squealed and slammed like a heavy wooden door with rusted hinges. Jacob grabbed Alice's arm and whispered as loud as he dared. "Turn off the lantern. Someone's down here."

"Who?" Alice asked as quietly as she could while she snuffed the light.

Jacob slid around Alice and shrugged as he headed toward the nearby square of light. The new hallway narrowed, and Jacob realized it wasn't a hallway at all, but an old ventilation shaft. It was a rectangle, not unlike the shafts his dad had shown him in the mines, but this one was carved into the stone with more care than any he'd seen before.

Jacob walked as softly as he could. Voices grew louder as they approached the light. An old rusted grate separated the room and the shadowed shaft in which Jacob and Alice were hidden.

Snippets of the conversation became audible as they crept closer.

"… fool, they'll never …"

"… wrong. I don't think …"

Jacob and Alice inched their way forward until they could see the men inside and hear what they were saying.

The closest man faced away from them. Jacob guessed he was a blacksmith, with his wide shoulders, leather apron, and scorched pants. His voice was muffled, like he spoke through a breathing mask. "It's only been two weeks, and our food stores are depleted to the point we will no longer be able to support the people who matter." When he stopped talking, a loud click sounded before the man took a deep breath.

"*You're* the fool, Newton," said the other man, who stood whip thin in a pinstriped suit and a tall hat. He rubbed a broad mustache as he spoke. "The fact these families are poor does not mean they don't *matter.*"

"You know what does matter?" the first man asked. Jacob guessed he was the man named Newton. "Feeding our people matters, Benedict. Cutting down on the massive backflow of sewage matters. All of our systems are overtaxed. Soon the boilers that provide heat will fail, and we won't be able to run so much as the city lights. Our walls will lock plagues and death inside with us." Something hissed, and it seemed to come from one of the men. "You expect Highlanders to go into the mines?" He waited a beat, and there wasn't a response. "No, of course not. We need to get these people out and back to work."

"It's not safe," the second man said. "I won't send these people out to their death. We'll secure the Lowlands, at least build them safe passage, and then they can return to the mines."

"They aren't important. Send them out now to cull the herd and balance our food shortage. Finishing the railway and restoring the trusses are what's important. We need to reopen trade with Dauschen. You think those bugs just *decided* to show up here?"

"What?" the thin man asked. "What do you mean?"

Silence seemed to close in all around them.

"If Dauschen allies itself with the Deadlands," Newton said, "none of this will matter."

"What aren't you telling me?" The thin man made an exasperated noise. "Never mind. I won't send these people to their deaths so you can have fuel for your lights."

"You will, Benedict," Newton said as he leaned in close to the other man, "or you'll join them."

The thin man, Benedict, grunted and doubled over. It took Jacob a moment to realize the man had been punched. Newton stomped away. The door squealed again when he threw it open. When Newton glanced back at the thin man, Jacob saw the mask over the lower half of his face— silver with four spikes along the jaw—a breathing apparatus he'd only heard tales about. Alice's hand almost crushed his own. Newton was the city smith.

Jacob's leg started to cramp. He shifted it slightly. Jacob overbalanced and threw his hand out to catch himself. He felt the loose brick move beneath his fingers. He lunged for it as it fell, but the brick bounced through the largest opening in the grate.

The crack as it hit the stone floor below was thunder in the quiet dark. Something metallic rattled and clanged nearby.

"Who's there?"

Jacob froze when a shadow appeared at the grate.

CHAPTER NINETEEN

Alice's fingernails dug into Jacob's shoulder. Neither of them breathed.

"Damn bugs get higher every day," Benedict said. He slammed his palm against the grate a moment before Jacob heard retreating footsteps.

"Wait." Shadowy fingers reached through the grate and Jacob stared, horrified as that nimble hand wrapped around the vacuum flask. He must have dropped it when he dove for the brick. Jacob leaned farther back into the shadows beside Alice.

"Do you recognize it?" Benedict asked, handing the flask to the city smith.

Newton rolled the flask between his hands and narrowed his eyes. "It was certainly made with some skill."

Jacob turned his head. Alice's eyes were as wide in the shadows as his must have been. He heard something creak below them, and the door opened.

"Send a patrol down," Newton said. "It might be nothing, but I'd rather be sure of it." The heavy door slammed closed once more.

"I think they're gone," Jacob whispered. "Thought we were going to get caught."

"They want to send us out to die," Alice hissed. "Just so they have fuel for their damn boilers?"

Jacob blinked. He'd almost never heard Alice curse before. She saved it for special occasions, which generally meant when she was very, very mad.

"Let's go," Alice whispered. "I don't want to get caught by the patrol they're sending."

Jacob nodded and followed her into the darkness. He kept his left hand on the stone wall as they felt their way through the narrow tunnel. It took longer in the darkness, but they made their way around the huge stone pillar and the underground lake until they could no longer see the light from the grate behind them.

"Lantern should be safe now," Jacob said.

He couldn't *see* Alice in front of him, but he heard the rustling of her backpack and the quiet squeak of the lantern's handle before she clicked the igniter. The lantern burst to life like a sun. Jacob squinted against the brightness. Alice pointed the lantern out across the lake. Something shifted up on the far wall and Jacob shivered. It didn't look big, but he was tense enough that anything could make him jump.

They passed the wood coffins and continued up the sloping path. The pale stone coffins were a welcome sight as they made their way back through the twisting corridor of the dead. Alice paused at the mummies. She shined the light on them briefly and then walked back toward the entrance to the catacombs.

"I'd rather be with the mummies than those men," Alice muttered.

"Me too." Jacob was shaking when they finally made it back out of the catacombs. They'd be safer back in the train station. He was sure of it. "We need to get out of here."

Alice nodded. The motion was jerky, and Jacob thought she might be just as scared as he was. "What if he recognized Charles's flask?"

Jacob didn't answer, but the thought hadn't left his mind.

It wasn't much longer before Alice's light shone across the underground station. The table where they'd eaten was void of the dust that entombed everything else. Their footprints carved a living map, showing everywhere they'd walked before.

"Let's just go home," Jacob said.

Alice nodded and led the way past the broken carriage and back to the hallway with the collapsed staircase. Jacob glanced at the poster they'd seen when they'd first arrived. He wondered just how long the train station had been abandoned.

"I'll go up first," Jacob said as they stared up at the hatch with the spring bolt.

"What if those men are waiting for us?" Alice asked.

It was one of the reasons Jacob wanted to go up first, but he didn't say that to Alice. "I doubt this is the only way into the catacombs. Besides, do you really think they saw us? I think they would have said something if they had."

Alice nodded and aimed her lantern up at the hatch. Jacob climbed first, pausing with the heel of his boot hooked onto one rung and his ear close to the old spring bolt. Nothing but silence sounded overhead, so he pushed the hatch open. The relief he felt at the darkness blossomed in his chest.

"Clear," he said, pulling himself into the cellar of the old inn. He pulled the hatch back and held it while Alice followed him up.

"Let's get out of here," Alice said, sweeping her lantern around the room once before snuffing it.

They made their way over to the cellar door and snuck out as quietly as they'd come in.

CHAPTER TWENTY

THE STREETLAMPS BLAZED OVERHEAD BY the time Jacob had walked Alice home—with a promise to meet at Bat's in the morning—and started back to the house. He stood beside his sleeping parents, contemplating waking them to tell them what he'd heard in in the catacombs. Instead he wandered down to the workshop. The lights were out. No one was awake. Did he just wait until morning? Would that be too late?

He sat down for a while before tucking *The Dead Scourge* under his pillow, unwilling to let it out of his reach before Charles had seen it. His fingers ran over the copper hinges and the raised silver skull. Sleep finally took him before he could decide on whether or not to wake Charles.

When morning broke, half-blinding Jacob as he squinted across the room, he was surprised to see the doctor packing his bag and leaving the room.

The doctor nodded at him.

"You made it out of the Lowlands?" Jacob asked. "I'm glad."

"As am I." The doctor had a nice smile, but he looked uncomfortable, or anxious. Jacob couldn't place it.

He turned and looked at his parents after the doctor left. His father stared at a small bottle of medicine. His mother had her hand on his shoulder, but she was keeping her distance. Jacob knew what it meant. She only kept her distance like that when his dad was angry about something.

"What happened?" Jacob asked.

His dad looked up. "They raised the price of my medicine. Doc says the supply line has been cut off, and what's still in town is going to get more expensive."

"I was afraid of that," Charles said as he walked into the room, wiping his hands on a dark towel. Charles tucked the oily rag into an open pocket on his leather vest. He turned his head, as though he meant to see through the walls, all the way to the Lowlands.

"Supply and demand," Jacob's dad said. "Or it's just another instance of the Highlanders holding us down."

Charles sighed. "I normally wouldn't argue with that, but what do they gain? If the Lowlanders all get sick, it's going to spread into the Highborn people as well." Charles harrumphed. "I don't care how thick-headed Parliament can be; they don't want that."

Jacob barely kept his mouth shut about what he and Alice had overheard, but his dad was already upset, and he didn't want to make it worse.

"Maybe you're right, Charles," Jacob's mom said. "Either way, what can we do? We barely have the money to afford Peter's medicine as it is."

Charles looked at Jacob and cocked an eyebrow. Jacob looked away. He understood what Charles was saying without saying it. *Don't even think about stealing again.* This was one time he'd have to let Charles down. His dad needed medicine, and nothing was going to keep it from him.

"Did the coins from Festival help?" Jacob asked, glancing between his parents.

"Of course they did," his mom said. "They bought a full bottle. Thank you for that."

His dad gave her an odd look before nodding in agreement. Jacob knew what it meant. It helped, but not enough.

Jacob took a deep breath and looked at Charles. "Can I show you something in the lab?"

Charles shrugged. "Sure, let's go. Alice is waiting in the lab." The old man turned and led the way out of the room.

"Alice is here? Why didn't you tell me?"

"I just did."

Jacob tucked *The Dead Scourge* under his arm and followed Charles down the hall and out into the little lab. When the door opened and Alice looked up from the workbench, Jacob asked, "When did you get here?"

"Did you tell anyone what we heard?"

Jacob shook his head.

"What you heard where?" Bat asked, his bulky form filling the doorway behind Jacob a moment later.

"That's not important," Jacob said. He pulled the book out from under his arm and slid it onto the bench beside Charles.

Charles glanced at it and then his head jerked back toward the table. "Where did you get that?"

"It's …" Jacob glanced between Alice and Bat. He didn't think it would hurt if Bat knew about their find. "There's an old bookstore in the abandoned station by the catacombs."

"How did you even—" Bat started to say, but Charles silenced him with a sharp look over his wire-rimmed spectacles.

"Well then," Charles said. "I suppose you found your way under the streets."

Jacob nodded. "This book, though, it's written like they were actually there. In the Deadlands."

Charles slid the heavy book off the desk and ran his fingers over the silver skull. "That's because he was, Jacob. Some things … some people believe there are things that should be forgotten and lost to time."

"Like the Forgotten in the book?" Alice asked.

Charles sighed and flipped through a few pages. "Yes, like them."

"Miss Penny never taught us about them," Alice said.

Jacob nodded his agreement. "All she ever taught us was the men who lost the war died in the deserts."

Charles slid the book back to Jacob. "Son, you'll learn that people tend to omit the things they're most ashamed of. Or most terrified of. The Forgotten were exiled at the end of the war for their crimes." Charles glanced up at Bat.

"If you call having a difference of opinion a crime," Bat muttered. "Those men didn't deserve what they got."

"Neither did their families." Charles turned back to Jacob. "Read the book. I knew Archibald in the war. He was a good man. I hope he still is."

"What happened to him?" Alice asked.

Charles laced his fingers together and leaned on the workbench. "His book was declared an act of treason. It told a story different from the one our government had written into our history books, and they didn't take kindly to it. Oh, I can understand that on one hand. It was only a few years after the war, and we were holding the city together by threads at best."

"What did they do to him?"

Charles looked at Alice and then returned his gaze to the bench. He rolled a small bronze cylinder between his fingers. "They sentenced him to exile in the Deadlands."

"In the book it sounds like there are people out there, though." Jacob opened to the first pages. "It sounds like they have metalsmiths."

"They do," Charles said. He looked at Bat.

Bat cursed. "Yes, they do, but they're madmen."

"They are … different," Charles said.

"Keep that book hidden," Bat said to Jacob. "I doubt many people would realize what it is at a glance, but I don't want to see you in trouble over it."

"I'm surprised you don't just take it from him," Charles said, eying Bat.

The larger man shook his head slowly. "Our history shouldn't be lost to our children. They should know the good and the terrible." Bat turned around and walked back inside the house.

Charles watched him go. The old man's forehead wrinkled, and Jacob had only seen it like that when Charles was thinking hard. "He's changed."

"Bat?" Alice asked.

Charles nodded. "He's always been a government man. Used to work close with Parliament." Charles tapped the bronze cylinder on the workbench and set it down. "I'm honestly surprised he didn't take that book."

"Why?" Jacob asked, running his fingers over the old hinges.

"To burn it."

"What?" Alice stepped over beside Jacob. "That's crazy. Why would anyone want to burn a book? Much less an old history book."

"Some people would consider it dangerous, Alice."

"It's just a book," she said. "It can't be nearly as dangerous as the men we heard talking in the catacombs."

Charles jerked his head up and his eyes locked onto Alice. "What are you talking about?"

Alice looked at Jacob. He shrugged. Jacob wasn't sure what they should say and what they shouldn't, and Alice's guess was as good as his. Alice's guesses were usually better than his, actually.

Charles rested his back against the bench while Alice spoke. His eyebrows slowly drew down as she made it further into the story, telling him about the man named Newton and the plan to send the Lowlanders outside the walls.

"Gods," Charles said as he leaned over and pushed the door to the house open. "Bat! Bat, get back out here."

Bat's footsteps echoed on the wooden floors as he approached the lab. Jacob could tell he had been there before the door had opened.

"Who's Benedict?"

"Who?" Bat asked. He looked down for a moment and then

shrugged. "I'm not familiar with the name."

"He was with a large man, probably the city smith himself from what the kids have told me."

Bat shook his head slowly. "Maybe one of the smith's apprentices? I honestly don't know."

"With a top hat and a pinstripe suit?" Charles said. "I doubt that very much. Alice has told me a very disturbing story." Charles paused and glanced at the kids before turning his attention back to Bat. "It sounds like the man in the top hat was against it, but someone is planning to remove the Lowlanders from the city walls."

"That's insane," Bat said with a wave of his hand. "I can't believe they'd do that. I know there's segregation in the city—hell, there's a bloody wall that literally divides us all—but to throw people back into an unprotected town?" He shook his head. "I just can't believe it."

"I heard it too," Jacob said. "We're not making it up."

"They've no reason to lie," Charles said. "The kids gain nothing. What motivation is there?"

Bat ran his hand through his hair and frowned.

"Tell Bat what you heard Newton ask, Alice. He needs to know."

"He asked the other man … I don't remember exactly how he said it, but it was something like 'Do you think those bugs showed up on their own?'"

Jacob stood up and pointed at Alice. "Oh, remember what else he said? If Dauschen allies with the Deadlands, then none of it will matter."

Bat took a step backward like he'd been punched. He stared at Charles. "Who could herd the bugs like that?"

Charles nodded. "The only answers that make any sense terrify me."

CHAPTER TWENTY-ONE

J ACOB AND ALICE SPENT MOST of the day in the lab. *The Dead Scourge* lay open on the workbench and they both read, shoulder to shoulder, until Jacob's mom interrupted them for lunch, and again for dinner.

Charles left early in the morning, but he returned that night, shortly after Alice went home. Jacob was still in the lab. He'd read over half of *The Dead Scourge* in one day, and he had a million questions for Charles.

Jacob twisted the knob on the back of another arm brace, locking the brackets in place between glances at the book. He crouched down under the bench to find the tensioner, sorting through leather bags and wooden buckets full of all sorts of mostly useless things.

"What do you need?" Charles asked as he stepped into the lab.

"Tensioner. I think Bat moved it."

"No, no, that was me." Charles reached up to the top shelf of the little bench and lifted a flat piece of gray metal. Hidden behind the lip of the shelf as it was, Jacob never would have seen it.

"Thanks." Jacob began twirling the handle to loosen the vise before locking the tensioner in place. "Did … did you ever see any of the Mechanical Men in the Deadlands? During the war?"

Charles smiled. "I see you've made some progress on your book."

"Yeah, but did you ever see any?"

"I did, as a matter of fact. You know, they never liked that name though. Call themselves Biomechs."

"Biomechs?" Jacob asked as he looked the mechanical hand over.

Charles nodded. "It's a name from an old story, about a man who was half human and half machine. He strived to stay human, but kept replacing parts of himself with machinery. Philosophical nonsense, but not a bad story."

"Could someone survive like that?" Jacob asked.

Charles tapped the glove and pulled it off the tensioner. "Well, you've helped make people almost a full quarter machine, haven't you?"

Jacob looked at the webwork stretched along the brace as the hand closed on its own. "I hadn't really thought of it like that."

"I don't mean it in a bad way, Jacob. You've helped do some real good with these contraptions. Samuel told me they're sending a squad of wall repairmen into the Lowlands tomorrow with a few Spider Knights. Makes me think what you and Alice overheard was exactly right."

Jacob's smile fell when he remembered the catacombs.

"Thankfully, they're at least sending some folks out to look at the walls," Charles said. "I'm going to go with them, and I'd like you to come too."

"Charles," someone said from the doorway to the house. Jacob looked up and saw Bat leaning against the frame. "He's only a kid. You can't take him into that mess."

Charles took a deep breath, his gaze moving between Jacob and Bat. "We need parts, Bat. I can't afford them here, and Jacob can help me gather what we need in the observatory."

"What about the city smith?" Bat asked.

Charles shook his head. "Unless you want to hand over fifty gold, I doubt we can get what we need."

Bat leaned back and whistled. "Hell, we could buy a new Jacob for that."

Jacob frowned. He didn't find that terribly amusing.

Charles snapped a spring onto the tensioner and locked the thumb mechanism in place. "If what I'm afraid happened is actually what happened, most of the Lowlands will be clear already. Don't get me wrong, I'm not saying it will be completely safe, but with the knights we should be fine."

"The kid has talent," Bat said.

Jacob was much happier with that statement than the thought of buying a new Jacob.

"Now," Charles said, squeezing Jacob's shoulder, "we just need to convince your parents to let you go strolling around the Lowlands."

"We really don't have to. I can sneak out."

Charles chuckled. "I'd rather not have your mother strangle me in my sleep."

"Now you're just being optimistic," Bat said. He smiled and started into the house.

✧   ✧   ✧

"ABSOLUTELY NOT."

The look on his mom's face told Jacob all he needed to know, and he slumped into the high-backed chair. "We'll be with the knights. Samuel will be with us too. We'll be safe!"

Jacob's dad touched his mother's arm, and she glared at him.

"He would be invaluable helping me at the observatory," Charles said. "We need more parts to build the arms Jacob designed and the legs I've been working on. A good supply run could give us the springs and brackets to build nail gloves too. They'll be instrumental in the rebuilding of the Lowlands."

"Buy the parts," she said.

Charles rubbed his beard. "I would, if I could. They are terribly expensive from the city smith, and I don't have the raw materials to make them myself."

Bat cleared his throat. "If I may?"

Jacob's mom narrowed her eyes, but nodded.

"If Jacob and Charles aren't able to retrieve the parts from the observatory, I will feel obligated to buy the parts from the city smith. What Charles hasn't told you is the fact they will cost upwards of fifty gold."

"Fifty gold?" Jacob's dad asked. "You could feed a family for a year on that."

"Close to it," Bat said. "So, my offer is this: let Jacob go with Charles, and I will pay him five gold for his services."

"That's enough money to pay for Dad's medicine for two months," Jacob said. He kept his voice level, but it was an effort to hide his excitement over Bat's offer.

"I'll look after Jacob." Charles moved his gaze from one parent to the other. "No harm will come to him while he's with Samuel and me."

Jacob didn't think Charles had even asked Samuel yet, but Jacob was smart enough to keep his mouth shut.

"I don't know …" his dad said.

Jacob's mom took a deep breath and squeezed her forehead. "You ask me to risk my son to save my husband."

Bat laughed quietly. "I'm fairly certain, even if you say no, Jacob will be sneaking off to join Charles."

Jacob's mom showed a weak smile, and his dad acted like he was covering up a cough, but Jacob was pretty sure it was a laugh.

"Promise me," she said as she looked at Charles.

"On my life."

She nodded.

Jacob could scarcely believe it, and he crossed the room to throw his arms around his mom and dad. Excitement warred with dread as the realization of what lay outside the city wall flashed across his mind.

"Enjoy your adventure, son," his dad said.

"Thanks." Jacob gave his dad another hug and then walked back to stand beside Charles.

"Alright," Charles said. "Let's get packed up and ready to go." He ushered Jacob down the hall and out into the lab. "I'll get the saddlebags emptied out. I think that will give us enough room to carry what we need."

Jacob took everything out of his backpack. He hesitated with his hand on *The Dead Scourge*, but he decided to leave it behind. It was pretty heavy, and it would take up room they might need.

Charles strapped the holster for the air cannon across his back alongside a slim backpack. He slid the gun in and out, making sure it still had clearance. "Keep these on," he said, tossing two flimsy lengths of metal and leather to Jacob.

"What are they? They look like my sliding gloves."

"Sliding gloves?" Charles said as he shook his head and smiled. "It's armor. You can snap it onto your gloves and then hook it into the straps on your vest."

Jacob looked down at his vest, unsure of exactly where he'd be hooking it. He looked at one end of the metal sleeve, and then the other. Three hooks folded out from inside. "Oh, I get it." He slid his arm into one sleeve and fumbled with the hooks until they were securely fastened into his vest.

Charles gave it a tug. He nodded when it didn't budge. "It'll save you from some nasty bites if it has to, but it's best not to test it."

"You really think we're going to run into invaders?"

"Yes," Charles said. He handed Jacob a long metal pipe about as thick as his thumb. "I know Alice is better with a spear, but now you can tell her all about this one. Don't point it at anything you don't want dead when you hit that button."

"Are we heading out tonight?"

"I'm too old for that kind of excitement. Besides, the repairmen aren't leaving until the morning. I don't want to be out there without the knights."

Jacob started taking his armor off. He set it on top of his backpack on the workbench. Since he wasn't taking it with him, he carried *The Dead Scourge* back into the house to read before starting his restless night of sleep.

CHAPTER TWENTY-TWO

"S TORM'S ROLLING IN," CHARLES SAID as his gaze crept skyward.

Jacob looked up and frowned at the layers of clouds. Light pierced the overcast sky above them, but far in the distance, the world was lost to darkness. Jacob adjusted his backpack and made a mental note to grab a poncho before they left for the Lowlands.

"Let's get everything loaded onto the steambike and meet Samuel down by the gate."

"Mom packed some snacks for us," Jacob said. He slid his backpack off and stuffed two sandwiches and a bundle of jerky into it.

"That was awfully nice of her," Charles said. He closed the saddlebags and pulled out a Burner. He checked the water level in the steambike's boiler, screwed the cap back on and then hit the igniter. It wasn't long before Jacob heard the water boiling, and steam worked its way out of the exhaust.

Jacob stuffed a poncho into his backpack. "You want one?"

Charles shook his head. "Little rain never hurt anyone."

Jacob didn't disagree, really, but it looked like a *very* nasty storm moving in. He put a vacuum flask filled with water in his pack and pulled the buckles tight.

"Here," Charles said.

Jacob glanced up just in time to see something leather and shiny headed for his face. He barely got his hands up in time to catch it. "Goggles?"

"For the steambike. It's a bit windier than I remembered. Hard to keep your eyes open without them."

Jacob had seen goggles like them before with their dark leather straps, brass frames, and yellow-tinted glass. "Are these zeppelin goggles?"

Charles chuckled and adjusted the load of packs and guns on his back. "They are at that."

"Where did you get them? There hasn't been a zeppelin in Ancora in … in … years?"

"Sounds about right. Not since the last embargo with Dauschen. Of the few airmen we had here, most of them moved to Dauschen. Ancora always was more of a train town."

Jacob remembered Miss Penny telling them about almost every citizen of Dauschen being pilots. Even the kids were raised to pilot airships. "Is it true what they say? That you could fit a hundred people on the largest airships, the zeppelins?"

"At least," Charles said with a broad smile. "I rode on a few of them during the war. Maybe you'll get to see them one day if our government ever gets its head on straight." He cinched the ties on one of the larger pockets on his vest. "Let's go meet Samuel."

✧   ✧   ✧

THE WORLD WAS SOMEWHAT TINTED through Jacob's new goggles. He kept his arms wrapped firmly around Charles's waist. The streets of the Highlands were a friendlier fare than the cobblestones of the Lowlands, but it still felt like Charles was trying to shake his brains out through his stomach.

They swerved down the street, dodging carriages and beetles and the occasional hapless pedestrian. Some people looked on them with shock, some with awe, and a few with what seemed to be fear. Jacob almost sighed in relief when the steambike began to slow near the westernmost gatehouse.

Charles glanced over his shoulder. "We're here. Pretty smooth ride in the Highlands. Can't say the same for our trip through the Lowlands, but we'll worry about that later."

Jacob blew out a breath and slid off the steambike, carefully avoiding the flames beneath the boiler. Charles took his backpack off and hung it on the steambike's handlebars before heading to the gatehouse.

Jacob followed, happy to be off the bike for however short a time. "Where are we going?"

"I want to talk to Samuel before we leave," Charles said. He paused in the middle of the courtyard and then walked toward a cluster of Spider Knights. They were saddling their mounts, getting ready to escort the repairmen into the Lowlands. A dizzying blur of arachnid legs erupted below the mounts when the spiders shifted from side to side. Jacob guessed they'd been locked up in the stables too long and were itching to run.

"Samuel!" Charles shouted as they approached the knights.

Several of the men looked up. It only took a moment for Jacob to recognize his friend and Bessie.

Samuel raised the facemask of his helmet and smiled. "What are you doing here, old man? We're about to head into the Lowlands. Take stock of the damage."

"We're coming with you."

"You and … Jacob?"

Charles nodded as he shook hands with Samuel. Bessie flexed her legs, raising her eyes up over Jacob's head before touching his shoulder with a furry leg. She crouched back down, and Jacob patted her between the eyes.

Samuel frowned and adjusted his gloves. "I don't think this is going to be a place for kids. Or old men, for that matter."

"I can assure you, this old man isn't going anywhere except the Lowlands today."

Samuel sighed and leaned close into Charles's ear. "Why do you want to take the kid? It's not going to be safe."

Jacob knew he wasn't supposed to hear that, but he wasn't going to let it slide. "I can take care of myself."

Samuel glanced at him.

"See?" Charles said. "He'll be fine."

Jacob pulled on his armored sleeves and slid the hooks into his vest, glad he'd worn one of his heavier shirts underneath, as the wind had a bite to it. The fact Samuel didn't want him to go hurt a little, but he also knew Samuel just didn't want to see him injured.

The Spider Knight started to protest again, but Charles cut him off.

"Unless you can help me identify and pull all the parts we need, I need Jacob."

Samuel rolled his neck in a small circle and looked at Jacob. "Fine, I'm not going to argue with you. Just stay close to me, will you? I'm not explaining to your mom why you're dead."

Bessie shifted quickly from one side to the other, smacking Samuel in the head with an unfastened buckle.

"Well," Samuel said as he snatched the loose buckle and fastened it, "I think Bessie's okay with that. Give me a minute to talk to my captain. He's not going to be happy about it."

✧   ✧   ✧

It wasn't long before Samuel returned from the eastern gatehouse, an odd expression on his face. Jacob wasn't exactly sure what it meant.

"You look flabbergasted," Charles said.

"I … he … he said it's fine," Samuel said. "Apparently … you made an arm." Samuel shrugged.

A tall man with dark hair and a thick mustache walked out of the gatehouse. All the eyes in the courtyard shifted to him. He wore a gold-lined uniform set with more medals than Jacob had seen in his entire life.

The man held the attention of all those around him without words, only an undeniable presence.

"This is the boy?" the captain asked. His voice rang in deep, basso tones as he leaned down slightly to look at Jacob. Jacob wasn't short—he was actually tall for his age—but this man was a mountain.

"Sir?" Jacob said, barely squeaking the words out.

The captain extended his hand and almost crushed Jacob's with a firm handshake. "Thank you."

It was about then that a little boy walked out from behind the mountain. He was small with brown hair and an arm made of metal.

"Peter!" Jacob said. "Shouldn't you be at the hospital still?"

"I have to go back, but they let me leave for a little bit."

"How are you doing?"

"Good. The arm you made me is the next best thing to having my own. The other kids want one."

The captain ruffled Peter's hair. "He's my boy, Jacob. I can't thank you enough." He turned and looked down at his son. "You should get back to your mother. She's waiting at the hospital."

"Bye, Jacob!" Peter said.

Jacob waved as the boy walked away, escorted by one of the knights.

"I was afraid he'd be teased for the loss of his arm," the captain said, bringing everyone's attention back to him. "People can be cruel creatures." He rubbed his hands together and looked at Jacob. "And some people can be selfless, generous souls."

Charles squeezed Jacob's shoulder. "He is." Charles glanced between Jacob and the captain. "Usually."

The captain smiled. "Samuel tells me you're going into the Lowlands today. The sentries on the towers tell us it's mostly clear, but there are occasional signs of movement. Be on your guard, and stay with the knights. If I didn't know of your intentions to build more arms, I would never allow this."

Charles ran a hand over his beard. "The horde of invaders that broke into the city—I want to see them too, and I want to see where they ended up."

The captain gave Charles a thoughtful look. "Most of my knights will be guarding the wall repairmen. I'll keep a small detachment with you, but that's all we will risk."

"Sir," Charles said, before he gave the captain a perfectly formed salute.

The captain eyed Charles for a moment, and then returned the salute. "Call me Lewis. Best of luck." He turned to leave and clapped Samuel on the shoulder. "Take care of them."

"Sir."

Samuel turned back around and grimaced. "Looks like I'm not getting rid of either one of you."

"Not unless you're a terrible Spider Knight and let us get eaten," Charles said with a broad smile.

Samuel narrowed his eyes and slammed his facemask down.

Charles leaned closer to Samuel and spoke quietly. "The conversation Jacob and Alice overheard … it could mean trouble."

"Bat thinks so too," Samuel said. His voice sounded muffled slightly by his armored facemask, but the mesh slits on the front made it easy enough to hear.

"If …" Charles started to say, but then stopped to think. He looked at the townsfolk milling around them. "If people *decide* to move back to the Lowlands soon, we need to know what's waiting out there."

Someone began barking orders up near the gate. A line of knights formed with the Spider Knights behind them. In the middle were the wall repairmen with carriages filled to bursting with pulleys and scaffolding.

"Stay with the repairmen for now," Samuel said. The gates creaked open and he led them into the formation.

CHAPTER TWENTY-THREE

T HE CITY GATES OPENED, AND the full devastation of the Fall sprawled across the Lowlands before them.

"Gods in heaven," Charles said. He pushed the steambike outside the city wall. "Get your gloves on."

The forward movement of the entire party slowed to a crawl. The beetles pulling the repairmen's carriages jostled and shifted, unaware of why they were suddenly stopping. Jacob reached out toward the ruins of the Lowlands, and slowly let his arm fall back to his side.

"It's … it's gone."

He stared at the rubble of what had once been the lower wall. A few connected bricks still stood, jagged shadows against a calm, cloudy sky. Black carapaces and gleaming blue legs were cut, dismembered, and shattered among the remains of the buildings.

Jacob felt a pressure behind his eyes before he realized there were tears running down his cheeks.

"Jacob," Charles's voice grew firm, drawing his attention. "Get your gloves on."

Jacob nodded as he unbuttoned his thigh pocket and slid the metal-scaled gloves out. He stared at the mesh web as he pulled it over his fingers one at a time. The metal looked dull in the cloudy sunlight when it snapped into his armored sleeves.

"We'll see worse before this is over," Samuel said. He sidled up beside them on Bessie. "I'm glad so many of the homes survived. There's a lot of debris for the bugs to hide in. Be on your guard."

Jacob watched Bessie stalk toward the fallen wall with Samuel on her back. Jacob's eyes trailed from the Spider Knight to the ruined buildings around him. A few homes had survived, yes, but it seemed like there were just as many left on the ground in so much rubble.

The group of repairmen started moving quicker, their wheels rumbling across the cobblestones and crunching up bits of debris and pieces of invaders. Charles and Jacob followed. They made it down the gradual incline, into the courtyard with the fountain, before Jacob saw the first man.

He didn't look so different, lifeless in his armor and face down as he was. The body was too thin, his flesh already taken by the scavengers that ruled over the dead in Ancora.

Beyond that nameless soldier, past the fountain, lay a crater littered with the bodies of Red Death. The remnants and shells of the invaders that had almost caught them on the steambike sent a shiver down his spine.

Charles whistled. "You took out a horde of those things with that mine you dropped."

One of the repairmen glanced back. "The boy did that?"

Charles let out a humorless chuckle. "That he did."

"Damn."

The winds shifted, and the thick, gagging scent of decay filled Jacob's mouth until he almost retched.

"Easy," Charles said. "You'll get used to it after a time."

Jacob wanted to scrape his tongue and rinse his mouth out with Charles's firewater.

Bessie wandered back over to them. The spider seemed twitchy, rotating quickly from one angle to the next, and Samuel grimaced as he patted her head. "Did you want to check any of those Reds?" he asked when they weren't within earshot of the others.

"Not enough left," Charles said. "If I'm right, there will be more of the blasted things."

Samuel nodded, his silver faceplate glimmering in a ray of sun while he urged Bessie toward the front of the line. He exchanged words with a knight near the front before scampering ahead, down the hill that eventually would lead them to the Square.

The road took them close to one of the collapsed buildings. The legs of a dead Widow Maker curled around what looked like the heavy black crown of a chimney. Jacob choked and turned away when he saw the scattered skeleton of a woman beside it, parts still settled inside a pale blue dress. His eyes started to burn again when he felt Charles put an arm around him.

"It's okay. Nothing can hurt her now. Do you need to go back? No one here would think any less of you."

One of the repairmen stood by the skeleton for a moment, hunched over, and lost his lunch. He coughed and choked and hacked before wiping his mouth and cursing.

"No," Jacob said. "I want to help."

Charles squeezed him, and the reassuring gesture almost made Jacob cry again. The rubble across the road shifted. The spear slung across Jacob's back almost sprang into his hand. He faced the cascade of falling wood and bricks that clattered and bounced into the street.

Something moved. A glint of black. A hint of red. It moved again, and enough of the building fell away to reveal a Red Death. It was injured, and when it saw the group of knights, it screamed in that shrill, terrifying wail.

One of the knights started toward it.

"No!" Charles said. He slammed the metal wedge beneath the steambike and unholstered the air cannon on his back. "Don't step on the bricks. It's not stable." He racked the slide three times. The Red Death had worked itself out far enough to raise one of its wings.

Charles pulled the trigger.

A deaf silence followed the boom.

All that remained of the Red Death was a smear of yellow blood and chunks of its black carapace.

"What the hell did you shoot that with?" one of the knights asked.

"Science." Charles spat on the ground and holstered the air cannon.

Jacob stayed close to Charles as they rounded the bend. He occasionally glanced up to watch the Spider Knights prowling over the buildings and debris. Jacob always found it fascinating how the knights moved, leaning and standing in their saddles so their mounts could climb or descend a sheer wall without losing them.

"A lot of the wall is still intact here," one of the repairmen said from the top of his carriage. He pointed to the west. "Wouldn't take much to reinforce it, but that won't do much good with the higher walls gone. I think we could—"

"Hold!" a knight at the front of the line shouted.

Jacob stared. There was a pile—a mountain—of Red Death and Widow Makers and those weird Walker-looking invaders where the bank used to be. His eyes traced the scythe-like arms of the Mantises. They were impaled in the invaders, and some were in their own kind. Widow Makers had died with their fangs in Walkers and Red Death, and … people.

Clothes and skeletal limbs lay strewn among the carnage. Bright fabrics and old blood mixed with the dead invaders, all encased in a rancid stench.

A repairman fell to the ground and put his head in his hands. "Gods … so many."

"This is it," Charles said before he cursed so loudly and at such length that every knight turned to look at him. "This is one of the frenzies. Samuel!"

The Spider Knight nodded and said something to the knights closest to him. Jacob could see them making hand gestures, but he couldn't understand what they were saying until Samuel shouted back from across the Square.

"Let us check the dead. We'll clear it for you."

Charles nodded.

Jacob hadn't realized just how high the mountain of dead bugs was until Samuel stood beside it.

"Stay by me," Charles said. "If too many of those things are still alive, we'll need to make a fast escape."

Jacob didn't get a chance to so much as nod before the first Widow Maker scrambled over the hill of corpses. Its obsidian legs gleamed as it shifted in the sunlight. The Widow Maker could have been mistaken for a sculpture of black gemstones if it weren't moving.

The knights recoiled and circled the mound of dead. The Widow Maker raised its front legs and crouched.

"Prepare yourselves!" one of the Spider Knights shouted.

Bessie and the other Jumpers began beating their legs on the ground in a steady rhythm—one two, pause, one two, pause. Jacob had seen small Jumpers tap out warnings with their feet, but he'd never seen the Spider Knight's mounts do it.

The Widow Maker shifted, following the Spider Knight beneath it. It never saw Samuel and Bessie climbing the building behind it. Bessie leapt. Samuel's halberd pierced the Widow Maker's head with a crack and then Bessie returned to the earth in two quick hops off the mountain of carcasses. The rhythmic tapping of the Spider Knight's mounts subsided.

"Come on," Charles said, pushing the steambike forward. "It's clear."

A few moments later, two of the knights shouted, "Clear!"

Samuel lowered his faceplate and dangled a Sweet-Fly in front of Bessie's eyes. She delicately plucked it from his grip and began grinding it up. "Looks like the rest are dead."

Charles wedged the stand under the steambike again and looked over the mound of dead. "I want to be wrong about this, Samuel."

"We're going to check the wall," Ambrose said. "This section looks mostly intact to the southwest. If it is, we may just need to worry about the walls closer to the city wall."

"Split the knights?" Samuel asked Captain Lewis.

The captain nodded and began shouting orders. By the time he was done, over half the Spider Knights and the city knights had gone to the west wall with the repairmen. Samuel and a handful of others stayed behind with Charles and Jacob.

"I know those men are the priority," Charles said, stepping up beside the mountain of invaders. "Thank you for leaving us a guard."

"Samuel would be a pain in my neck for a year if I left you two out here to die," Captain Lewis said. "I distinctly remember having to listen to his complaints for a month after we had to abandon a cat to a nest of Walkers. How long do you need?"

Charles looked back to the pile of carcasses and death. "As long as it takes."

Captain Lewis chuckled and nodded. "Scream if you need us, tinker."

Charles watched Lewis saunter away on his mount before glancing up at Samuel. "I rather like your captain."

"He's alright. Most days." Samuel winked at Jacob and hopped down off Bessie. "Now, what exactly are we looking for?"

"You'll know it when you see it, I'm afraid. It'll be attached to some of the bugs' heads."

Jacob had seen Red Deaths in his classroom before, but they were small and dead and no larger than your average Pill-Bug. Alice's family had raised some giant Pill-Bugs, sure, but most domestic Pills never got too large to carry around. Miss Penny had kept some of those hatchling Red Deaths in large jars, preserved in some kind of stinky fluid.

Jacob reached out and touched the shell that hid the wings of the dead beetle. One wing was missing, so only half of the creature's trademark red skull stared back at him. The shell felt slick and surprisingly thin, with a few ridges and bumps. He pushed on it, and something cracked beneath it.

"Let's get this over with." Charles peeled back small segments of a Widow Maker's broken legs and tossed them into the street. Pieces of a Walker went next, and Charles grunted when he tried to roll a segment of a Walker out of the pile. It was at least four feet high.

Jacob and Samuel stared at him for a moment. Then Samuel stepped up to help pry the pieces loose.

"Keep an eye out, yeah?" Samuel said to the other knights. "And watch for fangs! We don't need anyone dying."

Only a few called back, but Jacob figured the rest were helping keep watch too.

The chitin and bodies were all dry on the outside of the mountain, but as they dug deeper, things grew moist, and the stench grew ever more foul.

Jacob gagged when a piece of a wing dragged some slimy bits of blue goo out of the pile with it. He let go of the wing, but the blood and innards kept it stuck to his hand. "Gah, this is so gross."

Charles leaned over and looked at the mess stuck to Jacob's hands. "Ah, you have part of a silk sac." The old man bent down and picked up a broken bit of a Walker's leg. He scraped it along the palm of Jacob's glove until the wing and the ball of silk beneath it stuck to the leg instead of Jacob. Charles flipped the entire mess farther into the street and went back to work.

Jacob opened and closed his hands a few times. It was a little sticky, but not as bad as he'd thought it would be. The scene repeated itself a dozen times, knights cursing as they got stuck in Widow Maker silk and blood and gunk.

"I always did want to be a knight for the glory," Samuel shouted from a little higher up the mountain of dead bugs.

The other knights around them laughed. Jacob smiled and glanced at Charles. Charles didn't laugh. He stared at something.

"What is it?" Jacob asked.

"Your spear," Charles said quietly. He eased the air cannon into his hands. "Now."

Jacob's motions were not so slow. His arm whipped up, pulled the spear off his back, and slid the trigger forward in one quick, smooth motion. A three-bladed head snapped out the front of the rod, propped up on reinforced fingers of steel, while the butt of the spear lengthened.

Jacob didn't have time to think as the mountain of dead things began to shift. A great maw appeared in the hole Charles had been working at. Rows of teeth, each the length of Jacob's finger, filled the cavern of the worm's white, maggot-fleshed mouth.

All he heard were screams.

CHAPTER TWENTY-FOUR

"CARRION!" ONE OF THE KNIGHTS screamed as a sea of the flesh eaters shot forward from the crevices of dead bugs, each as long as a man was tall and thick as a small Pill-Bug.

Instinct was all that drove Jacob's thrust. Somewhere his brain had registered that Charles only pumped the cannon twice, that if he didn't move, they were both going to die.

So he moved.

He leaned forward and jammed the triple-bladed spear up through the bottom of the Carrion's pale mouth. He felt the spear clank and bend when it hit row after row of the beast's teeth, finally exiting the top of its head in a burst of grayish black slime.

Jacob jerked the spear back out of the Carrion Worm. It slid easily through the gleaming flesh, coming free before the bulbous body tumbled the short way to the ground, cracking the brittle legs and shells beneath it.

The Spider Knights were fast, so very fast. Bessie leapt backward when the worms attacked, giving Samuel time to free his halberd. The weapon made quick work of the Carrion, but not all the knights on foot had been so lucky.

Charles swung the air cannon around and focused on one of the knights, who was on his back, his sword laid across the maw of a great worm. That sword was the only thing keeping him alive, and the knight was losing the battle. Charles adjusted his aim, and the air cannon thundered when he pulled the trigger.

The worm was relentless. Even with a quarter of its body missing, it pushed down on the knight.

Charles pumped the air cannon again and stepped closer as the knight screamed. He raised the gun to his shoulder, and half the worm's head vanished in the boom that followed.

The knight rolled to the side, coated in grayish black gore. He took three steps up the mountain of death and lunged. His sword cut through the head of another worm, and the creature died instantly.

Movement all around them stopped. The spiders were restless after the battle, pacing from side to side while their knights tried to calm them.

"It looks like everyone's okay," Jacob said.

Charles glanced down at the boy and shook his head. "No, son. No, they're not. I never should have brought you out here." He raised his eyes to the hill of carcasses.

Samuel stood there, looking down at the shiny armor beneath the bulk of a Carrion Worm. Blood—red, human blood—stained the worm and the body beneath it. Samuel shook his head. "Jones is gone."

"Jones," the knights around them echoed. It was only that one word. There would be time for mourning later, but on the battlefield, it was only ever that one word. Jacob heard stories that knights would use the names of their fallen comrades as a battle cry. He never imagined it could be such a terrible sound. This was not the glorious scream of an army bent on revenge. It was only sadness for the loss of their friend.

Samuel reached down and pulled something out of Jones's hand. The Spider Knight half slid, half walked down to Charles and Jacob. Bessie circled the dead bugs, coming to stand beside her knight.

"Is this what you're looking for?" Samuel asked. He held a small metal box out to Charles.

Charles took it, held it in his hand, and frowned. He turned the rectangular box over and over. Jacob could see dents and scratches and what looked like marks from fangs and mandibles.

Samuel turned to the worm Jacob had killed, and looked as though he meant to kill it again. "Carrion." He toed a stray chunk of the worm. "That means …"

"Plague Bugs," Charles said. "I've only ever seen so many Carrion Worms when there were Plague Bugs."

Charles pried the back of the box open and pulled out a few wires. "Damnit, it's a transmitter." He held up a short, fat glass tube. Two metal bars and a copper wire coiled inside of it. Every few seconds, a burst of dim blue light flashed in the tiny gap between the metal. Charles ripped it out of the transmitter and stared at it. The flash died, separated from whatever had been giving it power.

"We need to find the other half. It's going to be embedded in the bugs."

"Charles!" someone shouted from across the Square, closer to the wall repairmen. It was Captain Lewis, and he was heading toward them.

"Captain?" Charles asked.

The captain didn't say anything else until he got closer. His steel boots clanged against the cobblestones as he came to a halt. "I think we found it."

It was a small thing, with a bit of gore splashed across it. Square, not much different in appearance than the transmitter.

Charles cursed and took the device out of the captain's hand. "The transmitters inside the walls drew them close." He squeezed a tab on one end of the gray box and popped the rear panel off. "Once they were close enough, a signal went out to the head units. It sends the bugs into a mating frenzy."

"That would make them more aggressive," Samuel said.

"That's an understatement." Charles poked through the innards of the receiver with his index finger. "It makes them unbiased killers. Winner gets a mate, everything else dies. Except there's no mate to win, so they just kill everything."

"How do you know that?" Jacob asked.

Charles froze and stared into the receiver. He cursed so long and so hard, even Samuel took a step back before the old man smashed the receiver on the ground. "It's my own design."

Jacob recoiled at the words. "*What?*"

Charles sighed. "We used them in the Deadlands War. Set up ambushes for supply lines. There was a general who thought we could do more with the transmitters. Mount them on cities and let the bugs tear our enemies to pieces. I never let them do it."

Samuel crossed his arms and barely suppressed a shiver. "I can see why."

"You can't control the bugs," Charles said. He curled his hands into fists. "You can lead them to a transmitter, but you can't stop them. They'll kill everything and everyone. Combatants, civilians, children. I never gave them my designs for fear of something like this."

Samuel picked up the crushed metal housing. Some wires and a magnet hung out of the side. "Someone figured it out."

"That they did, boy. That they did."

"It was probably done in the lead time before Festival," Samuel said. "No one would have looked twice at a stranger."

Charles looked up at the captain. "You need to find the rest of the transmitters. As long as their power supply lasts, they could outfit more bugs with receivers." He wiped his hand off on a scrap of relatively clean cloth. "The receivers are dangerous too, but less so than the transmitters."

"They'll be in the piles of dead bugs?" the captain asked.

Charles nodded.

"Well, we need to clear the Carrion Worms out as it is, so we'll keep watch for the transmitters." He turned and started to walk away.

"Captain Lewis."

The captain turned back to Charles.

"Are you aware of any rumors to send the Lowlanders back into this mess? So they can work the mines?"

The captain grimaced and looked at the tower of dead bugs before returning his gaze to Charles. His voice was barely above a whisper. "You know I can't speak of Parliament's secrets, so tell no one what I say here." The captain paused and added, "Swear it as a man of honor."

"I will not speak of it, or of the source. This I swear, by sword and blood."

The captain nodded. "Good enough." He crossed his arms and bit his lip. "Charles, you seem a good man, and Samuel speaks highly of you and Jacob. I can never repay you for what you've done for my son, but this puts my family at risk …" He trailed off and narrowed his eyes before taking a deep breath. "Perhaps I heard a rumor."

"What rumor?"

"There's a man I know," the captain said. "I won't say who, for I swore an oath of my own, but let us say he is powerful. I've heard tales he's colluded with Dauschen. His supporters will tell you he's merely trying to forge an alliance, but there are whispers of darker things. A man—a man who died mere days after telling me—said our unnamed politician was set upon destroying the Lowlands."

"I know the politicians aren't fond of us in the Lowlands," Charles said, "but that seems rather extreme."

"Destroy the Lowlands and set up a trade hub," the captain said. "They'd make more in taxes in a month of trading with Dauschen than they do in a year from the Lowlands. If the Lowlands are cleared, all they need to do is bring the train back into service."

Charles cursed.

"What?" Samuel said. "That's insane. You can't just wipe out a whole city."

The captain lowered his head. "I thought so too, Samuel. I thought my informant was mad, but look at the evidence. The first part of the plan was to unleash Plague Bugs in the Lowlands."

"War-mongering fools," Charles said as he cracked his knuckles. "All they do is send our children to their deaths. For what? For gold? Are those the men you want to serve, Captain? Men who will send your son to his death to line their pockets?"

The captain visibly stiffened, but he didn't meet Charles's eyes. "They offer protection here, Charles. Protection for our families. What choice do we have?"

"Hard choices. The easy choice is rarely the right one."

The captain stared at Charles for a moment, and then nodded. He took his leave without another word, walking toward the group of wall repairmen.

"If they intend to run us out of town," Charles said, turning back to Jacob and Samuel, "I plan to make as many arms and legs as possible before they do it. Give these people hope, and give them something to fight with."

Jacob saw the captain glance back at Charles's words, and the captain's shoulders seemed to hunch forward ever so slightly.

"They won't run you out, old man," Samuel said. "They're just going to run out everyone like Jacob and his family."

"Run them out?" Charles said before he spat on the ground. "Feed them to the Carrion Worms, more like. Jacob, saddle up and get ready to go. We're heading to the observatory."

"You can't still be serious about that," Samuel said. "We've seen Widow Makers and Carrion Worms! We have no idea what's between here and there."

"Oh, I think we have some idea," Charles snapped. "Are you coming?" He hoisted the leather backpack onto his shoulders.

"Dammit, old man," Samuel said. His eyes trailed from Charles to Jacob. "You're seriously taking the kid?"

"The *kid* knows my lab as well as I do. Maybe better. I'm definitely taking the kid."

"It's not worth it," Samuel said.

"Worth it?" Charles asked. "Those of us from the Lowlands are running out of money fast. It's been kind of the vendors inside the city walls to lower their prices, but once demand outstrips supply … I've seen what hungry men can do."

"Can't you just buy the parts off the city smith? See if he'll loan them to you?"

"No," Charles said. "I can't. We have history, and you know damn well he's a cheap bastard." Charles waved his hand, dismissing Samuel's words. "Now you sound like Bat, always banking on a generosity that could fail you at any moment."

"Come with us," Jacob said, looking up at Samuel. "Charles can cut you in on any sales to the Highlanders."

Samuel sighed and his gaze traveled up the mountain of dead bugs. "It's not the money, Jacob. I don't want to see either one of you get hurt just to go pick up some junk from the observatory."

"It's the only way," Charles said. "I have all the springs I need back in my old lab, and enough fittings carved out to make a dozen gloves. It would cost me fifty gold to get those parts from the city smith. Bat wasn't exaggerating."

Samuel cursed and stared at Charles. "Fine. Fine! I'm coming with you. If you get any of us killed, I'm going to haunt you for the rest of your life."

Charles grinned through his beard. "Well, that won't much matter if we're all dead."

CHAPTER TWENTY-FIVE

THE CAPTAIN HADN'T BEEN HAPPY when Samuel relayed their intent to move forward with the plan, regardless of the Widow Makers and Carrion Worms. Lewis didn't want any of them to go, but he hadn't tried to stop them either. He'd wished them luck.

"Why didn't he try to stop us?" Jacob asked, unable to contain his curiosity any longer.

"He needs the reconnaissance," Samuel said. He bounced slightly in Bessie's saddle. The spider was taking her time, staying close to the steambike's warmth, while Charles bobbed and weaved between fallen buildings and shattered carriages.

Jacob squeezed his arms around Charles when the steambike swerved around a dead beetle. It was one of the huge horned beasts he'd seen in the courtyard around the Hall. He couldn't tell if it was the same one, but it was dead nonetheless. Not far past it was a white carriage, broken into a dozen sections.

"Oh no." Jacob shut his eyes and looked away, but he could still see the skeleton in the brilliant, shredded white dress. The lady who had gifted him the money to play Cork, he was sure of it.

"What is it?" Charles shouted. He slid the throttle to the side and accelerated through the courtyard.

"I just … I think I knew her."

Charles nodded, but he didn't say another word. The steambike slowed slightly as they came to the other side of the Hall.

"Don't stop," Samuel said from his perch on Bessie's back. The Spider Knight was off to their left, scampering over a random pile of bricks. Bessie adjusted her weight the instant the rubble shifted, never losing a step or tossing her rider.

Jacob stared past Samuel and Bessie, his eyes following the trail of limbs and carcasses that led up to the front door of the Hall. The mountain of carnage almost reached the peak of the entryway.

"Gonna be a hell of a cleanup," Charles said as he glanced at the dead bugs before turning his attention back to the road. "I was thinking about checking the lift, but now I'm thinking we should get to the lab and get out."

"As fast as possible," Samuel said. "I'm going topside to make sure there isn't anything waiting between here and there."

Charles nodded.

Samuel tapped a simple pattern across Bessie's legs, and the spider leapt to the side of a building. Samuel leaned forward to keep his balance as Bessie scaled the wall and disappeared over the peak of the roof.

The cobblestones grew rougher the farther they traveled into the Lowlands. Neither of the steambike's riders tried to speak as the tires bounced and dipped over the street. Charles slowed and turned down two alleys. Jacob and Charles didn't see any more of the dead mountains as they flew down the hill and started up the incline that would take them to the observatory.

Bessie danced along the rooftops, Samuel's armor gleaming in the sunlight where it wasn't caked in gore. He pointed to the opposite side of the homes and drew his hand across his throat.

Charles cursed. "Means we've got company." He opened the throttle and didn't speak again.

The steambike felt like it was trying to rattle the teeth right out of Jacob's head. "Thank the gods," Jacob said under his breath when the dome of the observatory grew larger in front of them, and the bike coasted to the door.

Samuel followed up right behind them and slid off Bessie's saddle. He patted her head and tapped her front leg twice.

Jacob knew it was the command to have her stay put. Samuel didn't normally give her any commands. She just stayed close by. The fact that Samuel had given her one now unnerved him.

"What's over there?" Charles asked. He worked at the lock on the front door. The mechanism began moving and sliding, retracting the bolts all around the door while Samuel spoke.

"Red Death, and lots of them. I don't think they're dead at all. It doesn't look like the wall is down completely, which is a pleasant surprise."

"May have come up through the underground," Charles said. "Some of the old tunnels are still accessible."

"Under the second level?" Jacob asked, his voice rising in pitch.

Samuel watched the road behind them, but he spared Jacob a glance and a nod. "That's why I told you to stay out of there, kid. The tunnels run from the observatory all the way up to the castle."

Jacob looked back toward the city wall. The castle—what the Lowlanders liked to call Parliament—was obscured by fog and distance. He hadn't forgotten the sounds he'd heard with Alice in the catacombs. Something had been down there with them, and chances were good it had been some of these bugs.

The final bolt snapped open and Charles swung the heavy door inward. It was dark inside the observatory, the sunlight only reaching a short way past the door. Jacob shivered as he stepped inside.

"Let me get a lantern," Charles said. He moved quickly through the darkness. Jacob could just make out his shadow at the workbench before the lantern light sent a pair of Jumpers scurrying up the scaffolding. "Samuel, watch the door. We don't need any surprises, invaders or otherwise. Jacob, you know what we need. Let's start filling up the saddlebags."

Jacob scrambled up a ladder fashioned from wood and rope until he was on the third level of scaffolding. "How many heavy springs?" he yelled down at Charles.

"I can hear you just fine, boy. No need to shout." Charles sorted through drawer after drawer in the workbench, pocketing various tools and placing others in a leather sack at his side. "Grab two bricks."

Jacob pulled the tightly wound bricks of springs out and dropped them onto the pile of mesh at the base of the scaffolding. Each brick held one hundred heavy springs. Jacob hesitated, and then threw a couple more bricks down just to be safe.

"Why do you even ask?" Charles said. He moved on to a barrelful of braces and brackets. The metal squeaked and sang as he sorted through it.

Jacob knew they needed more of the small brass brackets to make the hands. They were on the fourth shelf.

He put one foot up on the rope tied around a crossbeam and pushed himself up to the edge by an old, somewhat rotted crate. Jacob cursed, his feet dangling precariously off into the air before he finally rolled onto the shelf.

Charles looked at Jacob over the rim of his glasses. "That's what the ladder's for. Your mother won't appreciate me bringing you back in pieces."

"I've done that a million times," Jacob said. He pried open one of the larger crates. There were only two nails holding the lid down, so it didn't take much effort. The brackets clinked together in the old potato sacks. He threw two sacks to the floor and then a third for good measure.

"I'm grabbing ten bricks of the light springs," Jacob said, moving around to the next crate. The shelves here were uneven, and weren't tall enough to stand on, so Jacob had to slide through a narrow gap in the scaffolding in order to crawl onto the shelf with the springs. Something landed on his arm, and he jerked to the side, banging his elbow on a small wooden box and sending it off to shatter on the stone floor.

Metal and bearings bounced across the floor in a thunderous chorus.

"You okay?" Charles asked, squinting up at the shadowed shelf on which Jacob was perched.

"Yeah, a Jumper got the drop on me." Jacob held his hand out and the spider hopped off his arm, onto his palm. He let the spider jump up to another crate and vanish into the darkness behind it.

Jacob made quick work of the light springs, emptying all but two of the tightly wound bricks onto the mesh below. He made his way to the other end of the shelves and slid down the ladder. Something caught his eye on the wooden box he'd broken—an old emblem. Jacob bent down to wipe the dust off. A skull, like the one mounted on *The Dead Scourge*, peered back at him from a patch nailed to the wood.

"Charles?" Jacob said as he picked up the lid to the box.

"Come on now, Jacob. We're almost done packing. What is it?"

"It's a skull patch."

Charles cursed. "Did it break? What was inside the box, I mean. Did it break?"

Jacob lifted the rest of the box and stared. Hidden in the destruction was a ring of brass. Jacob picked it up, only to be surprised at its heft. He turned it over in his hand. Two brass bands sandwiched a glass circle and what looked to be spirals of copper. Some kind of light swept around the inside, and it almost looked like a miniature lightning strike.

"What is it?"

"Deadlands technology," Charles said. He lifted the device out of Jacob's hands. "It's something like the turbines that keep the city lights running at night, but on a much smaller scale. We shouldn't leave this here."

Charles walked back to the bench and wrapped the mechanism in mesh and a rough cloth before placing it in one of the saddlebags. Jacob loaded the springs and brackets and braces into the saddlebags until they wouldn't hold anything else.

"Fill your backpack with as much as you can," Charles said. "We'll have to make do with what we have."

The heavy steel door slammed against the wall and Samuel stood like a shadow, lit by the sunlight behind him. "We need to go *now!*"

"What is it?" Charles asked. He cinched the saddlebags closed and threw Samuel the last two bricks of springs.

"Death is on the move."

CHAPTER TWENTY-SIX

S AMUEL JAMMED THE SPRINGS INTO the large pockets on Bessie's saddle. He flipped open a smaller pouch up near the back of her head as he settled onto her back. Jacob watched the Spider Knight raise the whistle to his mouth. He sounded a run of five high notes in a quick staccato. He waited a beat and then repeated it in a lower octave.

Jacob knew enough to know what it was, and as soon as Charles finished tying the saddlebags down and stashing the steambike's stand, he threw his arms around the old man's waist. He briefly released his grip on Charles with his left hand so he could lower his goggles.

Samuel had sounded a warning, only it was a warning that there were too many enemies to fight, and everyone else should retreat.

"Hold on tight," Charles said. "This is going to get bumpy."

Samuel swore and pointed toward a shadow that pulsed and swelled and seemed to be oozing toward them from the poorest part of the Lowlands. "I'll try to draw them off, but Bessie can't outrun them for long."

Charles pulled a black leather satchel off the steambike and tossed it to Samuel. It hit the knight's hand with a smack. "There are only three in there. You hit that igniter, drop it, and get that spider running like hell's at her heels."

Samuel nodded and slung the satchel over his shoulder. A cloud of steam rose from the brass exhaust when Charles adjusted the throttle. He slid a wide pair of goggles over his glasses and looked at the Spider Knight.

"See you in hell, kid." Charles released the brake, and the steambike rocketed down the hill.

Jacob's teeth rattled, even though he didn't think he could clench his jaw any tighter. The metal in the saddlebags made a tremendous racket, and he knew it would draw in the Red Deaths. It wasn't long before his mind registered the awful, screeching whine of the beetles over the calamity of the steambike's cargo. Samuel and Bessie leapt and bounded across the nearby rooftops.

The sea of red skulls and black bodies came into terrible focus when they reached the bottom of the hill. Jacob looked to the left, down the street where he'd seen that dead Walker not so long ago, and the Red Deaths poured up the hill in a never-ending, churning wave of darkness. One of the creatures was no match for a squad of Spider Knights, but hundreds of them? They were virtually unstoppable.

Charles pitched the bike to the right. The tires squealed on the stones, protesting the sudden change in direction. Jacob wondered why until he saw the tip of another horde scrambling over the homes and falling into the street, littering the path in front of them.

"East road," Samuel screamed as Bessie twisted and ran across the roofs. He turned his gaze to the north, and his head snapped back toward Jacob and Charles. "Fast as you can!"

Jacob had his head against Charles's back with his eyes watching Samuel, so he knew what was coming when the Spider Knight pulled the first metal orb out of the black satchel around his neck. He knew what the igniter felt like when it clicked into place, even though he couldn't see it move at that distance.

Samuel dropped the bomb before he leaned forward, and Bessie shot ahead of the beetles, scarcely touching the rooftops as she bounced along.

The earth shook as the bomb sent up a fireball twice the width of the street, filled with legs and heads and obsidian chitin. The roar of the explosion drowned out every other sound, and at once the world became nothing but noise—and in that noise, an unnerving silence.

Jacob did his best not to scream as a house behind them collapsed in the shockwave of the explosion. Charles took the curving east road at speeds only a madman would attempt. There was a time when Jacob would have found the wind tearing through his hair exhilarating, but now it only added to the terror.

The steambike swerved to the right and the Hall came into view. That mountain of bugs still sat on its doorstep, but it wasn't so silent now. It heaved and shifted, and the maggoty flesh of the Carrion Worms pulsed at its surface.

A glance to the southwest showed him that sea of darkness, stained with red skulls. As many as Samuel had killed, there were four times that number pouring into the courtyard. Charles took a sharp turn, the steambike's tires squealing and bouncing and protesting across the cobblestones before he slammed the throttle open.

They rocketed forward, the screams of the Red Death following them up the hill that would take them back to the Square. Jacob couldn't see Samuel, and his stomach fluttered as he searched for the Spider Knight. He kept his head swiveling back and forth while Charles began dodging the rubble and carcasses that led into the Square.

Samuel appeared on the roof by the bank. Jacob saw him hit another igniter as Bessie reached the ground. The black metal ball bounced off the mountain of dead bugs, and Samuel hunkered down in his saddle while Bessie charged across the ground.

Jacob didn't watch the fireball as it went up. He felt the earth shake, but he kept his eyes on the city wall. It stood closer now, so close. He could see two Spider Knights standing outside as they closed in on the gates.

"Get inside!"

Jacob could hear Charles scream for the guards to move, even though Jacob was looking back at Samuel and the mass of darkness pulsing behind him.

"Start closing the gates!"

Jacob saw the knights spring into action as the steambike blasted past them. Their cries echoed Charles's own to close the gates. Charles slammed on the brake and swore as he and Jacob skidded onto the smooth stones of the city, narrowly missing a pair of knights standing in the courtyard.

"Where's Samuel?" Jacob asked as he stripped off his goggles, hopped from the bike, and jogged back to the gate. Relief washed over him when Samuel shot through the ever-narrowing opening.

There was no ceremony or slowness. The gates boomed shut, metal smashing into stone and rattling everyone's ears in the courtyard. The huge bolts slid home, creating an impenetrable barrier moments before the waves of Red Death broke and smashed into the wall. Their high-pitched cries mimicked that horrid sound when Miss Penny scraped metal across the chalkboard to wake up the class.

"Is everyone back?" Samuel asked. He slid off Bessie's saddle and looked back at the wall. "Did the captain make it back?"

"Almost everyone," the captain said as he laid a hand on Samuel's shoulder. "Was that your whistle?"

Samuel nodded.

"You saved a great many men today. The Red Deaths were drawn to that whistle like nothing I've seen before." The captain squeezed Samuel's shoulder and then let his arm fall. "How did you know you could call the horde and still escape?"

Samuel shook his head and said, "I didn't."

The captain looked at him for a moment and said, "Thank you," before he turned around and walked to the eastern gatehouse.

"What now?" Jacob asked.

"Let's get everything back to the lab," Charles said. "Then I'd like to have a chat with the captain and whatever repairmen we can find."

Charles and Jacob climbed back onto the steambike. The streets were almost empty. A few people stood in the windows, watching them go by, but almost no one stood outside.

Jacob watched the windows and storefronts as Charles maneuvered back to Bat's place. "Where is everyone?" The screech of the Red Death echoed in the distance.

"If I was to guess, I'd say they sounded the alarm after Samuel signaled with the whistle."

"You really think the whistle was why they came after us?"

"I don't know." Charles put his foot down before sliding it back and flipping the metal stand underneath the steambike. "Give me a hand with the doors."

Charles had installed a puzzle lock on the lab door, with Bat's approval. Jacob slid the nine brass tiles around until the springs inside clicked. The bolts at the top and bottom of the door retracted, and Jacob pushed one side open while Charles slid the other out of the way.

"Alice?" Jacob asked as he held the door open. She looked up from *The Dead Scourge* and almost leapt to her feet.

"You're okay?" She threw her arms around Jacob and squeezed as though she meant to remove every ounce of air from his lungs. She released him and shuffled away before asking, "You're both okay? I heard there were … I heard some of the repairmen didn't make it back."

Charles snuffed the Burner beneath the boiler on the steambike and pushed it inside the lab. A trail of black smoke rose against the pale wall, pooling and spreading across the ceiling until it dissipated.

"One of the knights didn't make it either," Jacob said. "I saw him, and then …" He shook his head.

"Heard there was trouble."

Jacob looked toward the doorway and smiled when he saw his dad standing upright. He didn't look as tired as he normally did, or maybe it was the lighting in the lab.

"The boy did great," Charles said, hefting brick after brick of the springs out of the saddlebags. "We'll be able to build more prosthetics than we have time to build."

Jacob squeezed past Charles as the old man bent down to open the lowest of the saddlebags. He hugged his dad, and felt a little safer when his father ruffled his hair.

"It's almost dinner time. Bat has ribs he bought from the butcher. You won't want to miss it." His dad started to walk away.

"How's Mom?"

"She's much better now that she knows you're safe. We were out on the balcony and saw you coming up the street."

Jacob hesitated, looking between Alice and Charles, and the hall that would lead to his mother.

"Help Charles put everything away," his dad said. "Your mom can wait a few more minutes to chew your ear off. Alice, I'm sure Bat won't mind if you wish to join us."

"Thank you," she said, "but only if it's okay with Bat."

They spent ten minutes quickly arranging supplies and stacking them into neatly organized towers. Everything was ready for them to start building when they were done, though it would take a while to remember exactly where they'd placed each item.

"Let's get some food," Charles said. "I'm sure Samuel will still be at the gatehouse after dinner."

The door to the hall closed, and Jacob stared at the heavy wooden door before slowly turning around. "Mom's going to kill me."

Alice and Charles both laughed.

CHAPTER TWENTY-SEVEN

JACOB SAT BY HIS MOTHER at the knotted wooden table. Alice sat across from him, and they exchanged glances all throughout the first course. He was surprised that none of the other houseguests were there, only Bat and Jacob's family and friends. The empty places at the table made the high-ceilinged room feel like a Hall.

"The potato salad is delicious," Jacob said, looking at the head of the table.

"Thank you, Jacob." Bat scooped up a heaping spoon of the rich salad and refilled his plate. He looked a bit too big for the chair in which he sat.

"Charles?" Alice said.

The old man looked up.

"In the book it says that the people in the Deadlands kept Fire Lizards as pets. Is that really true?"

"I don't know that I'd call them pets." Charles chewed up a bite of potato and swallowed. "They were on friendly terms, you could say. Some of our spies lived with families that would feed the lizards. No one was crazy enough to let one into their home, that I'm aware of. Some were trained, yes, but mainly to ambush their enemies. Well, to ambush *us,* as a matter of fact."

"What about the firestorms?"

Charles nodded. "Firestorms are quite real in the deep desert. There are geysers of oxygen, you know. Sometimes they catch fire, and sometimes a valley will fill with the gas until a spark or a lightning strike sets it off." Charles pointed his fork at Alice and winked at her. "That's when you run."

"Have you seen the old cities?" Jacob's dad asked. "My father used to tell me stories before he died in the mine collapse. I always wanted to see them."

Charles took another bite, his eyes flicking between his plate and his glass. Jacob knew that look. He was debating how much to say. Charles swallowed and took a drink of water before he nodded.

"They aren't really cities anymore. There are ruins of steel and iron that stretch even higher than the city wall, but those are the lands of Widow Makers and Tree Killers. They are burned out, and the Dead-lands are a fitting home for them."

"Imagine the people, though," Jacob's dad said. "An entire city of people living in that desert?"

"It likely wasn't a desert when people lived there," Bat said. "Look how fast the invaders have grown and changed. Red Deaths the size of a carriage? Widow Makers with fangs large enough to run a man through? Two decades past, it was unheard of. Who's to say what that desert was like a hundred or three hundred years ago? However long ago the city fell."

"Why doesn't anyone know what happened?" Jacob asked. "The people had to have gone somewhere."

"No one knows," Charles said. "I've heard theories—oh, there are always theories. A giant beast swallowed the city, the entire population was lost to war, or the first firestorm burned everything to the ground. Truth is, we may never know."

"Do you think it was the Forgotten?"

Charles shook his head. "That city was long dead before the Forgotten were banished from Ancora. There are ironbark trees and cacti taller than houses where men once laid stone roads."

Jacob had almost forgotten to enjoy his ribs he was listening so close-ly to Charles. A dead city. "I'd love to see it someday."

Jacob's mom let out a sigh. "You and your father. I swear, you'll both be the death of me."

His dad smiled.

Charles wiped his hands on a cloth napkin before setting it on his plate. "Well, if you would excuse us, I'd like to talk to Samuel about our adventure today."

Bat pushed his chair out. "Before you go …" He disappeared into the kitchen around the wall and came back with a tray of round chocolate balls. "I picked up a few truffles from the candy maker today."

A flurry of hands snatched up every last candy when Bat set the tray down. The big man wore a bigger smile when his guests gushed about the flavors and textures.

Alice shoved a second truffle into her mouth, and Jacob thought she might drool. "Thank you so much. I've never had a real truffle before."

"My pleasure," Bat said. "*Now* you can be excused."

Alice laughed and slid her chair back.

"Did you need a hand with the dishes?" Charles asked.

Bat shook his head. "It'll be dark soon. Best if you go now and get back early."

"You aren't wrong," the old man said. "Jacob, Alice, let's go."

"Charles?" Jacob's mom said as the trio walked toward the lab.

Charles looked back and waited.

"Thank you for keeping him safe. I hate to think what could have happened if he'd snuck off on his own."

Charles nodded.

Jacob continued down the hallway and pushed the heavy door to the lab open. He hated it when his parents talked about him like he wasn't right there in the room. He was old enough to know what risks were worth taking.

The door closed behind them. Charles glanced at it and then back to Jacob. "Good of you not to talk back to your mother. Keep a level head, boy, or one day you'll smart off to someone who would just as soon put you down."

Somehow Jacob didn't think Charles meant someone who would be mean to him. Charles meant someone that would kill him. Jacob wasn't helpless, but the old man did have a point.

Alice flipped a page in *The Dead Scourge* and brushed her hair back.

Charles paused and stared at the workbench. A moment later, he slid the nail glove off the top shelf and placed it in his backpack before slinging it over his shoulder.

"What do you need that for?" Jacob asked.

"It's not me who needs it. Come on, you two. Let's find Samuel and Ambrose."

✧   ✧   ✧

IT WASN'T LONG BEFORE THEY were back in the courtyard by the gatehouses. Many more people gathered there now. Word had obviously spread that it was still safe inside the walls, and the terrible cries of the Red Death were nothing more than a baleful sound.

Charles knocked on the door to the eastern gatehouse and waited. A few moments later the door swung in. Samuel wasn't there. Jacob didn't see any of the Spider Knights, only a handful of city knights. The whole room smelled like tobacco and ale and sweat. Jacob wrinkled his nose, looking around the stone room and the long oak table in the center. At the far end, with his hands splayed across a map and his head hanging low, stood the captain.

"Did you really need to bring kids in here?" the captain asked. He glanced up before folding over the map on the table. His voice was deeper than it had been earlier that day. He didn't sound angry, but he didn't look happy either.

"He's my assistant," Charles said, putting his arm around Jacob's shoulders.

The captain narrowed his eyes. "And the girl?"

"She's my assistant," Jacob said as he put his arm around Alice.

Alice rolled her eyes and blew out a noisy breath through her nose, but she didn't protest. Jacob was pretty sure he'd be hearing about it later.

The captain rubbed his face. "What is it you need, tinker?"

"We're looking for Samuel," Charles said, his eyes sweeping the room. He frowned slightly. "And the wall repairmen. I thought they'd be here."

"They're off at the Wild Horse. The Spider Knights took the men out after I asked them to leave." The captain turned another map over on the table and looked up. "I'm sure they'll drink to Jones and his *glory*. Now, if you don't need anything more …"

Charles gave a curt shake of his head. "Thank you for your help earlier, and just now."

The captain nodded as Charles turned around and led Alice and Jacob toward the Wild Horse Inn.

Jacob said nothing and followed Charles back out into the evening light of the courtyard. They were near one of the streetlights when something clicked and whirred until it became a constant, steady hum. The streetlight burst into brilliant life as they walked beneath, scattering shadows across the cobblestones.

"Charles?"

"Hmm?" he said as he looked back at Jacob.

"Why did the captain have a map of Dauschen?"

"I saw that too," Alice said. "It had squares and crosses all over it."

"You kids have good eyes." Charles took a sharp right, heading toward the row of shops and inns set into the eastern block. "Not out here." He weaved his way around an elderly couple as they started to climb onto a carriage before he stopped in front of an old four-story stone building.

A tall, iron-wrought horse hung above the door. Its mane looked caught in a breeze as the horse reared up on its hind legs. A gust of wind sent the sign swinging slowly on its anchor. The metal rungs squeaked as they shifted on the pole.

"This is it," Charles said. He mounted the short staircase to the front door and put his hand on the equine handle. "It's time you saw the Wild Horse."

CHAPTER TWENTY-EIGHT

SOUND EXPLODED FROM THE ENTRYWAY when Charles pushed the door open. Jacob had been to taverns with his father in the Lowlands, but as he stepped inside the Wild Horse Inn, he knew this was a different world.

"They welcome everyone at the Wild Horse," Charles shouted over his shoulder. "You won't need to keep your head on a swivel here." He paused and bent down to Jacob. "Of course, they probably should be watching out for you, eh?" He laughed and thumped Jacob on his back.

"Men," Alice said, exasperated. She crossed her arms and followed close to Charles.

The bar was off to the right, a bizarre mix of the grandest, most run-down, most elegant thing Jacob had ever seen. The bar back stood at least fifteen feet high and some fifty feet long. One of the bartenders slid along the back on a copper and steel ladder set up on rollers. He flipped two bottles down to another bartender, who caught them without looking.

The second bartender poured both bottles with one hand. A blue liquid and a yellow liquid splashed together and merged into a thick green syrup. He repeated the pour four more times in four separate glasses. He added a splash of seltzer water to thin them before sliding them out to a patron with a nod and a mustached smile.

Another bartender hit a square panel by the shelves, and the shelves began to rotate. The top shelf of bottles slid back, and the bottom shelf rose until the top finally reappeared at the bottom.

Steam and smoke came out of a large window in the corner. A man in a tall white hat slammed a mallet into a gong and yelled, "Order up, fourteen."

Jacob laughed as he watched a bartender put a basket of food on a tray beneath what looked like a child-sized steam locomotive. He pulled a long-handled switch on a panel below the train, and Jacob saw the track above their heads shift. The bartender pushed a button that dropped the gate in front of the locomotive and sent it powering around the track.

Jacob couldn't look away while the tiny engine puffed and chugged along the rails. The tray slammed into a pillar above a table, and one of the men stood up to pull it down while the train continued back to the bartenders, only to be corralled by its gate once more.

"Jacob!"

He looked away from the train, and Charles motioned him over. Alice sat next to Samuel in a high-back booth with another Spider Knight and a small group of repairmen. Her eyes were stuck to the train too. The repairmen were quiet, and some were clearly shaken.

Above all of the chaos and whispers and drunken bellows, an organ played in the corner opposite the bar. It was a mad assembly of horns and whistles and brass and ivory that bent to the organist's every whim. Flaps and valves opened at seemingly random intervals to fill the room with a lively, sweeping jig. A few of the more intoxicated patrons danced on the small stage by the far wall.

"Jacob," Samuel said, standing up to let Jacob and Charles slide in next to Alice.

"You all want a drink?" Samuel asked.

"Do I need a drink?" Charles rolled his eyes up to meet Samuel's.

The Spider Knight frowned, and then nodded.

"Then I'll have a drink."

"You kids want something?"

"I'll have a Sweetwing Tea," Alice said.

Jacob almost gagged. "They make that out of Sweet-Flies."

"How many times have you had my mum's stew? I know you know she puts Pill-Bugs in it."

"That's different. They aren't Sweet-Flies. Give me honey any day."

Alice narrowed her eyes. "Grow up."

Samuel laughed and turned around. "Bartender! Three Dragon's Bane, a Sweetwing Tea, and a Sweetwater."

One of the bartenders held up five fingers to confirm the order.

"How bad were the walls?" Charles asked when Samuel settled back down.

Ambrose swirled his drink and blew out a breath. "Before that new wave of Red Death did some more damage, they were already gone to hell and back. It'll take months to straighten those walls out, if not longer. Need a battalion of knights just to hold the damn things off so we can work."

"How long will it take to put up some temporary blockades?" Charles started folding a cloth napkin over and over again.

"For what?"

"Cordon off part of the city. Build the wall back in stages."

The repairman beside Ambrose shook his head. "Too long. Just getting the lumber together and building the barrier for one city block could take weeks if we're under attack."

Charles nodded. "I have something that might help with that." He awkwardly removed his backpack in the narrow booth, elbowing Jacob in the head and Samuel in the ribs. "Sorry, sorry." He pulled out the glove made of mesh and metal.

"What is *that* going to do for us?" Ambrose asked as he leaned forward. "They're great, but they're slow to reload."

"We improved the loading mechanism. The new gloves are going to let you build faster than you thought possible." Charles slid the glove on slowly and flexed his fingers in the mesh, forming a fist. "Hmm, angle's a little awkward here, but ..." He slammed his fist into the stack of thick boards he'd made.

Jacob could barely make out the whine of the springs above the organ in the background when the glove sent three nails deep into the wooden boards with a snap. Charles pulled a lever across his wrist, and another round of nails slid up into the springs. He turned the wood over and slammed his fist into it again.

The repairmen all stared at the little block of wood. Six nails, fully driven to their heads, decorated the pale wood. Ambrose picked it up and ran his fingers over the nails.

"Is this ironwood?"

"It is." Charles pulled the mesh glove off. Its brackets hung limply beneath the nail-driving mechanism when it wasn't attached to a hand. "I'd like to see you buy a few of these. I'm sure the city would subsidize it for you. It's one of the better inventions I've had in a while, if I do say so myself."

"It's brilliant," Ambrose said.

"I should have a model that can drive rivets through steel in a few days. The run we made to my old lab in the Lowlands gave me the heavy springs I needed."

"Charles, we could build the walls in half the time with these tools," Ambrose said. "Do you think the new glove you're building will penetrate stone?"

Charles didn't hesitate before he said, "Easily."

Ambrose nodded slowly. "We could use it to drive the anchors. Use this to build the temporary walls. Rebuild a block at a time, as you suggested. This could actually work. Even our best carpenters take at least three hits to drive a nail." He shook his head. "This takes all of that away. I'm telling you, it could actually work."

"Take this one," Charles said as he pushed it toward Ambrose. "I'll make more, but before you buy them, make sure it will do what you want it to do. What you need it to do. Hold on a second."

He raised his hand to stop one of the bartenders making their rounds of the tables. The man was dressed in a roughly stitched leather jacket made to resemble one of the Highlanders' suits.

"Sir?"

"Is Baddawick in?" Charles asked.

"I believe so, sir. Would you like me to fetch him?"

"I jolly well would."

"As you say." The bartender tipped a hat he wasn't wearing and continued on to the next table.

"'Jolly well'?" Alice said with a hint of amusement in her voice.

Charles smiled. "I love this bar."

"Who's Baddawick?" Alice asked. "That's an unusual name. The only Baddawick I've ever heard of was the man who designed one of the big steam locomotives."

"One and the same. He does like to take all the credit, but he didn't do it alone."

Samuel leaned forward and lowered his voice, so only their group could hear him as he interrupted. "I know you have the same question we have."

Charles raised an eyebrow. "The transmitters?"

Samuel nodded. "The attack wasn't natural, which means someone planned it."

"I'm sure Parliament knows that by now," Charles said. "They have a ready culprit in Dauschen. Who better to blame than the city that laid an embargo against Ancora?"

Samuel blew out a breath. "Between that and the transmitters, who wouldn't suspect Dauschen of trying to start a war? Do you think it *could* be them?"

Charles shook his head. "I doubt it. There's only one other living man I know of who's seen the design for those transmitters, and he's not in Dauschen. However, I doubt that fact would be enough to dissuade

Parliament from taking action."

"What are they planning?" Ambrose hissed. "Could they be stupid enough to attack Dauschen?"

"Frightened people do stupid things," Alice said.

"You're damn right," Charles said. He sighed and looked in the direction of the man walking toward them with a tray on his shoulder. "I do hope those are ours."

CHAPTER TWENTY-NINE

"Gentlemen," the bartender said, sidling up beside the table. He glanced at Alice and added, "and miss." He hit a button on the edge of the table and a pillar rose out of the wood. The bartender set the square tray down on top of it, said "Enjoy," and walked away.

Jacob started to reach for the Sweetwater, but Charles stopped him.

"Just wait."

Jacob was going to ask why, and then the tray broke into smaller trays. The pillar beneath extended a dozen mechanical brass arms, each with a precariously balanced drink or section of tray on top.

"How in the …" Jacob's words trailed off as everyone picked their drinks up. When the weight lifted, the arms retracted to make the tray whole once more. It leaned a bit to one side, and then some more, until the tray stood vertical.

"That's amazing!" Alice said.

"Not done yet," Charles said.

Jacob wondered why Charles was leaning away from the tray, until it launched into the air.

"Incoming!" one of the bartenders shouted.

Alice laughed and slapped Jacob's arm as the nearest bartender caught the tray and set it on the shelf.

"Baddawick's a madman," Ambrose said, but his smile betrayed his words.

Jacob watched the post vanish into the tabletop while he tried not to look at the long, thin wing sticking out of Alice's drink. He focused on enjoying his Sweetwater and leaving Alice to enjoy her tea. At the Wild Horse, Sweetwater was dark and bubbly and tasted more like candy than the watered-down version in the Lowlands.

"This city isn't prepared for war," Charles said.

"War?" Ambrose asked.

Charles nodded. "The Lowlands must be reclaimed, and the walls rebuilt, if Ancora is to stand a chance. If those plans are for maneuvers against Dauschen, their designer is risking war. Ancora isn't ready for war."

"Maybe a skirmish," Ambrose said between sips of his Dragon's Bane. "I don't think it would escalate to war."

"No one thought the trade embargo with Dauschen and banishment of the Forgotten would result in the Deadlands War, either."

Jacob and Alice exchanged glances. They'd both read *The Dead Scourge.* They knew how the Forgotten had forged their own city in the Deadlands. The Forgotten had used the resources Ancorans once thought impossible to harvest to start trading with Dauschen. The embargo had drawn a line in the sand, and the Forgotten had taken their reparations in blood.

"Before my time," Ambrose said. He swirled his drink and set it down before he laced his fingers together. "War isn't my concern, and I think you know that. I want to repair the walls and keep the Lowlands as safe as they can be."

"I think some men want to watch the Lowlands burn," Samuel said, glancing between Ambrose and Charles. It made Jacob think back to the conversation he and Alice had overheard in the catacombs.

"You're both right," Charles said as he leaned forward. "But either way, the Highlands can't support the sheer quantity of refugees it's harboring. Ambrose, this is why I want you to use the gloves, and rebuild the walls faster than anyone thought possible. If Samuel's right, and this was some twisted ruse to eliminate the Lowlands, the walls are their best hope. If you're right, Ambrose, and I'm just a paranoid old man, they still need the walls to keep the Lowlands safe. The sooner the better."

Ambrose nodded slowly and crossed his arms. "It's reasonable, Charles, and it's a perfect excuse to fortify the Lowlands without raising suspicions about your own suspicions. I'll put in the request to have Parliament pay for the gloves, too." He slammed the rest of his cocktail and winced. "Gods, but I hope you're wrong."

The table grew silent for a time while everyone finished their drinks. Jacob watched the bartenders move around the room. He'd come to realize that each table had its own built-in surprises.

One shot little arcs of water over the inn's patrons at random intervals. The streams of water seemed to vanish right into the woodwork. Jacob figured there were funnels or pipes or something catching the streams, but he couldn't see anything.

Alice bumped him with her elbow and pointed at a far booth, closer to the bar itself. A post, not unlike the post in their own table, rose and extended half a dozen arms. This time, though, each arm had a hose connected to it that moved forward until it bumped a glass, rose slightly, and dispensed refills without the bartenders having to lift a finger.

"I love this place," Jacob said.

"I thought you might," Charles said before he sipped the last bit of his drink.

"Jacob, look!" Alice tugged on his sleeve and pointed across the room again. "They have a picture man."

It wasn't every day they saw a working camera. In the Lowlands, maybe they'd see a picture man on Festival days, but that was usually about it. This camera was set up on a tripod, not far from the booth that automatically refilled the drinks. A painting hung on the wall of the old Hall in the Lowlands. Jacob recognized some of the founders of Ancora. Miss Penny had drilled the history of their city into his head well enough to remember a little bit.

"How much do they cost?" Jacob asked. "I don't think I have enough."

"Go on, you two," Charles said. "I'll take care of it if Baddawick doesn't."

It didn't take long for Jacob and Alice to weave their way across the room, slowed only by their tendency to gawk at the machinations of the Wild Horse and the occasional bartender hurrying out to a table. Jacob watched the locomotive steam by overhead one more time as they slid into the nook where the picture man had been standing.

"Where do you think he went?" Jacob asked.

Alice shrugged. "Maybe the restroom?"

"I bet they have an amazing restroom here." Jacob blinked as he thought about what he'd said and looked up to meet Alice's eyes.

They both burst into laughter.

"That's not something I think I've ever heard before," she said, her laughter trailing off. She propped herself up on her toes and leaned over the middle of the picture man's wooden tripod. "I've never seen a camera like that."

"I know," Jacob said. He took up a position opposite Alice and pointed toward the wood in the center. "They usually have that bellows-looking thing here, but this one has extra sections."

"Extra lenses," someone said from behind them.

Jacob turned around to see the picture man standing behind them, sipping his drink.

The man was about his parents' age, maybe a little younger. He looked tired, and his suit was wrinkled, but there was a spark Jacob couldn't quite place, in the wide eyes and narrow smile.

"You kids want a picture?"

"You know," Alice said, "we aren't *that* young."

"Of course not, ma'am." He was loud, talking over the sudden crescendo in the music before it fell away a bit so they could speak in normal tones again.

Jacob laughed and swatted Alice's arm. "Ma'am. Now you sound as old as Miss Penny."

Alice narrowed her eyes and looked back to the picture man. "We'd love one. The table with the old man and the Spider Knights is paying for it."

"Oh, don't worry about that," the man said. He set his drink down and adjusted his hat. "If I can give you Lowland kids something to smile about, that's payment enough." He turned around and opened a chest.

Jacob and Alice glanced at each other.

The man smiled. "Frankly, I figured *you* were from the Lowlands," he said with a nod toward Alice, "because you've actually been nice to me and your friend. Most of the Highborn girls that come in here want to be treated like the Queen of Dauschen."

"Have you been there?" Alice asked. "To Dauschen?"

"I have indeed, little miss." He pulled a slim plate of metal out of a larger trunk by the wall. "It's a beautiful place, don't get me wrong, but I'd never want to go back."

"Why?"

"Well, lots of reasons," the picture man said with a humorless laugh. "You think it's tough in the Lowlands?"

Jacob nodded. He didn't think it was tough, he *knew* it was tough. Some kids didn't even have half of what he had, and sometimes his family would go for an entire day without food.

"It's not, kid. I mean, sure, it's not as nice as the Highlands, but it's not a living hell either. Parts of Dauschen are so poor, they can't afford wood for a funeral pyre, much less pay for a burial. They burn their dead in mass pits, they do. Poor kids that starve to death on the streets while the monarchs sit on a gilded throne that could feed them for a century."

Alice's face hardened. "That doesn't sound so different at all."

The picture man blinked. "Why would you say that?" He paused and frowned. "You have food and shelter in the Highlands. You may have Highborns who don't think you belong here, but that's a far cry from Dauschen.

"You think the Highlands are better than them, don't you?" Alice asked. "That's … I don't even know what that is."

The man frowned and glanced away for a moment. "I only meant to say you don't have it so bad in the Lowlands. Well, when the wall's up at least. Be thankful for what you have, a roof over your head, and food in your stomach. There's always someone who'd give anything to have what you have."

"People should be thankful for *who* they have," Alice said. She looked up and smiled at Jacob.

"That they should, little miss. That's enough talk. I think my drink's gone to my head. Now, you two line up on that wall, right in front of the camera."

Jacob stood in front of the painting where an ancient, impossibly tall building towered so high it looked like it went straight up through the ceiling. Alice stood a little ways to his right, studying the founders and the leaders from the Deadlands War immortalized on the old wall.

Up close, Jacob could see the dead across the bottom of the painting. Men that looked like half machine and half flesh, suits of armor so complex they made his head spin, even in a painting.

Something smacked into Jacob's upper back, drawing his attention away from the painting's carnage. He turned his head slightly and found a furry gray body with eight eyes staring back at him. The Jumper twitched and hopped up onto his shoulder, where it seemed perfectly happy to stay.

"You want I should get rid of that?" the picture man asked.

Jacob shook his head. "He fits. We like Jumpers."

Alice smiled when the man frowned. He clearly wasn't so fond of Jumpers. "I bet he really wouldn't have liked our Pill-Bugs." Alice smiled and ran a finger over the spider's head. It pumped its legs up and down a few times in response. "I guess they're all gone now."

Jacob put his arm around Alice and gave her an awkward half hug.

"Okay, you two stay as still as you can. It's a new camera, and it's pretty fast, but you'll need to stay still for a bit."

Jacob and Alice froze as the picture man ducked behind his camera. The Jumper scampered out onto Jacob's elbow and stared forward.

Alice laughed. "I think he wants to be in the photo."

"Looks good! Don't move!"

A click and a whir sounded when the picture man pushed the large brass button. Jacob almost jumped when the entire side of the camera opened and a panel of lights swelled into a golden glow. He watched the gears shift, and the panel retracted.

"You're all set," the picture man said. "You want I should make two copies?"

"We're done?" Jacob asked. "But that was … that was so fast."

"It's a new model. I don't think it takes quite as good a picture, but it gets the job done. Plus, you kids don't have to stand there for half the day." He smiled and slid a cartridge out the bottom of the camera.

"What's that?" Alice asked.

"It stores the negative. Don't have to worry about the light ruining it. I'll be back in a few minutes. You kids can wait at the table."

"He's going to develop them now?" Alice asked as Jacob released her shoulder. "We had a family photo last year and it took a week to get it back."

The Jumper scampered back up Jacob's arm and curled its legs over his shoulder. "I guess we'll see."

Jacob looked back toward Charles and the repairmen. A man stood beside them with a full head of wild white hair. It stood up in every direction imaginable, held in place by the strap of a mad pair of goggles. The man turned his head to the side, and Jacob could see the goggles were like Charles's. A dozen lenses shot off the leather and metal frames.

"That must be Baddawick," Alice said.

"Let's go meet him." Jacob took Alice's hand and led her around the tables, past the organist—who'd switched to a slow, dark serenade—and back to their table.

CHAPTER THIRTY

CHARLES STOOD UP WHEN JACOB and Alice made it back to the table. He motioned for them to slide back into the booth. They did. Charles joined them on the wide bench. The Jumper scampered down Jacob's arm. He raised his hand up close to the wooden beam behind the booth, and the spider made short work of the distance. It vanished into the shadows above.

"I suppose it's only a matter of time before the city smith steals your idea," Baddawick said.

Charles nodded. "Wouldn't be surprised if someone already drew up some plans for him."

Baddawick harrumphed and set the nail glove back down. "It's an excellent design. How many nails can you load in the cartridge?"

"At this size, you can get about thirty in."

Baddawick nodded. "Well, you should only need about thirty to get one of those temporary panels up." He nodded again, sending his hair bobbing and weaving above his goggles. "You realize they could use this for homes, too?" Baddawick leaned in. "Now that's where you could make some real money, my friend."

Charles laughed and flipped the glove over, exposing the mesh beneath the braces. He glanced at it and then back to Baddawick. "I'd rather take money from the men who don't need it. I'm working on another model. Picked up the springs yesterday, in fact."

Baddawick raised an eyebrow. "Always the humanitarian, eh? I remember when you were just a soldier following orders, when we both had a little less white up top." He paused, and his eyes trailed back to Jacob. "I heard a strange rumor. Some folks say a boy leapt off the city wall and lived. Had huge wings like a Devil Moth." He threw his arms out to the side and wiggled his fingers.

The old man's face didn't wear much of an expression, and Jacob wasn't sure why. Charles took a deep breath and shook his head slightly. When he spoke, he sounded normal, if a bit quiet. "They weren't quite that large." Charles turned his head and winked at Jacob.

"Was it one of the old gliders? Like the mercenaries we met in the Deadlands?"

Charles nodded. "A lot more portable than those monsters they used to haul around." Charles motioned for Baddawick to lean closer. "We added some hinges and spring locks, mounted the controls on a backpack."

"How heavy?"

"Light enough for Jacob to carry on his own. He climbed the staircase to the top of the wall while he was wearing it."

Baddawick ran his hand through his hair. "I'd almost forgotten how good you are, Charles. I'd like to see that one day." He glanced between Charles and Jacob. "Well, well, introduce me, won't you?"

Charles turned toward Jacob and the others.

"This is Alice," Charles said as he gestured to her. "She has most of the common sense that Jacob's missing."

"You may have guessed that this is Jacob," Charles said, nodding at Jacob. "I'm training him myself, as a matter of fact."

"So," Baddawick said before he started smiling, "Charles teach you how to make square wheels?"

"What?" Jacob said.

"It's an old joke," Charles said. He rubbed his forehead and returned Baddawick's smile with a small laugh. "We did know some gullible people back then."

"That we did," Baddawick said. "That we did."

"You've seen the prosthetics some of the kids have been wearing since the Fall?"

"The Fall?" Alice asked. "They already named the attack?"

Baddawick grimaced and nodded. "People like to label things—especially grim things—with a catchy name." He turned his attention back to Charles. "Yes, I've seen them. Simple, but quite useful."

"Jacob designed them," Charles said as he squeezed Jacob's shoulder.

"Really?" Baddawick drew the word out and looked at Jacob with a far more discerning eye. Jacob stared back, feeling defiant, but he wasn't sure why. "You do have talent, boy. I saw the captain's son."

Baddawick began shaking his finger at Jacob. "You know what's most amazing? The captain's son didn't think you crazy. He actually found you quite likable. Wouldn't shut up about it, actually." Baddawick mumbled the last words, and Jacob barely caught them over the buzz of the bar and the organ music all around them.

Baddawick leaned into the table, barely speaking loud enough for Charles and Jacob to hear. "The city smith knows the boy invented those?"

"I just put some spare parts together."

Baddawick fluttered his hand to quiet Jacob. "He knows, yes?"

Charles nodded, a small frown pulling at his lips.

Baddawick shuffled closer, his voice not much above a whisper. "I've heard rumors he's into something bad, and he considers you a threat." Baddawick eyed the table. "All of you."

"Are you suggesting we leave?" Charles asked.

Baddawick nodded. "Leave Ancora, lest you want to face the city smith. You know Parliament worships the beetle dung on that man's boots, Charles. A conflict with him will be the end of you all. Whether the Fall was an attack on Ancora from the outside, or an attack from within, dark times are coming."

Charles drummed his fingers on the tabletop, a shadow darkening his brow. "You're not wrong." He nodded and glanced at Jacob and Alice. "We'll be ready. I'm not breaking up anyone's family unless it's absolutely necessary."

"Prepare them for the worst. It was a pleasure to meet you both, Jacob, Alice." Baddawick stood up straight and his voice returned to its previous volume, rivaling the melodic runs belting out of the organ's pipes. "You always were a bastard, Charles. Come by for drinks anytime, I'll always charge you double."

Baddawick winked before he walked away, circling booths before stopping to whisper something to the organ player. Jacob followed his path until the old inventor vanished through a doorway.

Jacob looked back at Alice. She'd been watching Baddawick too. He shrugged once Baddawick was gone.

"Well," she said. "He's interesting."

"He's disarming," Charles said. "He can be manipulative, but if he's on your side, you won't mind a bit." He turned back to Jacob and Alice. "Let's get your pictures and get home before your parents decide I'm a bad influence."

He passed the nail glove across the table to Ambrose. "Take this. Show it off to your supervisor, and then come by my lab. You know Bat, yes?"

"Samuel's uncle?"

Charles nodded. "Yes, my lab is in the old stables he was using for storage. Come by tomorrow and I'll get you some cartridges of nails. See about getting the city to pay for enough gloves to section off a block of the Lowlands per day."

Ambrose nodded. "Shouldn't be difficult." He pried the cartridge out of the top of the glove, revealing the spiral of nails inside before snapping it back together with a click.

"If it *is* difficult," Charles said as he lowered his voice, "let us know who and what their reasons are."

"I will. You'd have to be a fool not to see the value here." Ambrose extended his arm and shook Charles's hand. "Either way, I'll see you tomorrow."

✧   ✧   ✧

IT WAS LATE WHEN THEY made it back to Bat's house. Jacob thought Charles might fall asleep while he regaled his parents with stories of all the contraptions plastering the Wild Horse.

"I think we'll have to go there," his mom said. She leaned against his father.

"A camera that can take a photo in under a minute?" his dad asked. "Sounds like one of those old fairy tales in your books."

"Fairy tales don't have cameras, Dad." Jacob pulled his backpack up off the ground and unbuttoned the main flap. "Here." He held his arm out with the little gray metal frame the picture man had given them.

His dad leaned forward and took it from Jacob's grip. His eyes moved from the photo to Jacob and back.

"And they developed it already?" his mom asked, leaning in closer to see the photo of Alice, Jacob, and the Jumper. "Oh, Jacob, look at the colors!"

"It's a new kind of camera," Jacob said. "The picture man said they have a new film that lets them do color. He said a lot about mixing three colors and chemicals and … I don't know, but it looks neat, doesn't it?"

Jacob yawned.

His dad handed the picture back, and Jacob looked at it again. Alice wore a big smile. The Jumper had huge eyelashes, as Alice liked to call them, and the pattern on its fur made it look like a smile. Jacob's arm was around Alice, and he rather liked how they looked together. Him with his short, scruffy hair, leather vest, and a worn pair of denim pants, and her with a looped leather shirt, or loops as the Highborn kids called them. Pockets alternated with wide straps down her shirt and ended above a darker leather skirt.

Jacob knew they were leftovers from the Highborn kids, but they were new to the Lowlanders. Jacob was pretty sure all of the kids would be asking their parents for loops when they got home. You could fill those pockets with just about anything.

"Why don't you get some sleep," Jacob's mom said.

Jacob's first instinct was to argue that he wasn't tired, but he was actually very tired. He nodded and stood up. Bat said two of his guests had left to stay in the Castle, which left a few extra beds open for Jacob and his parents. The thought of not sleeping on the couch or the floor enticed him.

"Sleep is a fine idea," Charles said as he stood up and walked down the hall, somewhat leaning over like he was ready to fall into bed.

Jacob watched him go and then nodded. "Okay, I'll see you in the morning." He gave each of his parents a hug. His dad squeezed him hard enough Jacob had trouble catching a breath until the hug relaxed.

He made his way to the spiral staircase and started up to the top floor. He supposed it was an attic, really, with the narrow rooms almost fully contained in each dormer. Bat had called it something else. Jacob tried to remember as he stepped off the stairs and squinted in the dark hallway.

"A gable dormer. That was it," Jacob whispered to himself as he pushed the iron handle down and pulled the heavy wooden door open.

It didn't take long for Jacob to make himself at home. He slid his backpack onto the top of the cedar chest in the corner. Only a sliver of moonlight and the yellow glow of a distant streetlamp lit the small space. Jacob opened the first in a series of drawers beneath the bed. A yellow-green glow rose up from the jar of glowworms when he set them inside.

He hesitated, and set the jar on the cedar chest instead. Even the dim light glinted off the silver skull when Jacob pulled *The Dead Scourge* out and laid it at the foot of the bed. He was tired, no doubt, but Alice had told him about some of what she'd read later in the book, and nothing was going to stop him. He wrapped a blanket around his shoulders after tossing his clothes into another drawer, propped himself up on his elbows, and began to read.

> There was only one man guarding the gates to the great city of the Deadlands. A field of death—man, beast, and machine—was strewn around him. He did not move, no, he only waited. When we were close enough, he asked what our purpose was.
>
> I had been sent to treat with the Deadlands nation, and I told him as much. It was when he nodded, in that simple gesture, I realized he was not entirely a man. The brass and copper I had taken to be armor disappeared into his flesh. Pistons moved at his neckline, and something shifted and spun beneath his jaw.
>
> It was not until I set foot in the Deadlands that I learned what they called themselves: Biomechs. They were the men and women who had taken metal into their own bodies, some to repair hands or feet or limbs, others to gain strength.
>
> Atlier, one of our own smiths, was fascinated with the Biomechs. The rest of us were intimidated at best, and terrified at worst. Never had I seen such power as what we saw from the Biomechs in the battle of the Deadlands nation. Raw, terrible power.

Jacob read until the light from the glowworms started to dim and he realized they needed food. He leaned over the bed and opened a drawer, pulling out a small box of dead flies. The glowworms weren't particular about what they ate, really, but they did tend to glow better on a steady diet of flies.

Jacob added the food to the jar, and the glowworms immediately began to eat. He set the lid back on and levered the wire lock across the top to hold it closed before shutting the light away in the drawer.

He left *The Dead Scourge* on the edge of the cedar chest. There were questions to which he wanted answers. Charles had been in the Deadlands War, and Jacob wondered if the old man had seen Biomechs with his own eyes.

Tomorrow, he'd find out.

CHAPTER THIRTY-ONE

CHARLES WASN'T AT BREAKFAST THE next morning, but Jacob's mom told him the old man was working out in his lab. Jacob stuffed his face with eggs and a soufflé he was fairly certain had some kind of flies in it. Some things shouldn't be crunchy.

Charles was hunched over his workbench when Jacob walked out. He loaded a heavy spring onto the tensioner and lined up the metal brace for another prosthetic. Charles glanced up when Jacob swung the oak door closed, the metal bars hitting the frame with a clang.

"Morning, Jacob." He turned his attention back to the mechanical hand.

"I thought you'd be working on more nail gloves."

"I was, earlier," Charles said, nodding to a small stack of gloves.

Jacob picked the top two up. There were three altogether. "Are they already done?"

"Not quite. I need to outfit the cartridges with springs and followers so we can load them. You want to give me a hand?"

Jacob started digging through a wooden bucket under the bench. He'd seen Charles stash the thin metal strips the day before. Jacob pulled out the long iron box that held the followers, and pushed the bucket back under the bench with his foot.

He set about mounting a spring catch in the smaller vise on the other end of the table. It would be almost impossible to set the follower properly if he didn't have the catch. Jacob forced the cartridge down over the spring catch until it clicked. He made sure the spring was properly aligned before slipping the follower in through a little slit in the side. One of his favorite things was letting springs fire bits of metal and wood around the room.

Charles raised his eyebrow when Jacob looked up.

"Duck," Jacob said, and he ripped the bolt of the spring catch out the side. The spring exploded with enough force to throw the cartridge across the room where it slammed into the door with a thunk.

Charles looked at Jacob and tried to hide a smile. "Good thing Bat doesn't mind a dent or three in his doors."

Jacob walked over to the door and picked up the cartridge. "Can we start loading them?"

Charles glanced back at him. "You *want* to load them? I didn't think you enjoyed the menial tasks." He turned his attention back to the workbench. "I hate loading those cartridges. I need to build something that can feed them automatically. Maybe mount it on the bench." He nodded to himself. "A curved bin would work. Like a magazine but much taller."

"How would it push the spring back?"

Charles sighed. "I don't know yet. I'm just complaining, Jacob. If you want to load the magazine, you go right ahead."

Jacob pulled his stool up beside Charles and dragged a blue and red can of nails closer. He picked one of them up and twirled it between his fingers. "They don't really look like nails."

"True. They don't have heads until the springs drive them into wood. Even then, it's not as clean a head as a fully manufactured nail." There were three quick clinks as Charles adjusted one of the braces with a small hammer and chisel. He blew a few metal shavings out of a wrist joint and tested its movement again.

"Charles?"

"Hmm?"

"Did you ever see a Biomech in the war?"

The old man's hand slowed in its movements, gently wiping the dust and dirt off the black mesh of the new prosthetic. "I saw many Biomechs, Jacob. Understand, some of the Deadlands people used biomechanics to repair a lost arm or leg, much as you designed these prosthetics. Others though … other men were hungry for power, and would give almost anything to obtain it."

"What kind did *you* see?"

Charles leaned back on his stool and raised the magnifiers on his glasses. "I saw all of them, Jacob. I saw a man without legs who could run as fast as a Fire Lizard, and a woman without an arm that could lift a carriage with one hand. And I saw the madness. The crazed men who worked their machinations into their own bodies. Not to replace or repair a wound, but simply to make themselves *better*."

"Did they?"

"In a way, I suppose. They made themselves very good at killing, Jacob, letting fear drive them to extremes. They killed our friends, they killed themselves, they killed the Fire Lizards. The Forgotten wore the Deadlands banner, and by the gods they earned that damned skull."

"Are they still like that? Even after the war?"

"Some, I am sure." Charles tightened a length of metal in one of the vises. "The city of Bollwerk has grown to be a much more civilized place than you'd expect."

"How do you know?"

Charles fell silent. Jacob could see the small frown etched across the old man's face, and he knew better than to ask him anything else. They worked in silence for a time, until Jacob thought it would be okay to speak, or perhaps until his hunger had impaired his judgment.

"Do you think they were wrong to create them?"

"The smiths?" Charles asked.

Jacob nodded.

"No." Charles set his tools down and turned to Jacob. "There is very little in this world that's inherently evil. Even the most evil men you can think of didn't start out that way. Most men don't become what they intended to be."

"What do you mean?" Jacob asked as he crossed his arms.

Charles pinched the bridge of his nose. "I didn't always want to be a smith, much less a tinker. Tinker is a label given to a smith when people think he's lost his mind. My mind is very much intact, thank you."

Jacob muffled a laugh, and didn't say what came into his own mind.

Charles smiled. "Yes, well, now we're getting off topic. My point is, I wanted to be an organist. I wanted nothing more than to play the organ at Festival and sit in the Great Hall behind the castle walls. It wasn't a crazy dream, Jacob. I was good. I was damn good, but then the Deadlands War came, and the world became something else.

"Do you miss it? The organ, I mean?"

"There are days, yes, when my mind is stuck in the past. You have a passion, don't give it up. You'll need it to keep the shadows at bay when this world goes wrong."

Jacob didn't know what to say. Should he say sorry? He didn't think Charles would like that. Charles was not a man to accept pity, especially from someone a quarter his age. He thought it would be safer to stay quiet, or change the topic entirely.

Jacob looked up at Charles. The old man stared back, but Jacob didn't feel like Charles was seeing what was in the room. His mind was somewhere else. Charles held up the prosthetic, tested the knob that controlled the hand, and nodded.

"That one done?" Jacob asked.

"Yes, let's get back to the nail gloves. We're going to need the money from those, I'm afraid."

"Don't you think we should donate some of them?"

"The city is paying for the repairs and the tools." Charles stretched out one of the thick springs and latched it into a hook. He lowered one of his lenses and began inspecting it for any weaknesses, prodding and pulling on the metal spiral. "If it was Lowlanders having to pay for their own repairs, yes, I'd give them as much as they needed for free. But we'll need money if we have to run, Jacob."

The thought of taking a trip with Charles excited Jacob. The old man was full of stories, and it seemed like every day he had a new one to share. Jacob worried about his dad, though. Could his parents make the trip? And what about Alice? And what about the other Lowland kids he knew?

Jacob's thoughts took a dark turn as he thought about what Charles was saying, what he'd read about in *The Dead Scourge*, and what the men had said in the catacombs. If Newton convinced Parliament to force the miners back to work, before it was safe, they'd have a revolt. The Lowlanders were mostly unarmed behind the city wall, so Newton would get his wish either way. They wouldn't have to feed the dead.

Charles and Jacob didn't say much else through throughout the day. Jacob's mom and Bat came by a few times with snacks, but almost the entire day passed inspecting springs and assembling cartridges. It was evening before someone knocked on the outer door to the lab.

CHAPTER THIRTY-TWO

"Get that, would you?" Charles asked.

Jacob set down the mesh glove he'd been stitching to one of the braces. It really didn't need another row of stitches, but he was going to lose his mind if he had to load so much as one more nail cartridge. Jacob reached out to the lock on Bat's door, a simple button in the center of the wrought iron brace. He pressed it and a series of gears moved together, retracting the bolts that were sunken into the floor.

Jacob was surprised to see that the streetlamps were already on. His mom had said something about dinner when she brought the last round of food for them, but he hadn't really thought about how late it was getting. He was surprised they hadn't seen Alice yet either.

Ambrose stood outside the door. People walked by on the street behind him, and even a few carriages rattled by. Ambrose waited for Jacob to get the door pushed open a few feet before stepping inside and helping him close it again.

"Probably best not to put your gloves on display with the doors open," Ambrose said.

"Agreed," Charles said. He released the tensioner and lifted another nail glove off the device. "What did the city have to say?"

Ambrose frowned and cracked a knuckle on his left hand. "You have your gold, for as many as you can produce."

Charles nodded. Jacob expected him to smile or celebrate, but all the old man did was nod.

"And?" Charles asked. "If you came here with nothing but good news, I'm sure you wouldn't look so nervous."

"I'm not …" Ambrose started before he sighed. "It's just … the city smith was there. He had his hands on the glove."

"Oh?" Charles said. "And is that prat going to create his own version now? And by 'his own,' I mean copy mine exactly?"

Ambrose frowned. "He said he recognized the make of the cartridge. I'm pretty sure he knows you designed it, but I swear to you I didn't tell him."

Charles froze. "Well, that may accelerate our timetable to some degree. The city still agreed to pay me?" Charles asked as he turned around and gripped the edge of the workbench.

"Yes."

"Would he …" Jacob started. "Could he recognize your vacuum flask?"

"Probably," Charles said.

Jacob grimaced and squeezed his forehead. His words tumbled out in a rush. "I dropped it in the catacombs. Benedict picked it up. He said something about knowing it was a tinker's work, but not sure whose."

"Damn," Charles bit off the word.

"I'm sorry," Jacob said. "I didn't mean to drop it or—"

Charles held up his hand. "It is no fault of yours." He glanced at Ambrose, and then at Jacob. "There is bad blood between us, me and the city smith." Charles pulled off the gloves he was wearing—with little square bits of rubber worked into the fingers—before rubbing his face.

"How so?" Ambrose asked as he narrowed his eyes. "I know you're not fond of the smith. Hell, none of us are."

"You know his full name is Newton Burns?"

Ambrose nodded.

Jacob recoiled. Newton Burns was a name that tainted the pages of *The Dead Scourge*. His slaughter of the enemy—be them soldiers or families—earned him an apt title. He may have been hailed as a hero in

Ancora after the war, but the writings of Archibald in *The Dead Scourge* painted him as a monster.

"You know he was a killer in the war?"

"I've heard the stories," Ambrose said. "You kill or you die."

Charles let out a humorless laugh. "I always hated that motto. Newton was a murderer, Ambrose." Charles crossed his arms took a deep breath. "Some of us tried to stop him during the war, tried to have him put on trial. Parliament eventually pulled him away from the front lines, but they were slow to do it. He never saw a trial for his war crimes. The ways he killed, and the people he killed … I always worried he'd come after me and mine for our interference."

"He's looking to make an example out of someone," Ambrose said. "Crime has risen since the Lowlanders moved into the Highlands. He's convinced Parliament that a public punishment would set things right."

"Why do they even listen to his rhetoric?" Charles almost spat the words.

"He has influence," Ambrose said quietly. "His wife's brother runs the local police, and he's well connected with the knights. The men and women I know in Parliament still feel he was a hero in the Deadlands War, and his opinion carries a great deal of weight because of it.

"The Butcher of Gareth Cave," Jacob said, his voice not much above a whisper.

Charles and Ambrose both turned to him.

"Where did you hear that name?" Charles asked.

"It's in *The Dead Scourge*. Archibald, the author, he wrote a lot about the Butcher. There's a whole chapter in there. He's … he's a monster."

Jacob shivered as he realized who he'd stolen from over the past couple years. Every time he took something from the city smith's workshops … If he'd been caught, what would have happened?

Ambrose reached down to the back of his heavy work boots. The old leather was separating a bit, and Jacob wondered what he was doing as he peeled it down the length of his calf. Coins clinked together in the leather satchel that Ambrose had hidden away.

"A false boot?" Jacob asked.

"One of my favorites," Ambrose said with a smile. He pulled a clasp locker closed. Some of the kids called them zippers, but Jacob always preferred its proper name. "Now then," Ambrose said, hefting the coins and bouncing them in his hand. "This is one hundred gold."

"A hundred?" Jacob shouted. He'd never seen that much money in one place before.

"How many does that cover?" Charles asked.

"Five gloves."

Charles nodded slowly. "We were able to assemble seven today. Take five and come back in two days with five hundred gold."

Jacob almost fell off his stool.

"Take some extra cartridges with you today. Prove to them how useful they can be. Put that bastard smith in his place." Charles tossed one of the gloves into the air and Ambrose caught it.

"That shouldn't be a problem," Ambrose said.

"The money or the smith?"

Ambrose only smiled as he stacked the nail gloves into a leather backpack.

"I'll have some heavier gauge gloves for you next time," Charles said, "but they're only for you and the repairmen. I won't charge for them, and you shouldn't let Parliament see them. They'll fire bolts that can fasten steel to stone, but they could also be used as a weapon." Charles laced his fingers together and met Ambrose's eyes. "I did not build these things to kill."

"Finish as many as you can by tomorrow night. I'll bring the gold, but do me a favor?"

Charles raised an eyebrow.

"Pack your things. Whatever you need to make an escape. Whatever you may need to set up shop somewhere else. Just … just be ready."

Jacob watched Ambrose leave and then locked the door behind him. He shivered, remembering stories of what Parliament did to those considered traitors. Jacob pulled his stool closer to the bench.

"Let's get a few more done tonight," Charles said. "Then I'm afraid we better get some packing done."

Jacob and Charles didn't speak much that evening. They assembled gloves as fast as they could until Jacob almost fell asleep on a box of nails.

Charles sighed and released the tensioner as he finished the spring box for another glove. "Let's get some sleep."

Jacob yawned and nodded, following the old man into the house. He set the glowworms out and started packing, making sure to include some Bangers and Burners in his backpack. It wasn't until he finished some time later that Jacob realized he was thirsty. The plush rugs and carpets silenced his footsteps when he started back down the spiral stairs.

He was almost at the bottom before he heard the voices. Jacob crouched in the shadows on the landing at the second floor. A Jumper scampered by on its way to snack or sleep or whatever it was Jumpers did in the dark places of the city. Jacob strained his ears, and could just make out Charles's words.

"I've already talked to the girl's mother, and now I'm asking for your blessing. If what Samuel just learned is in fact coming to pass—and I fear it's true, considering what Ambrose said—they *are* going to come after us."

"You're asking us to let you take our son away from the protection of the city walls." Jacob's mom was almost hissing at Charles.

A lower, quieter voice said something, and his mom fell silent. In Jacob's heart, he knew his dad was speaking. He couldn't see his mom and dad. Only Charles's white hair was visible from Jacob's hiding spot.

"He's right," Charles said. "The trade routes have been shut down. I'd take you both with me if you were well, but you're not. Bat managed to buy enough medicine to get you through a month, but then what? You won't be able to get more where we're going, and I believe you'll be safe here once we're gone.

"Damn you, Charles." Jacob could hear the tears in his mother's voice. "If they come for him, you take him with you. You keep him safe."

"No one is safe, Mags," Charles said.

"Then as safe as you *can* keep him," she said, biting off the words.

"On my word."

Charles's footsteps echoed when he started down the hallway. They grew louder at first, and then trailed away into the distance.

Jacob's parents were whispering, but he couldn't hear what they were saying. Why wouldn't they be able to come too, if Jacob and Charles had to leave? His dad was better. Was he really still sick?

Jacob crept back to his room and stood in the doorway, no longer worried about being thirsty. He didn't know what to do, but he remembered something Charles used to say. You can never have too much knowledge. Jacob picked up *The Dead Scourge*. What Charles and Ambrose had been saying put an awful new angle on one of the most terrible chapters Jacob had read. The Butcher was the city smith, and the city smith wanted to make an example out of him. The city smith wanted them dead. Jacob wanted to know more about the man. It didn't take long to find the first chapter that mentioned him.

> The Butcher of Gareth Cave. Some simply called him the Butcher, and some dared not say his name aloud, as though he'd become an omniscient specter who could find them at any time, in any place.
> Little did I know, I'd already met the Butcher when I was much younger. I'd shared a classroom with him in Ancora. Our families worked the mines together. It wouldn't have been a stretch for me to call him a friend, but whoever he'd been before the war, that boy was dead. The man I'd met, the Butcher, knew only death in his heart and steel in his hands.
> While I was taken aback at the acceptance and penetration of Biomechs in the Deadlands culture, the

Butcher saw it as an abomination in the gods' eyes. His fear of them became an unyielding hatred.

Gareth Cave was what we'd call a blacksmith's shop in Ancora, but it was also a hospital run by an old inventor who knew more about Biomechs than anyone else in the Deadlands. We were in Gareth Cave when it happened, when the Butcher earned his name in blood.

A small girl, maybe ten, maybe younger, sat patiently beneath the blade and wrench of the old inventor. She only winced while the man pivoted her leg, detaching it from the mount in her thigh. After changing a myriad of parts, the man reattached the limb and had her test the new leg by kicking a steel plate. It buckled like it had been hit by a battering ram, and the girl giggled.

She was the first to die. An axe to the forehead. The Butcher had been a smith for a few years, and he had more than enough strength to split the girl's skull and follow through into the old inventor's chest. There was silence in the cave following the shock of those murders. It hung in the air like a fog, until a woman screamed.

The Butcher broke her neck and then crushed her husband beneath his boot. The Biomechs there were in various states of disrepair, and though they may have been more powerful when healthy, the Butcher slaughtered them in their weakened and wounded states. I can still hear the sounds. The terrible screams, the bodies breaking, and the men shouting for him to stop. The Butcher began killing our own men, his own Ancoran blood, when they tried to stop him. He gunned them down.

I ran from that nightmare, and it is a shame that will haunt me until the end of my days. Had I tried to stop the Butcher, I would have died, but there are many days I feel that is the fate I should have embraced.

In the end, Gareth Cave was no longer a welcoming refuge for all peoples of the Deadlands. It was a grisly tomb.

Remember what he did. He is no hero.

Jacob closed his eyes. His imagination ran wild, showing him the Butcher on a rampage in the hospital, killing Peter, and the doctors and the nurses and Bobby, all because he'd made them new limbs of metal.

Sleep did not come easily.

CHAPTER THIRTY-THREE

T HE NEXT DAY PASSED JACOB by in a blur of nails, springs, and mesh. They'd finished fourteen nail gloves by the time the sun started to creep below the city walls and the light seeping through the cracks in the door became an orange fire.

Jacob pushed his fingertips together and frowned.

"Sore?" Charles asked as he pulled the spring box together for the fifteenth glove.

"Yeah. I think it's from loading all the cartridges and leveling the followers."

"You just need to build up some calluses. Then you can do this all day."

"I'm pretty sure we just did this all day," Jacob muttered.

Charles laughed. "I can't argue with that."

"You really think Ambrose will bring five *hundred* gold?" Jacob asked.

"I do. Ambrose is well aware of the time his builders could save. His family has lived in the Lowlands for almost a century."

Jacob could scarcely contemplate how long a century was. That would be his father's grandfather's grandfather? He squinted as he tried to figure it out, finally giving up with a shake of his head. "Do you mind if I go out for a bit?"

"What for?"

"Well, I need to rest my fingers, and I haven't seen Alice at all today."

"Worried about the little miss?"

Jacob frowned and flicked a nail across the bench. A glass jar clinked when the nail bounced off it and rolled away. "Did you talk to her parents last night?"

Charles froze in the middle of wiping his hands off on an old oily rag. "You heard that, hmm?"

"I was coming down to get a drink. I heard most of it."

"Yes, I spoke with them. The city smith knows my work, and because of that flask, it's a solid theory he knows it was you in the catacombs. That puts Alice in danger too."

Charles crossed his arms and stared at Jacob. "I don't want to sound cruel, Jacob, but you are one of the best-known pickpockets in the Lowlands." Charles ran his hand over his beard. "That makes you ideal examples for a public punishment."

Alice's family was tied up with Lowland politics in some way, but Jacob had never given it any real thought. Jacob raised his eyes to meet the old man's gaze.

"I think you understand, yes?"

Jacob nodded. Depending on whom the Butcher knew, he'd know Jacob had been a pickpocket, or still was.

"It's the perfect excuse to come after you, Jacob." Charles leaned against the workbench. "Now, go find Alice. Tell her what you heard here."

Jacob didn't say anything else. He slipped his leather backpack over his shoulders, unlocked the door, and left the lab to Charles and his awful revelations.

✧　✧　✧

JACOB FIGURED THE BEST PLACE to find Alice would be at her inn. It may have taken him a while to find the inn with the carved dragon above its door the first time, but now he knew right where to go. He didn't stop at the front, instead heading straight to the third door from the end. Jacob paused for a moment before knocking, looking up and down the street.

He knocked three times. The tiny door within the door squeaked open, and relief flooded Jacob when a pair of blue eyes appeared.

Alice narrowed her gaze and slammed the peephole closed. The door swung inward a moment later. "Come on. No one's home. We can talk in here."

As soon as the door closed, Alice's voice rose. "What did you do?" she asked as she poked Jacob in the chest with her index finger. "Charles has my parents convinced I need to run away from the city all because I know *you*."

"I didn't—"

"Clearly you did, or I wouldn't have a backpack and purse filled with so many clothes and so much food I can barely lift them. What in the world happened? Did you get caught stealing?"

"No," Jacob said. "It's the city smith; he knows it was us in the catacombs. He recognized Charles's work."

Alice seemed downright furious, and scared. "It doesn't matter now, does it? I'm all packed and ready to leave at a moment's notice. Do you have any idea where we're going?"

"No, I don't."

"My mom thinks Charles might be overly paranoid."

Jacob glanced to the side, briefly eying an old vase in the corner while he made up his mind. He stepped forward and gently grabbed Alice's arm.

"Look, Alice, it's not Charles being paranoid. The city smith is the Butcher of Gareth Cave."

"How do you know?" Alice asked as she folded her arms and frowned.

"His full name is Newton Victor Burns."

She blew out an exasperated breath. "How do we even know the book is true? Archibald could have been a crazy person. Maybe he was just laying blame?" Her words sounded empty to Jacob, and she wouldn't meet his eyes.

"You don't believe that."

Alice sighed and flopped onto the couch by an overstuffed backpack and her leather purse. "No, I don't." She leaned over and patted her backpack. "I loved the story of the Butcher when I was a kid. It was all bravery and heroes and good killing evil."

"Sometimes the history books lie."

"I know." She stared at her hands folded in her lap. "I don't like it when people lie, Jacob." She glanced up. "Don't lie to me, okay?"

"I won't."

Jacob wasn't sure what to do when Alice stood up and wrapped her arms around him. He placed his right arm around her gently, and when she squeezed him harder, he hugged her back.

"Why aren't our parents packing?" she asked, stepping away.

"Charles thinks they'll be safer here with us gone. Bat said your family can stay with him if the Lowlanders get pushed out too soon. He'll protect them if war breaks out. I thought my parents were just staying because my dad's still sick, but maybe not."

"No," Alice said. "It would make them look guilty if they left. And what does he even mean by leaving? Where can we go?"

"I don't know, but I trust Charles."

Alice sighed and squeezed her eyes shut. "I do too."

Jacob waited for her to open her eyes and said, "If you have to run, meet us at the underground train station. We can meet there and then follow Charles."

Alice gave one sharp nod.

Jacob left her at the inn, and his mood was not improved. He started back to Bat's, wondering what kind of crazy person thought they could help reinforce laws by killing a kid. Oh, sure, maybe they'd only beat him publicly, lash him in the courtyard, but Jacob's imagination was far too vivid to believe that. He was sure he'd be tied up to a cross and fed to a Red Death or a Widow Maker. That's how they'd handled criminals in the Deadlands War.

He was so lost in imagining his own death, he didn't notice that the women in front of him had stopped walking. He smacked into one and she almost fell over.

"I'm so sorry," he said. "Are you okay?"

She straightened her hat and turned to look at him. "Mind your manners, you filthy steamborn wretch. I don't know why they still allow that filth here."

"Please, he can hear you, miss." Jacob didn't see who was speaking.

"We don't need their diseases." The woman's parasol caught the light of the streetlamp as she looked back at him once and frowned slightly.

Jacob was speechless. He felt like he should apologize for breathing her air, and nothing had ever made him feel so small.

"Your carriage, madam," a man dressed in a black leather suit said. He wore a hat, and silver-lined goggles were mounted on his head.

Jacob watched the lady climb into the carriage before he realized it didn't have legs. No bugs were at the front to draw it down the cobblestones.

The man closed the door behind the women and stepped closer to Jacob. He leaned down close to him and whispered. "Ignore the lady, son. She has quite the temper." He patted Jacob's shoulder and turned around.

"Sir?" Jacob said.

He looked over his shoulder with one hand on the carriage door.

"Is that a puffing demon?"

He laughed and pulled his goggles down before running his eyes over the length of the metal beast. "It is indeed, son. It is indeed."

Jacob stared at the contraption. He'd never seen one working before. He walked up to the side of the demon. It almost seemed a piece of art, the way the paint gleamed in the streetlamps, glinting off the curves of metal above the wheels. Jacob could hear the hiss of steam and flames as he got near the front of the demon, and he knew the engine must be beneath the curved metal sheet. He took a step back, so he could see into the driver's compartment, and watched the man push a lever to the floor and then turn a wheel. A burst of steam billowed out the back of the contraption and the carriage lurched forward.

Jacob couldn't stop a smile while he watched the legless carriage—a real puffing demon that ran on steam and pistons and gears—send bursts of vapor into the air as it motored down the street.

He spent the rest of the walk back to the lab torn between wondering why so many Highlanders seemed to despise everything about the Lowlands, and being awed by seeing an actual puffing demon.

CHAPTER THIRTY-FOUR

"Y OU OKAY?" CHARLES ASKED WHEN Jacob returned to the lab.

He nodded and flopped onto his wooden stool. "I saw a puffing demon, and it was amazing."

"So what's the problem, then? Afraid you'll never be able to invent something so grand?"

Jacob shook his head. "Some lady called me a 'filthy steamborn wretch.'"

Charles laughed and patted Jacob's back gently. "That's a name I haven't heard in many years. Wear it with pride."

"Why?"

The old man smiled. "Back in the war, some of the Highborn folks called us tinkers steamborn. Of course, it's 'steamborn filth' that gives them their greatest inventions. Don't judge them too harshly. Some progress improves humanity, and some progress improves only war. It only slips their mind that we gave them their running water *and* their puffing demons."

Jacob glanced over at the shelf where they'd been stacking all the gloves up. There were only a couple left.

"Did Ambrose come by?"

Charles nodded. "He wasn't going to come until tomorrow, but I think that man may be more paranoid than I am." Charles pulled out a leather satchel, much like the one Ambrose had given them before, and tossed it to Jacob.

It knocked his hand back into his chest like he'd caught a heavy rock.

"What's *in* this?"

"Five hundred gold."

Jacob almost choked. He carefully passed the satchel back to Charles.

"It won't bite."

"That's like ten years of my parent's wages, Charles. *I* wouldn't trust me around it." Jacob glanced at the floor and then back up to the old man. "Neither should you."

"Jacob, my boy, I'm trusting you with my life. One word could be the end of me. Five hundred gold is nothing."

"You're my friend."

"I am, and you are mine. I do hope you remember that when we have to flee the city."

"Where will we go?"

"I have a place in mind. Don't you worry about that."

"When will we have to leave?"

"Well, Ambrose is taking those gloves into the field tomorrow." Charles frowned. "The city smith never was a very patient man."

Jacob pulled an empty cartridge off the stack on the corner of the bench and dragged a can of nails closer. He started loading them in, one at a time. His fingers were still sore, but it wasn't quite as bad as it had been earlier in the day.

"I think Alice is mad at me," Jacob said. "She wouldn't be in this if it weren't for me."

"That may be true, but I'd guess she's more scared than angry. No one wants to leave their family and home behind, Jacob." He paused, reconsidering. "Well, most of us don't, anyway."

Jacob hoped Charles was right. He didn't want Alice mad at him. "Is Ambrose coming back for the rest of the gloves tomorrow?"

"That's the intention," Charles said. "We'll need to get a few more made. I just about have the heavy-gauge glove done." Charles grunted as he slowly released the tensioner. "A few of the heavy springs were bad, so it's taken a bit longer than I'd hoped."

He held the spring box up and turned it over a few times, changing out the lenses on his glasses before nodding. "I think it's ready." He leaned forward and picked up a larger cartridge and a case of bolts that Jacob hadn't seen before.

"What are those?"

"Ambrose calls them stone bolts. Used to call them anchors in the military." Charles held up one of the inch-thick bolts and the cartridge. "You be very careful with these. The nail gloves are dangerous, yes, but this could tear your hand off."

Jacob slid the case of bolts closer. They were heavy and a bit hard to drag across the wooden workbench. The metal case squeaked against the surface of the bench. Charles handed him a cartridge, and it was almost identical to the nail glove cartridge, only larger. Jacob leaned the first bolt against the spring and pushed it home.

"They're heavy. What's Ambrose going to use them for?"

"You've seen the plates the repairmen use to prop up their wooden walls, yes?"

Jacob nodded. He remembered seeing a wide metal plate on the ground behind the temporary barrier in the Lowlands. That already seemed so long ago. He felt like he was home in Bat's house with Charles and his parents.

"Good, good." Charles pulled out a long timber. It looked like someone had started carving it before the end had broken off. It was at least six inches by six inches and a good three feet long. Charles set it in the middle of the floor on its side, adjusted it a bit, and then crouched down beside the bench.

He rooted through some scrap iron under the bottom shelf until he came up with a length of gray metal. It wasn't rusty like the iron. Charles rapped it with his knuckles and said, "Steel." He laid it over the carved post, lining up the edges as best he could before starting to pull the heavy nail glove over his fingers. He curled his hand into a fist and gave the spring box a couple tugs before nodding.

"Pass me a cartridge."

Jacob handed him his current cartridge. It had four bolts loaded, and he wasn't sure if he could cram so much as one more onto the spring. "What are you doing?"

Charles slid the cartridge into the receiver and pulled the locking lever across the entire base of the spring box until it clicked. "I'm showing you why you don't keep this heavy glove loaded." He took his time, making a show out of moving his stool to the side and crouching down to line up the steel and the glove.

Jacob jumped when Charles slammed his fist into the steel sheet. He cringed at the squeal of metal as the spring box fired and the first bolt burst through steel and wood alike. Charles's hand barely moved at all as almost all of the force was absorbed by the buffer in the spring box. "I'm showing you how a little ingenuity and some common sense can build wonders."

Charles picked up the length of wood and steel and laid it on the workbench, steel side down. He pulled out a hammer and chisel and began chipping the wood away from the bolt. The wood smelled hot and charred as it fell to the floor.

Jacob leaned over and watched the end of the bolt come into view. "It's three times the size it was."

"Exactly. Best of all, it doesn't matter what's beneath the steel. The bolts hit with enough force to punch through steel, and the tips expand to lock them into wood, or metal, or stone."

Jacob reached out and ran his fingers over the deformed tip. He hissed. "It's a little hot." He stared at the warped bolt. "If that were stone …"

"It would make a hell of an anchor, Jacob. With enough bolts, I imagine you could mount a catapult on a watchtower. Not saying the watchtower could handle the force, mind you, but it could be done."

"Should we try to finish all the gloves tonight?"

"Ambrose already paid us in full. I'd like to finish them, but I don't think we have the time. Let's just see how many we can get into working order."

Jacob pulled out one of the pre-stitched mesh gloves and started snapping brass fasteners onto it. He counted out a perfect square, twenty by twenty, and snapped another fastener on. Charles would mount the spring box after Jacob finished. Then he'd be back to loading cartridges. Jacob frowned at the thought. He was almost as tired of loading cartridges as his fingers were.

A few hours went by while the pair worked at a relentless pace. "So, you found Alice," Charles said as he wrenched another spring box into place.

Jacob nodded. "I told her everything."

Charles looked over and watched Jacob for a moment. "I'm sorry you've been dragged into this."

"I'm more worried about Alice."

"Yes, well, boys tend to worry about the girls they like."

Jacob looked at Charles's eyes. The old man wasn't trying to mock him. There was no smile on his face. It was the same look his father got when he apologized for feeding Jacob peas. The image made Jacob laugh, just a little, before the thought of never seeing Alice again weighed him down.

"That girl knows how to look out for herself," Charles said. "If I'd ever had a daughter, I would have wanted one like her. Clever, idealistic, and kind."

"I guess," Jacob said. He started loading another cartridge. His fingers hurt a little, but it was a mindless task, and mindless was what he needed.

"It's best not to worry about it, Jacob. I won't leave you or your family to these wolves. We're prepared to run. We have gold, and supplies. There are a thousand places to hide in this city, and a million more outside the walls."

"Have you seen my folks?" Jacob asked.

Charles nodded. "They were running down to Market Street. Something about dinner. I wasn't listening too closely, to be honest."

"That's a good sign if Dad went too. He never leaves the house when he's feeling bad."

"Don't worry about them, Jacob."

"I can't help it."

"I don't mean this to sound horrible, boy, but if the city did anything to your parents, they wouldn't be able to use them as leverage to get to you."

"Why does it have to be me?" Jacob asked before he slammed a cartridge onto the workbench. "Is it my fault they fired my dad? My fault we couldn't afford to eat? You know what happens if you don't eat, Charles? You *die*. Was I supposed to sit there and watch my family starve? Is that what I should have done instead of stealing?"

"It's okay, Jacob," Charles said. He patted Jacob's shoulder. "It's not your fault."

Jacob wasn't as sure as Charles seemed to be. If Charles had really been so sure, why had they prepared to run? The thought wouldn't leave his mind while they assembled more cartridges and more nail gloves well into the evening.

The knock on the door came as the streetlamps burst into life, and the shadows of the city came calling.

CHAPTER THIRTY-FIVE

"S AMUEL!" JACOB'S HEART SANK AS he watched the knights push his friend onto his knees before slamming Samuel to the floor. The Spider Knight's arms and legs were bound in leather restraints. Blood leaked from his forehead. "What are you doing? Leave him alone!"

He tried to step toward Samuel, but Charles threw his arm out. "Stay back, Jacob. They're looking for an excuse."

"We don't need an excuse, tinker. This raid is sanctioned." Cold blue eyes turned back to Jacob beneath a shining silver helmet. There were three lines and a white bird painted onto the side. "Your parents are being interviewed by the police. Come with us, and we'll take you to see them." He held his hand out and smiled.

It wasn't a smile Jacob liked. It was the kind of smile he'd seen on a cat's face after it slaughtered a family of mice.

"Theft has become a problem in the Highlands," the soldier said, "and we're here to sort it out."

"I haven't stolen anything!" Jacob's hands curled into fists. How could they accuse him of something he hadn't done?

The door began sliding closed behind the men, and they didn't seem to notice. Jacob wasn't sure why the door was moving until he saw Charles leaning against the bench by the trigger Bat had installed.

"A lying pickpocket," the second soldier said, moving his halberd from one shoulder to the other. "You'll make an excellent example to all the other Lowland thieves."

"What is it you intend?" Charles asked. "What are you doing with

Samuel?"

"The Spider Knight is an accomplice," the soldier closest to Charles said. "Witnesses observed him passing information to known outlaws and he refused to reveal their whereabouts. We'll clear his name so long as you give us the thief, tinker. It's time he lost his hands."

Charles's expression froze. He looked cold, and it sent a shiver down Jacob's spine, even more so than the terror that followed the soldier's words.

The soldier closer to Jacob reached for him, and Jacob screamed. He didn't want to lose his hands. For what? For helping his father live? For helping feed his family? "No! Get away!"

The soldier grabbed Jacob's arm so tight Jacob thought his arm might break. "Let go!"

Charles swore, and before Jacob fully registered what had happened, the old man punched the soldier in his helmet. The crack of the rivet tearing through metal and smashing into the skull beneath was like someone had stepped on a giant Pill-Bug.

Jacob hopped away when the soldier's grip loosened, just before the man hit the ground, dead. Jacob could only watch as Charles whirled around to face the other man.

The second soldier scrambled to bring his halberd around, but it slammed against the rafters instead of finding its target.

"Always it ends in blood," Charles snarled. The whine of a spring and recoil of metal on metal echoed through the room as the next rivet found its home in the soldier's chest.

He tried to speak as the halberd clanged against the vise on the workbench and clattered to the ground, but the rivet had punctured something important. A red trail leaked from the edge of the soldier's mouth as he fell to his knees, and something like confusion washed over his face.

"I was not always a tinker," Charles said as he stepped behind the soldier. He placed a hand on either side of the man's head and twisted. A gristly crack filled the lab. The soldier's armor rang as it hit the stone floor. Only silence remained.

Jacob wanted to scream, but no sound came out. He stared at the blood on the floor. Charles had killed a man. He'd killed *two* men. To save Jacob?

"Why did you have to do that?" Jacob asked, his voice barely a whisper.

Charles squatted down beside Samuel and started slicing through the leather restraints. Jacob thought he could have used a key, but then realized the keys were probably under the soldiers. He didn't think Charles would want to touch the dead men any more than he did.

"I promised your mother I'd look after you. Bringing you home without hands wasn't part of the deal. You have a mind for machines, Jacob. I've always said it. I can't have an apprentice without hands." When Jacob didn't respond, Charles looked up. "There are casualties in every battle. We got lucky with these two fools, but sometimes the casualties will be on your own side."

Charles lifted the leather bands off Samuel, and the gag fell away. The Spider Knight gasped and sat up, rubbing his wrists.

"Thank you," Samuel said.

"We're going to have to leave the city. They'll be out for blood now."

Something boomed against the heavy oak door and men began yelling.

"Open the door! The city guard commands it!"

Three deafening knocks shook the door.

"I hope you can run," Charles said, looking over Samuel's leg.

Jacob followed his gaze to Samuel's calf. Blood seeped through the fabric and slowly dripped down his silver armor.

"I've had worse," Samuel said. "The most important thing is that we get away. I can worry about my leg later."

"Break it down."

Jacob heard the words, and a moment later, the door shook in its frame. The wood began to splinter around the iron bands and braces, and his heart leapt as he realized they weren't at all safe in the lab.

Charles cursed and threw a backpack over his shoulder. "I'd hoped to take the steambike, but I've no desire to kill those men."

"I doubt we could," Samuel said as he hefted a pack of his own.

"What about Bessie?" Jacob asked.

Samuel cinched a belt around his waist and adjusted the shoulder straps before testing his movement. "She's in the stables. No way we can get to her in the middle of all the city guards."

A jagged crack appeared in the door when something slammed into it again.

"Alice!" Jacob almost yelled her name.

"She already knows what to do," Charles said. "We'll get to the rendezvous and wait for her. She may already be there."

"So long as they didn't catch her," Samuel said.

Charles frowned, but he didn't object to Samuel's words as a web-work of yellow light appeared in the cracked door.

"Goddamned fools taking orders like the gods themselves ran this city." Charles cursed as he scooted an angled piece of metal into the doorway. "Anyone with enough sense to breathe should have enough sense not to cut off a kid's hands."

Jacob looked at the heavy springs and the spear-like spikes loaded into the holes across the front. "You're going to kill them."

"Shouldn't kill them," Charles said as he slammed a heavy nail glove against the metal and stone to anchor it, "but they won't be on their feet for a while, that's for sure."

The door cracked again, and Jacob screamed when a crossbow bolt shattered a glass jar beside his head.

"Run!" Charles yelled. "Now!"

Jacob struggled to get his backpack secured as they flung open the door to the house and ran, past the kitchen and through Bat's living room.

"Down the spiral," Charles said. "We can get into the catacombs through the basement."

"The third level?" Samuel asked. "That's too dangerous."

Jacob followed the pair into the darker depths of the spiral staircase.

"We don't have a choice," Charles said. Something clicked three times, and a small lantern burst to life in his hands.

Something thundered upstairs. Jacob could just barely hear it, but the screams that followed were unmistakable.

"Sounds like it worked," Samuel said.

"It'll slow them down." Charles slid a brick out of the cracked foundation and reached inside. "They'll think there are more traps, and do I ever wish there were."

Jacob heard a clang and a hum before stone ground against stone as a hidden door opened in the basement wall. Stones fell away from them and then slowly rolled to reveal a round, dark path.

"Go, quickly."

Samuel braved the darkness first. He had a short sword in his hand, and Jacob had no idea where it had come from. He saw Charles reach into the hole again before working the brick back into the wall. The doorway started closing, and the shadows felt like they were around his throat. Jacob's heart skipped a beat, thinking Charles was locking them into the catacombs, before the old man followed them into the narrow hallway with his lantern.

Jacob's breathing was still shallow, but at least he could see once Charles passed the lantern up to Samuel.

"Which way?"

"There's only one path. Once we're in the rotunda, go right. I pray Alice has found her way underground."

Samuel nodded. Jacob tried to get his breathing to even out, but his panic alternated between his parents, Alice, and the men who had threatened to cut off his hands.

Jacob fought back tears as they vanished into the darkness of the forgotten city.

✧   ✧   ✧

JACOB'S EYES ADJUSTED TO THE dimly lit corridor as they followed it up its gradual climb. "Is this the third level?"

"It's attached to it," Samuel said. "The gate we passed leads to the old tunnels the miners abandoned."

"I think that was only ten years after the war," Charles said. "Who would have thought your uncle had an escape route under his house so close to it?"

The floor broke into a brief series of steep stairs. No one spoke, balancing on the balls of their feet as they traveled higher. At the top of the stairs lay a shattered grate. Jagged splinters of iron caught the lantern light, and the path beyond seemed an endless chasm.

Jacob watched the pieces at his feet as he walked past, glancing backward until the gate vanished into the darkness behind them. "What could have done that?"

"Hopefully nothing we'll see today," Charles said.

"What the hell happened, Charles?" Samuel asked as he ducked through the third cracked support column they'd seen in the pitch-black tunnel.

"I'm not sure. A stampede of some sort could have done it, I suppose, but I'd expect to see piles of dead chitin left behind."

"No," Samuel said, taking a deep breath when the path's incline leveled off. "Why are they after Jacob?"

"I'm afraid it all comes back to the city smith," Charles said.

"He doesn't deserve that title," Samuel said before he spat on the ground. "The Butcher is far more fitting."

"Nonetheless, it is a story that started a very long time ago. I've stayed close to him, here in Ancora, watching for some sign of the monster I knew in the Deadlands War. I'm afraid I may have failed."

"Watch your step," Samuel said as the corridor opened into a wider tunnel. "We're at the old tracks."

Jacob stepped over the iron tracks as Samuel shined his light at the ground. The metal was old and rusted and looked ready to crumble. He wondered why the tracks here were in such terrible shape, when by the old station they almost looked new. Something fell and clanged in the darkness, echoing through the tunnel.

"Quiet," Charles said.

Jacob froze, the pounding of his heartbeat almost loud enough to drown out the distant footfalls of something scurrying through the tunnels. He grew more anxious as the rapid tapping of something large grew louder, vibrating through the tracks at his feet.

"Move," Charles said. "Through the gate up ahead. We lock it behind us. Go."

They broke into a jog, as fast as they dared without raising too much noise. The gate wasn't far, but even that short jog felt like the stuff of nightmares. Jacob knew at any moment something would drop from the ceiling, and that would be the end of him.

Charles fumbled with the lock on the gate for a moment before it squealed open. Something in the shadows echoed the scream of metal and then they were through.

"That's it," Samuel said. "We're back on the first level."

"What was that?" Jacob asked once they'd moved away from the gate.

"No clue," Samuel said. "I'm just glad it didn't catch up. Charles, you were saying?"

Charles glanced back at Jacob before returning his focus to their path. "There were a handful of us that swore to keep an eye on the city smith, or at least come calling if he followed a darker path. There are only a few of us left now. Some died of old age, but others were killed over the past year.

"Whatever his goal now, I'd guess he's trying to keep the truth about his war crimes hidden. He may suspect I've told Jacob, but I can't be sure."

"Light," Jacob hissed.

Samuel didn't so much as hesitate, his hand flashed out to the dial that would snuff the lantern, and darkness wrapped its arms around them a moment later. The darkness was a never-ending shadow until it reached a corner not a hundred paces away.

"Alice?" Jacob asked as quietly as he could.

"Could be," Charles said. "Samuel, keep your sword at the ready."

"You think?" Samuel snapped in a heated whisper.

They stayed close to the wall, outside the dim light. Jacob brushed against something slimy and it skittered away from him. He shivered and ground his teeth. He didn't mind bugs, but when he couldn't see what was touching him, he had no idea if it was something from which he should run screaming.

Samuel raised his hand in a closed fist, only a silhouette against the weak light. They crouched at the edge of the hall in a doorway that led out onto the old train station's platform.

"Alice," Jacob said, and he couldn't stop the smile on his face. She sat at the same wrought iron tables where they'd eaten, not far from the old bookstore.

"Shh," Samuel said as he picked up a broken stone. He threw it underhanded, and it cracked against the old dusty floor closer to Alice. She slammed a book closed and looked up, her eyes searching the shadows all around.

"Looks clear," Charles said. He stood up straighter as he walked out of the tunnel and into the light of Alice's lantern.

"Charles!" Alice said. She hopped up and ran toward the old man. "Is Jacob with you? Did everyone make it out?" Her voice cracked. "They came into the inn and they … they killed the innkeeper when she wouldn't tell them where I was."

Jacob stepped around Charles and stared wide-eyed at Alice. Dried blood edged a broad cut across her cheek. A brownish crimson stain marred her dress in the lantern light, smeared where she'd tried to scrub blood off her hands. A book lay on the ground in tatters, pages torn away and bloodied and left crumpled on the floor. He put his arms around Alice and hugged her as tightly as he could.

She was shaking, and a moment later he realized he was shaking too.

"I always wanted a grand adventure, Jacob—like Charles used to tell us about—but this is *not* what I had in mind." She sniffed and pushed herself away.

Jacob could feel the tears running down his face. "The soldiers said they have my parents."

"They'll be okay," Charles said.

"How can you know that?" Jacob asked, his voice cracking as terror warred with a terrible rage. "They killed an innkeeper? Why would they do that?"

"Our departure is the best thing we can do to keep them safe," Charles said. He squeezed Jacob's shoulder. "Parliament isn't going to hurt them so long as they can be used as leverage."

Jacob frowned and rubbed at his forehead.

"Where are we going now?" Alice asked. She slung her dark leather backpack over her shoulder. "They'll find us here eventually."

"We're going through there," Samuel said, pointing to the gate blocking the train tracks to the south.

Jacob looked at the giant dead invader in the tunnel and shivered. What would they do if they ran into one of those things and it was still alive? "I really don't want to get eaten by one of those."

Charles laughed, though there wasn't much humor in the sound. "Neither do I, boy. Neither do I."

"There's a spring close to the exit," Samuel said, looking over at Alice. "So long as it's not overrun, we'll get you cleaned up."

Alice nodded and seemed to be intentionally averting her eyes from her bloodied hands.

Something boomed in the distance.

Charles looked toward both ends of the train station and frowned. "I can't tell where that's coming from."

"I don't care," Samuel said as he started across the bridge. "Let's go."

CHAPTER THIRTY-SIX

THE DOORWAY ON THE OTHER side of the bridge was a long, dark staircase that seemed to vanish into the depths of hell. The archway itself mirrored the path Jacob and Alice had taken into the catacombs, but the stairs here were narrow, and seemed slippery the lower they got. Lantern light glinted on the water dripping down the walls and struggled to light the depths beyond.

"Why is there water on the stairs?" Alice asked.

"Groundwater," Charles said. "Nothing to worry about. There's a stream running through the mountain when we get lower. Some folks call it a river, but it's only a stream."

Another boom sounded in the distance, and the floor shook beneath their feet.

Samuel glanced back at Charles. "What is that?"

"I don't know, but I'd bet it's a bug."

Jacob felt Alice wrap her hand up in his own. She shivered and he squeezed her fingers tight.

"It's not one of those huge invaders, is it?" Jacob asked.

"It could be," Charles said, placing his hand against the wall. "If it is, we're safe here. There are no caverns large enough for the giants to reach this path. None of the giants have been seen in a decade. We should have another five years or so before the next brood. They hatch like clockwork."

"There's a gate up ahead," Samuel said. He hurried down the stairs. The Spider Knight shouted and jumped backward when something screeched and slammed itself against the gate. He lunged forward with the short sword and drove it through something with a crunch. He held the lantern up to the dead creature pinned through the gate and cursed. "Widow Maker."

"This high?" Charles asked. "I didn't expect them this high."

The blood coating the sword looked dark in the dim light when Samuel wrenched the blade up and out of the spider's head. "Stay away from the fangs. They're still deadly." He tried the handle and the gate only rattled in its frame.

"Here," Charles said. He stepped up beside Samuel. The old man pressed on a section of stone that looked like any other part of the wall, causing an unseen mechanism to groan and squeal. The gate rose slowly, and everyone ducked through as soon as it was high enough to pass under. The Widow Maker's carcass fell to the side.

"Do we need to close it?" Alice asked as she stepped carefully around the spider. Its legs were already curling up beneath it. "If it stays open, they'll know which way we went.

"The tracks we left in the dust will lead them here whether the gate is closed or not, but it will close on its own." Charles placed his hand on the wall and stopped. "Samuel, do you hear that?"

Jacob strained to hear what Charles was talking about. It wasn't a boom, but it was loud. It was constant and almost sounded like the water running through a fountain.

"Is that the underground river?" Samuel asked. "I don't remember being able to hear it this high up."

"You can't," Charles said. He narrowed his eyes and stared into the depths of the staircase. "Pass me the lantern, and let's get down to the third level. We'll know soon enough."

Charles paused and turned his head again.

"What is it?" Samuel asked before he passed Charles the lantern. He filled a small brass lamp with water from a rawhide canteen at his side. Jacob knew what the light was: an old carbide-mining lamp. It was small and the welds look repaired. Samuel waited a beat and then struck a flint across the striker mounted at the lamp's nozzle. A flame caught and flickered and then burst into life. Samuel clipped it onto his armor and it added a fair amount of illumination to the stairs.

Charles stared back up the corridor.

"What is it?" Samuel asked.

"Voices," Charles whispered, "where they should not be."

They all fell silent and listened. Charles snuffed the last of the light, and they waited in absolute darkness. Jacob flinched when he heard the clang of metal on metal and someone shouting in the distance.

"Be calm," Samuel squeezed Jacob's shoulder. "We have the advantage. Hands on shoulders, step left, step right."

Jacob stayed behind Charles. Alice kept her hand on Jacob's shoulder while Samuel led them into the black. Jacob kept his free hand running along the roughly hewn walls, feeling every crack and bump and jumping at anything sharp enough to feel dangerous. It seemed like half an hour, one careful step after another until Samuel said, "Hold."

They listened, and only the sounds of their own breathing wandering through the darkness to greet them.

"I'm getting the lantern out," Charles said. The click on the igniter sounded before a dim glow cut through the shadows. They moved forward again, traveling in the shaky light as the lantern swung back and forth in the old man's hand.

Samuel kept his sword at the ready, and it made Jacob jump at every shadow that shifted in the dim corridor. Alice wrapped her hand around Jacob's arm and stayed with him step for step until they reached another flight of stairs.

Jacob counted the steps until they surpassed a hundred. Slowly, the shadows became only shadows in his mind, and the thunder of the water was almost reassuring as it grew louder. They hadn't heard voices in a while. He knew the silence might be a product of the water's volume, but he didn't want to consider what that might mean.

The corridor stopped suddenly, spreading out onto another platform by way of wide stone stairs. It looked like an unfinished train station with a crumbling stone bridge, and storefronts so fallen into disrepair they were so much rubble.

Jacob yelped when he stepped forward and water ran over his ankles. The room was filled with a deafening roar, and the rapids and whitecaps of the river were frightening in the inconsistent lantern light.

"What the *hell*?" Samuel let out a string of curses unlike anything Jacob had ever heard. "This has *always* been a stream, knee deep at most."

Water raged through the cavern, lapping at the decaying stone bridge.

"There's no way this is natural," Charles said. He crouched at the water's edge and put his hand into the raging current. "We'll have to take the bridge."

"*That* bridge?" Alice asked, pointing at the cracked, collapsing stonework.

"Yes, we can't go backward. This is the only underground path that leads to the south."

"I'll go," Jacob said, taking a deep breath. "I'm lighter than you and Samuel."

"I don't like it," Samuel said. He adjusted the lamp mounted at his shoulder. "If he gets to the other side and something's waiting …"

"There's nothing here," the old man said, sweeping the lantern light from one side of the bridge to the other.

Jacob didn't say any more. He waded farther into the water where it was just above his shins. Even there, in the slower current, it threatened to knock him over. A few short steps brought him to the foot of the old bridge.

The top of the bridge was damp but clear. The railings had long since rusted and fallen away, clearly not meant to withstand the moisture in the cave. Jacob squinted and could just make out the far side of the bridge.

"It's intact," he said, turning to Charles. "Can you hold the light any higher?"

Charles raised the lantern as high as he could. Jacob took a few steps forward. The bridge felt solid. He continued to the halfway point and closed his eyes. Small vibrations moved through the old stone, probably from the rushing water more than anything else.

Jacob walked back across the bridge, crossing the water to stand with Alice. "I think it's okay."

Samuel glanced at Charles and shrugged. "I'll go first," he said. He walked into the water and adjusted the old miner's lamp.

"Here," Charles said. He held the lantern out to Jacob. "Keep it high." Charles stepped up onto the base of the bridge, but he waited until Samuel was safely on the other side before following the Spider Knight.

Jacob and Alice followed.

"I don't like this," Alice said. "I can't see anything."

"Here." Jacob held out the lantern.

"Thanks," Alice said. She took the light and held it up. "Are you coming with me?"

"You go first."

"If this bridge supported Charles, I'm sure it will support both of us."

"Just go," Jacob said. "You can put the light on the bridge for me at the other side.

"Come on!" Samuel shouted from the opposite shore.

Alice hurried over the wet stones and turned around when she reached the other side. Jacob followed, pausing in the center to glance over the edge of the bridge. As frightening as the raging river had seemed from the shore, it was even more intimidating from above. Jacob couldn't imagine anything escaping that churning mass of force.

Alice screamed. Jacob turned just far enough to see the flash of lantern light reflecting off an enormous, oblong eye. It was black and curved on the side of a wide, flat head, and Jacob threw himself to the side on instinct alone. The giant bug brought its head down, impaling a stone with a mouth that looked more like a dark, curved saber. Its tan forelegs surged forward like a scorpion's claws, narrowly missing Jacob's arm, before its bulk smashed into the bridge.

Its head rose again and released a deep chirrup before that terrifying saber smashed through another stone, scattering fragments into the river below as Jacob rolled off the other side of the bridge. His hands scrambled to find purchase, but the stones were too damp, too smooth. Samuel rammed his sword home through the creature's head before turning to help, but Jacob was already falling.

He didn't have time to scream before the raging waters closed over his head. He wanted to scream as the cold darkness of the river engulfed him, but he knew that would mean drowning. Jacob held his hands out to the side as the current turned him and tumbled him until something caught his palm. He thought it might be Charles or Samuel, but it was only a rock.

Jacob pulled as hard as he could, struggling against the river. He finally pulled his head above the water, a fraction of an inch, and gasped for air. He was almost in the center of the stream, and very close to the wall where the underground river disappeared.

"I see him!" Samuel shouted, and then he cursed. "Can't reach him."

"Jacob!" Charles said. "Hold your breath and ride the current." He said more, but Jacob's head dipped below the water, and all he heard was death rushing all around him. He caught part of what Charles had said when he resurfaced, "… empties into a …" and then his grip failed. Jacob heard Alice scream his name before he vanished into the river rapids. He wanted to shout, to warn his friends. They weren't looking up, and there were a thousand black eyes descending upon them.

✧   ✧   ✧

CHARLES KNEW THERE WAS A chance that Jacob could survive. Even if it was a slim chance, it was still a chance. The wail from Alice cut him to the bone, and he fought against the burning in his eyes.

"Come on, girl," Charles said as he wrapped his arm around Alice's shoulder. "We'll meet him at the bottom."

"That's a long way," Samuel said, raising his lantern from the crest of the bridge. Something gleamed at the edge of the light, black and thin and sinister.

"Run!" Charles yelled, sprinting at Samuel. He pushed Alice in the direction of the doorway in the far wall, sending her lantern light swinging around the room and up toward the ceiling. Charles swore as he tightened the mesh of a heavy nail glove around his right hand.

Samuel looked up, following the path of the lantern light. The Spider Knight didn't speak. He took two steps and leapt off the top of the bridge. Samuel grunted and grabbed his knee as he landed. Charles could tell it was awkward, and he silently prayed Samuel hadn't broken anything. A Widow Maker slammed into the bridge where Samuel had been standing. It crouched before leaping at the Spider Knight.

Charles bellowed and slid behind Samuel, his old knees protesting the sudden movement. His fist caught the side of the spider's head, and the heavy springs fired a bolt through its black carapace. Inertia carried the spider over Charles, where it smashed into Samuel before tumbling to a stop by Alice.

"Samuel!" Charles said as he glanced up at the ceiling of Widow Makers descending on them. "Get up and run!"

Samuel hopped up onto his feet and shouted as his ankle tried to give out.

"Run!" Charles grabbed the Spider Knight by his backpack and pushed him toward Alice before scooping up his lantern. The pair stumbled a few feet and then Samuel found his footing. The way Samuel was running, his ankle couldn't have been broken. It would probably be a swollen mess, but he could still run.

"Get down the stairs, Alice!" Charles looked behind them to see what

Alice was staring at. He couldn't see the bridge anymore. A sea of gleaming eyes and black bodies shone in the darkness as they descended onto the soldiers that had caught up to them. "Go, now! *Goddammit, run!*"

Alice blinked and turned her attention to Charles. She spun and dashed through the doorway ahead of them.

"There's a gate at the bottom," Charles said as he let Samuel hobble down the stairs ahead of him. "Find the emblem of the Spider Knights and push it. It's the gate release. Hurry!"

Charles heard the screams of the soldiers and the unholy cries of the Widow Makers echoing down the staircase. He didn't have to see the chaos to know the two forces had crashed against one another above that river of death.

"Where are we going!" The panic in Alice's voice was gut wrenching, but Charles knew he had to push her harder.

"If you ever want to see your blasted family again, *run!*"

He swallowed the guilt as he shoved her forward, and she sped down the stairs faster than he or Samuel could have hoped to run. She slammed her palm onto the emblem of the Spider Knights over and over until the rusted gate finally began to lift into the air.

"Crawl under!" Samuel shouted.

Charles glanced over his shoulder and saw the smaller Widow Makers come pouring into the stairwell behind them. Samuel turned to face them. Charles cursed and grabbed the Spider Knight by the collar.

"We're not dying today, boy!" He twisted and threw Samuel down the stairs.

Samuel didn't even get a chance to protest. There was still strength left in the old man's body, and adrenaline took care of the rest. Samuel bounced off the last step and rolled to a stop near the gate. He scrambled under it on his hands and knees as Charles ran toward them, fishing around in a leather pouch at his waist.

"Hit the gate!" Charles shouted as he dove beneath the rusted metal.

"There's no button!" Panic turned Alice's voice into a screech as she began slamming her palm across the stone walls.

"It's the outer gate," Samuel shouted. "There isn't one!"

Charles pressed the igniter on a Burner as he pulled it out of his pouch and dropped it to the floor with a crack before he dove forward, sliding beneath the stalled gate. "Then we pull it down!" He hopped to his feet and leapt onto the gate. The mechanism in the wall squealed, and it added to the bone-chilling cries of the young Widow Makers.

Samuel didn't need to be told anything else. He jumped up beside Charles and began jerking the gate as hard as he could, while the Widow Makers bore down on them. It only took a second before something shattered above them, and the heavy metalwork clanged against the stone below.

"Back!" Charles shouted as he dove away from the gate, hands over his head. Samuel followed.

The Burner detonated, slamming a fireball full of screaming Widow Makers up into the ceiling where it billowed out in gray and orange shadows.

Samuel dragged Charles to his feet and they half ran, half stumbled toward the light of Alice's lantern farther down the hall.

Charles could see the tears on her face, but said nothing as they turned a corner, leaving the Widow Makers to burn and throw themselves against the gate in their death throes.

"What was that?" Samuel asked once they started down another stone staircase.

"It's a Burner with a Banger at its center," Charles said. "One of Jacob's concoctions. Made it after he saw me building the real bombs."

"That was real enough for me," Samuel said.

Charles nodded as he wrapped his arm around Alice. His heavy nail glove still dripped with the blood of a Widow Maker, but it didn't stop her from wrapping her fingers around it. Charles sighed and squinted into the darkness below them. "Let's get the hell out of here."

CHAPTER THIRTY-SEVEN

J ACOB HAD HEARD SOLDIERS TALK about the certainty of death. He'd sat with them in inns and taverns as the old men regaled their audience with tales of glory and war and loss. Jacob had never understood what they'd meant by the certainty of death. He'd thought he understood, but he knew nothing.

As the air in his lungs escaped in a rush of bubbles and his chest began to burn with the need to take a breath, he came to understand the certainty of death. Lights and patterns shot across his eyes in the darkness, strange forms he knew should not be there. He squeezed his eyes shut as the current slammed him into a wall, and then he fell, wishing only to see his parents, his friends, and Alice one last time.

He felt something hard and unforgiving scrape the side of his face before the pressure of the water seemed to loosen around him, and it was finally too much. He opened his mouth and screamed, and the sound of his own voice in the void shocked him. Jacob gasped for breath, and it was immediately stolen away as his fall stopped abruptly. It felt as though he'd done a belly flop off the side of a mountain.

Jacob stopped moving and let his body rise. He'd always been a good swimmer, and as soon as he could tell which way was up, he lunged for the surface.

Relief was first on his mind when his lungs took a full breath. The air was thick with a spray of water, and it didn't take him long to realize he'd gone over a fall.

How far down am I?

No light reached his eyes. He knew the Burners in his vest were soaked and wouldn't work for hours. Maybe the glowworms? He slid his backpack off and fumbled for the jar. He was surprised it wasn't broken, but it was heavier than it should have been. No light shone when it cleared the top of his bag. He shook the jar and heard the water sloshing around inside. The glowworms were long dead.

Jacob cursed and popped the wire clamp off the top, starting to dump out the water and his only hope for light, when something Miss Penny had told him in class clicked in his head. He righted the jar, turned it over, and carefully drained most of the water.

"Ugh, this better work," Jacob said as he put his hand around one of the fat worms and smashed it against the side of the jar. It popped like a rotten fruit, and a dim light swelled around him. He washed his hand in the pool at his feet and snapped the top back on the jar.

Jacob swirled the water around inside and took a deep breath when the light from the dead worm brightened. He set the jar down and threw his backpack over his shoulders before picking it back up again.

"Right then." He looked around the room. The closest wall he could reach out and touch. It was a dead end to the right, but a thin trail followed the river to the left. Jacob took a deep breath and set off along the water.

He held the jar out as far as he could, but it started getting heavy very quickly. Jacob tucked the jar up against his chest and kept his right shoulder scraping along the stone. It was smooth for the most part, but it still caught at his shirt once and again.

Jacob counted the turns for a while, but they started to become gradual and steeper, and eventually all he could concentrate on was not falling down. He reached the bottom of the steepest slope he'd seen so far when the light faded from the second glowworm. The slope was steep enough that the river thundered over the edge like a waterfall. Jacob sat down at the bottom and finished chewing up a piece of dried, salted meat before he reached into the jar.

Something caught his eye in the distance. Something had moved, but it wasn't the river. How had he seen it without light? He leaned forward and choked back an excited yell. The cavern off to his left had a dim, greenish glow. It had to be worms, but what else was down there?

He left his last glowworm intact and began creeping around the edge of the cave until he was at the mouth where he'd seen the lights. There was no mistaking it. The worms farther in were fat, scrunching themselves up and surging forward along the walls and ceiling. But what had he seen moving in the darkness?

Jacob wasn't sure if it was worth the risk to go deeper into the glowworm cave. There were a lot of nasty critters that made a meal off the worms. He didn't have anything to fight off a Widow Maker. His thoughts trailed back to that sea of the awful things descending on his friends before he was lost to the river. Did they escape? Was he the only one left in the underbelly of the mountain now?

He shivered, glanced over his shoulder at the dark tunnel behind him, and forged ahead. The roar of the waterfall faded behind him. His eyes adjusted to the light from the worms, and he could see a narrow path beside the river quite clearly. The path widened more than he'd expected, and the footing felt far better away from the spray of the small waterfall.

The river didn't seem so threatening here. It moved slowly and made a peaceful echo in the cave. Jacob could see clearly when he stood beside a cluster of fat worms. He pulled the jar out of his backpack and rinsed it off in the river, leaving the last of the dead worms to ride the waters.

Jacob reached up and wrapped his hand around one of the fattest worms. It resisted briefly, clinging to the damp stone before relinquishing its hold. Something splashed in the water behind him. He didn't make any quick movements. He slowly turned his head while his heart hammered away in his chest.

A swirl of ripples vanished down the river, but nothing else moved. "It's only a worm. Must have been a worm." Jacob's motions became hurried. He grabbed two more worms before scraping algae off the walls and dropping it into the jar for the worms to eat. He returned the jar to his backpack. There were enough worms lining the tunnel that he didn't need the jar to see.

✧   ✧   ✧

SAMUEL'S LAMP FLICKERED AND WENT out. "That's it. I didn't bring extra fuel."

"Don't worry," Charles said as he raised the lantern in his hand. "Unless my memory's gone to hell, we're almost at the end of the line."

"We haven't seen Jacob," Alice said.

"I know." Charles almost whispered it. He thought they'd see Jacob at the second river crossing by the smaller waterfall, but he wasn't there. Only the body of the invader Samuel had killed and a dozen Widow Makers had washed up at the inlet.

And the knights.

Charles knew it was either them or the knights who would survive their escape, but those men hadn't deserved to die so horribly. The fact Alice had seen their shriveled, poisoned faces hadn't helped matters either. Charles suspected the heavily armored knights were either at the bottom of the river, or they had lived long enough to run away.

It was the younger knights they found with the Widow Makers. Just boys following orders.

"Charles," Samuel said.

When Charles looked up, Samuel's eyes flashed down to Alice and back up. He was asking a question. Charles shook his head. Even if Jacob hadn't made it, Alice didn't need that kind of news. She'd seen enough horrible things that day.

"Light!" Alice said when they turned a corner, and it was the first time she'd sounded something like herself since they'd lost Jacob.

"Watch yourself," Charles said. He put a hand on Alice's shoulder. "Bugs tend to gather in the entryways."

Samuel cursed and pointed at the path they were walking. Wet footprints led the way to the exit, following the chill in the mountain winds.

"Is it Jacob?" Alice asked as she leaned down. She deflated and said, "No, the footprints are too big."

"That means we have company," Samuel said. He raised his sword. "Be ready, and watch the shadows. Men can hide as well as any bug."

✧　✧　✧

JACOB KEPT ONE EYE ON the river and one eye on the path. It seemed like he'd been walking for over an hour since he'd heard the splash. Anymore he just felt tired and cold. The water had been chilly, but now it felt like there was a breeze, and it was anything but warm. His teeth chattered, and the sound echoed through the cave.

He walked on for a dozen more steps before his frozen mind registered what he'd been feeling. "Wind. If there's wind, there has to be an exit!" He'd only whispered the words, but they still bounced off the walls and whispered back.

Jacob forgot the cold in a burst of excitement, and a rush of adrenaline renewed his drive to escape the old tunnels.

He glanced backward and realized the glowworms were sparse here. The change had been gradual, and he could still see fairly well, but only darkness waited ahead of him. He had the new jar of glowworms out of his backpack and in his hand a moment later. They cast enough light that he could see clearly a few feet around him.

Something floated by on the river, and Jacob slammed himself up against the wall. He watched, barely breathing, as the body of a Widow Maker drifted past. It was dead, and he knew it had to be so if it was in the water, but it still sent a surge of fear down his spine. The shiny black carapace disappeared as fast as it had come, traveling past the circle of light around Jacob.

"The wind, remember the wind. Almost out of here." He turned a corner, following the path the dead Widow Maker had taken, and he almost shouted. It wasn't much, but a tiny dim light shone in the farthest reaches of the tunnel.

Jacob picked up his pace until a poorly placed step rolled his foot and he stumbled up against the wall. He held the jar up and looked at the water. If he'd stumbled the other way, he would have been back in the river, possibly with another Widow Maker. He took three deep breaths and moved on, chasing the light.

It wasn't long before he put the jar away. The river took a gentle curve to the right, and as he rounded the corner, Jacob could see a clear path to the mountains in the distance. He felt safe as the daylight grew bright enough to burn his eyes. Jacob welcomed the blinding sunlight with arms outstretched when he finally stepped out of the darkness. His boots crunched on a mixture of dirt and gravel near the exit. The roughly hewn walls took on a more refined texture, growing into a long trail of pictures and symbols carved into the stone.

Jacob ran his hand along the deep engravings. Knights and invaders and castles and steam formed scenes from a history of which he had no knowledge. It wasn't until he stood only a few steps from the exit that he recognized the skull. It sat near the top of the frame, almost identical to the skull on *The Dead Scourge*. Beneath it stood a sea of soldiers, each meticulously carved into the stone. Some were dulled, likely worn away by the winds and elements of the last several decades.

He leaned into the wall and stared at the Mech. One soldier was carved into the left edge of the panel, facing the tunnel. He wore the emblem of *The Dead Scourge* on his chest, and his helmet looked like the same skull. Jacob couldn't make out the style of armor, being carved in stone, but one of the soldier's legs was covered in thin rods and what looked like a series of three gears. They looked more like a symbol than anything else, as nothing was connected to them.

A weapon as tall as the man himself was propped up in his right hand. Made for ranged combat, Jacob had no doubt, but for what? It looked unwieldy and unbalanced. Jacob ran his fingertips over the skull before he turned and continued out of the tunnel.

Jacob had already stepped outside of the cave—wondering why a Mech soldier from the Deadlands was pictured on the stone mural—before he noticed the footprints. Wet footprints led from the tunnel before they disappeared in the gravel of the mountainside path.

He heard a crack and felt a pain in the side of his head before his world went black.

✧　✧　✧

"…THE HELL'S IN THAT KID'S backpack?"

Jacob slowly came to, awoken by the sound of someone mumbling. Something scratched at his back, and a moment later he realized he was being dragged along the gravel path.

"Kid shouldn't be so heavy. Could have just killed him out here, but no, it has to be a spectacle."

Jacob's first instinct was to kick out of the grip of the soldier who was dragging him by the ankle, but he held himself back. If he'd learned anything about combat from Samuel, it was to understand his situation before making a move.

Jacob turned his head to the side and stared. They were at another pool at the base of a waterfall. It was choked with the bodies of men and Widow Makers. The man dragging him was alone, talking to himself. Carrion Worms were already feasting on the nearby carnage, and it took everything he had not to vomit. Jacob squeezed his eyes shut and turned the other way before a horrific idea took hold.

He opened his eyes and turned to the pool. At the edge, within arm's reach, were upturned Widow Makers. He glanced up at the soldier and then back to the shiny black spiders. If he missed, and got so much as a pinprick from the fang, he'd die, but if he didn't grab it, he might as well be dead anyway.

The knight grunted and jerked Jacob forward. He felt a sharp stone cut into his back, but he didn't cry out. He focused on the fang, focused on what might be his only chance for escape. It was close now, and he reached out. His fingers touched the cold, dead chitin, and he wrapped his fist around it.

The Widow Maker's fang snapped off easily as the knight dragged him past it. It was larger than Jacob realized, almost a foot in length. A gust of wind carried sand and dust up from the gravel path and set the reeds around the waterfall whipping against the bank. Jacob tried to lean forward, but the knight started moving faster again, cursing the mountain winds.

"Stop!" The authority in the voice behind them was absolute. Jacob rolled his eyes back and almost cried in relief when he saw Samuel with his sword held high, standing beside Charles and Alice. He tucked the fang up against his leg, where it would be harder for the soldier to see.

"Simmons?" Samuel asked when Jacob's captor turned to face his friends. His sword fell a fraction of an inch.

"Stay out of this, you Lowland-sympathizing scum." Simmons glanced down at Jacob. "Awake, are we?" He dropped Jacob's foot and grabbed his forearm, wrenching Jacob up off the ground before wrapping his own armored forearm across Jacob's throat.

"Let him go, Simmons." Samuel's voice was lower than Jacob had ever heard it, and the threat was deadly.

"He has to pay for what he's done!" Simmons shook Jacob by the neck. "Parliament told us it's the Lowlanders' fault our trade routes have faltered." His voice rose to a scream. "It's *their* fault my little girl died without her damn medicine! And they'll pay for it, Samuel! They'll die for it!"

"Simmons," Samuel said as he took a step forward. "That boy isn't the cause of Ancora's problems, or your daughter's death."

"Stay back! He'll be off this cliff before you can even—"

Time slowed. Jacob felt Simmons start to push him toward the cliff-side. He saw Charles pull the air cannon off his back. He saw Samuel start to run, and he heard Alice scream.

Jacob's grip turned to stone around the Widow Maker's fang, and he snarled as he turned on Simmons. The fang slid up, underneath the seam where the helmet covered the knight's neck. There was a slight resistance before the fang pierced flesh and Simmons went still.

Jacob screamed incoherently as the soldier collapsed to the ground. Jacob tried to kick the fallen man, but Samuel grabbed Jacob's arm and pulled him away. The Spider Knight dragged him back to Alice. Jacob watched the soldier twitch, paralyzed by the spider's venom as it began to dissolve his neck. He only had a minute to live, at most. Charles didn't let him suffer.

The report of the air cannon echoed across the mountain valley. Charles stared at the dead man for a moment before he rolled the ruined armor off the side of the cliff. He walked back up to Samuel.

"Don't need to see that. They've seen enough."

Jacob didn't think he was supposed to hear what Charles had said, but he'd heard it. He didn't argue. He hugged Alice, and he wasn't sure who was shaking more. His rage turned to tears as he sobbed into Alice's shoulder. He'd seen enough to last him a lifetime.

CHAPTER THIRTY-EIGHT

ONCE THEY'D PUT SOME DISTANCE between themselves and the waterfall, Charles slowed and turned around. "Let's stop here. I need to rest these old bones a bit." An old stone table sat near the edge of the cliffside. So close, in fact, it made Jacob a bit nervous to sit on the end of the bench.

"I saw the Widow Makers coming off the ceiling," Jacob said. He winced when he touched his cheek. He knew he must look a mess after having his face dragged over the rocks in the river. "I wanted to warn you, but I was already in the river by the time I realized what they were."

Jacob had stopped shaking, but he was ready to sit down, or sleep for a week. Alice told Jacob about their journey through the mountain while they ate what might be the last sandwiches they'd ever see. The blank look on her face as she told the tale made Jacob uncomfortable.

"We made it," Alice said firmly. "You made it. That's all that matters."

"May not have made it if those city guards weren't after us," Samuel said. "A lot of the spiders got distracted by their conveniently canned meals."

Charles snorted a laugh. "That's a nice way of stating it."

"You'd think there would be a railing here or something," Alice said as she peeked her head over the side.

"There used to be one," Charles said. "Back when we didn't have so many invaders, people used to walk the mountain paths quite often."

"Where are we going?" Jacob asked. He looked up the mountainside.

It was almost a sheer cliff all the way up. He thought he could just make out the peak of the observatory, but it was hard to tell at such a distance. If he was right, they were below the far southern tip of the Lowlands. "We can't go back into the city."

Charles shook his head. "They found us in the catacombs faster than I thought possible."

"We weren't really in the catacombs," Alice said. "That's only where the dead are buried."

"Plenty of dead to call them catacombs now." Charles frowned and crumpled up the butcher paper from his sandwich.

Jacob started to throw his over the mountainside.

"Don't toss that," Charles said. "It's good for kindling. We'll need fire, especially as we don't have a tent."

"Why don't we just use Burners?"

"Sure," Charles said. "How many did you bring? Think we might need them for something other than lighting a campfire?"

"Already burned one today getting away from the Widow Makers," Samuel said. He folded his butcher paper and then did the same with the crumpled up papers.

"Where *are* we going, Charles?" Alice asked. "You never answered Jacob."

Charles hooked his thumbs under the edge of his vest and glanced over his shoulder as he started down the path. "The Deadlands."

"What?" Jacob said, exhaustion drawing the word out. "You're serious?"

"The Deadlands," Alice said. Even without inflection, her voice echoed back through the mountain pass. "And how do you expect to get us there alive? And how do you expect us to *stay* alive?"

"Only the dead cities are left out there," Alice said.

"There are more than the dead cities," Samuel said. "I've heard stories that Bollwerk was built on the iron corpse of Oase."

"Oase," Alice said. "I know that's the name of a lost city, but what's Bollwerk?"

"The last great city of the Deadlands," Charles said. "Perhaps not as grand as Ancora, but great nonetheless."

"The Mechs came from Oase in the war," Jacob said. He looked at Charles.

"That they did. Many of the Deadlands cities may have been destroyed in the war, but the Forgotten rebuilt at least one and named it Bollwerk."

"Hold up!" Samuel hissed. The steady crunch of their boots on the mountain path stopped, but it still sounded like heavy footsteps around them.

Jacob wondered why until he glanced up and saw a Walker coming down the cliff. It was at least twenty feet long, its legs churning and thumping across the rock face until it curled up on the path in front of them. Two antennae reached out and patted Samuel's shoulders before the Walker uncurled and scuttled down the far side of the mountain.

"The untamed Walkers can be dangerous," Charles said, "but they'll usually leave you in peace."

"It's the blue and orange ones you have to watch out for," Jacob said, as the awful memory of the Fall came flashing back to life, filled with stampeding legs and gore-soaked serrated mandibles. He'd seen more than one Ancoran left in pieces by one of *those* invaders. Jacob shook his head to rid himself of the image, but it was quickly replaced by the face of Simmons.

The look of surprise frozen on the soldier's face while the poison took hold after Jacob had stabbed him … It wasn't an image he'd be forgetting anytime soon. Jacob didn't like the fact he'd had to kill someone. The memory was visceral, even as it seemed distant. Charles may have shot the soldier, but Jacob had no illusions that the man would have died anyway. You do what it takes to survive. He'd learned that in his years as a Lowlander. This he had done to survive.

Charles and Samuel were talking among themselves, but Jacob didn't really hear what they were saying. He thought of his parents and whether or not they'd really be safe, and if his dad would get the medicine without Jacob's help. If Bat held true to his word, his parents would have enough gold to last quite some time. Jacob glanced at Alice, who looked into the distance at the shrouded mountain peaks, and worried for her family too.

And now they were going to the Deadlands? Jacob didn't like Alice being pulled into something so dangerous, but truth be told, he was glad she was with them. If they'd left her in the city, though? He almost growled as he rubbed at his face.

"At least we're in this together," Alice said. She squeezed his hand and looked back out at the mountains.

The trail took two sharp switchbacks before evening out again. They were narrow, and the sheer drop-off was dizzying. It was pretty obvious they were past the parts of the mountain path that were once frequented by Ancorans.

Charles and Samuel came to an abrupt stopped when they turned the corner and reached a flat section of the trail. Three men stood across the path. Two were shoulder to shoulder with halberds at the ready, blocking the trail behind the third. Jacob knew the man in front, and worry gnawed at his gut.

"I knew you'd follow the old trails," Captain Lewis said as he rested his hand on the hilt of his sheathed sword.

"Captain?" Samuel said. "Why are you here? *How* are you already here?

"He took the old lift," Charles said.

The captain nodded.

"Risky move, that. How'd you know it wouldn't collapse?"

"I had little doubt it was still functional. I didn't expect you to go underground."

Charles pumped the slide on the air cannon, and the captain started to draw his sword.

"Stay your hand. You move that slide again, and I'll run you through."

Jacob's heart sank. Any hope he'd had that the captain wasn't there to capture them evaporated.

Charles laughed, and it was a cold sound. "Run me through?" He pumped the slide again. "You'll be dead before you take two steps."

The captain unsheathed his sword, started forward, and stopped dead as the slide racked for the third time. Charles leveled the cannon at the captain.

"I have no desire to harm you or your men, but I'll kill you if you come for us. You sent knights to find us in the underground, to kill us all. How could you do that? How could you break the oath to protect all people of Ancora?" Charles snarled. "To twist it so violently that you can justify killing children and old men?" His voice rose, full of such venom Jacob barely recognized it. "On sword, on blood, you are an oath breaker."

The captain cursed and threw his sword to the side of the trail. "They have my son, Charles. Do you understand? They're going to kill my *son*."

"There are only a handful of tinkers who know how to build those transmitters, and only one as good as me. I intend to find him."

Captain Lewis narrowed his eyes. "What are you saying, Charles?"

"I can't allow you to imprison us, to *execute* us. I intend to break the alliance before it forms." Charles sniffed. "If Dauschen allies with the Deadlands, you're all dead anyway. What harm is there in letting us try to stop it?"

The captain said nothing.

"I give you one chance to restore your honor. Tell the knights we fled into the Lowlands. We snuck out with a group of repairmen."

"My son ..." The captain's eyes flicked from Charles to Jacob and back. He pushed the palm of his hand against his forehead and grimaced. "Gods be damned." He turned to the knights behind him and almost whispered the words, "Stand down."

"Sir?" one of the knights said as he glanced at his companion. He looked shaken, his halberd no longer poised to strike but lowered to the ground. "Our orders."

"You have new orders. Stand down and let them pass." The captain looked up to Charles and asked, "What of the city guard?"

"Dead," Alice said as she stepped around Samuel, a knife hidden behind her wrist. "You sent them into a nest of Widow Makers."

"It wasn't my order, girl."

Charles gently grabbed Alice's wrist and shook his head once.

"What did you do to stop it?" Alice snapped, jerking her arm away from Charles.

The captain frowned at her words. "Just leave. All of you leave. Charles, you know you can't return to Ancora after this. The city smith would put you to death."

Charles returned the air cannon to its holster. "One day, Captain, the city smith and I will have words. I rather think he'll find that to be a very bad day."

"Where will you really go?" the captain asked as the party passed him by.

"Into the Deadlands," Charles said. "I'm afraid that's the only place we'll find the answers to this mess."

"The Deadlands? Are you mad?"

"I've been accused of worse."

"And what will you say to the Steamsworn, Charles?"

"They are our allies," the old man said.

The captain hesitated. "And do you think the Forgotten will welcome your return? Do you think they won't remember what you did to them?"

Charles paused and looked back at the captain. "The Steamsworn understand war, my dear captain. The fact we fought against each other fifty years ago does *not* mean we can't be allies today. Let Parliament pull your strings for now, but try to remember your oath, your promise to protect all the peoples of Ancora. You were a good man once."

The captain said nothing as Charles turned away. Jacob glanced back before they rounded the corner of the trail. The captain stared at the ground, his shoulders slightly slumped. Jacob focused on the crunch of gravel beneath his boots. He didn't think the man wanted anything to do with cutting off Jacob's hands. The captain only wanted Peter back.

CHAPTER THIRTY-NINE

"WE SHOULD HAVE CAPTURED THAT Walker back up the mountain," Samuel grumbled as his armored boots rang against a large stone in the gravel path. "It feels like we've been walking for hours."

"Sure," Charles said. "We don't have a lasso, or a harness, or a saddle. I'm sure that would have ended well."

Samuel looked over his shoulder and smiled at the old man. "Leave me to my complaints, would you? I don't know what else to do with myself."

The air grew thick around them as they descended through a fog bank. Jacob couldn't see more than three feet off the side of the cliff, and he wasn't sure if that made him feel better or a whole lot worse.

"Why haven't we seen anything?" Jacob asked. "I thought we'd be fighting off hordes of invaders by now."

"Don't sound so disappointed," Charles said. "You don't have to impress Alice."

Alice laughed and bared her teeth at Jacob.

He started to protest, and then he watched Alice walking beside Samuel, laughing with him. Jacob could take a little embarrassment if it meant Alice could laugh.

Charles harrumphed beside him. "You're pretty smart for a kid."

"I didn't say anything!"

"My point exactly."

Jacob stayed with Charles while Samuel and Alice led the way through the dense fog. It wasn't long before the world became a lighter gray, and eventually they broke through the base of the cloud bank.

"Wow."

Jacob stared at the vista before them. A long trail led down the mountain, and from where they were, he could see the far mountain pass in the southeast that would lead them to the Deadlands.

"You can see the Bull's Horn," Alice said. She pointed off to the two ancient mountains that curved up around the pass, forming the horns that framed the road in the distance. "Looks different from down here."

"Charles," Samuel said. "We can't walk that distance in a day."

"Actually, it's about a day from the base of the mountain to the Bull's Horn. The pass into the Deadlands is an easy one. It's what's on the other side that worries me."

"We'll need to find a place to stay before nightfall," Jacob said. He looked toward the sun. It was already descending to the mountain range's far side. A pocket of wild Walkers streamed over the rocks below them, arcing out into the plain, only to disappear into another outcropping of rock.

"We have a few hours yet," Charles said. "Worried about the Red Death?"

Jacob nodded.

"Who wouldn't be?" Alice asked. "All we have is Samuel with his oversized toothpick and an old man with an air cannon."

Samuel ruffled Alice's hair, and she looked intensely irritated with the gesture. "I saw a girl with a blade tucked behind her wrist."

"That's better suited to cutting dinner," Alice said.

"Where are we going?" Jacob asked. "I mean, the Deadlands, I know, but what about tonight? We don't want to get caught in the open."

Charles glanced back at the sun. "We have a few hours, I think. Should give us enough time to get into Cave."

"We're taking the kids into Cave?" Samuel asked, and the surprise on his face made Jacob leery.

"What is Cave?" Alice asked.

Charles rubbed his beard. "You think of the Lowlands as the poorest part of Ancora, yes?"

"It is," Alice said.

"There are people who can't afford even the Lowlands, or at least they couldn't when the walls went up. They made their own district in the caves on the plain. It's not far from the mountain."

"It's just poor people?" Jacob asked.

"And people who don't want Parliament interfering with their business."

"Pirates and cutpurses," Samuel said as he eyed his gleaming Spider Knight armor. "Don't get too attached to the place, Jacob."

✧   ✧   ✧

Two more hours of hiking put them on the plains. Jacob held out his hands and let the tall grass brush his palms.

"It's beautiful," Alice said, pointing toward the Bull's Horn. "You can see a pod of giant Pillies in the field."

At first, Jacob couldn't see what she was pointing out, but then one of the gray stones moved not a hundred feet away. The antennae flipped into the air before the Pill-Bugs returned to grazing on the grass.

"They're huge," Jacob said.

"At least twice as big as mine," Alice said before she frowned. "Well, when I still had some."

Jacob squeezed her arm as he walked by. Alice had loved those bugs, and he knew she missed them.

"You could eat off one of those for a month," Samuel said.

"We're not killing a harmless Pilly just so you can snack," Alice said as she narrowed her eyes.

Samuel flashed her a smile and started moving down the flattened path through the grass.

"Almost there," Charles said. "See the door in the crevasse?"

Jacob didn't see anything but the rock. He let his eyes follow the path, and it ended near the mountainside. There, outside the field of grass, he could just make out a tall gray metal doorway. It blended into the stone on either side, almost impossible to see at a distance.

Charles hefted his backpack, adjusted the shoulder straps, and started forward. "Let's see who's home." It wasn't long before they were off the trail and standing before the entrance to Cave.

A steel knocker with intricate brass inlays hung from a rusted iron hook. It wasn't until he got closer that Jacob realized the brass was shaped like a skeletal hand clutching a steel orb.

"That's a …" Jacob frowned as he tried to think of the word. "What'd they call it, Alice? It was in *The Dead Scourge*."

"It's called a Devil's Hammer," Alice said as she reached up and slammed the weighted metal into a dented brass plate. The two quick raps sounded like a muffled gong, and the sound echoed behind the doors. "It's an old symbol from the Deadlands, adopted by the Forgotten."

Something slid within the door—some unseen mechanism—and then nothing.

"Are they not opening the doors?" Alice asked.

"Just give them a minute," Charles said. He gave the barrier a two-finger salute. He seemed to be looking at something higher up the door, but Jacob couldn't see anything out of the ordinary.

"Are the Forgotten here?" Jacob asked.

"I'm sure some visit the caves on occasion, but I doubt many of them would ever want to be so close to Ancora again."

Jacob turned around and looked up the mountain. Ancora hid behind a cloud bank, high above. He watched for a moment while the clouds shifted, offering glimpses of the peaks where he knew the city was nestled, before a noise drew his attention.

Another mechanism, louder and heavier, shifted within the door before a puff of dirt blew out beneath it. The right side swung open, only enough to allow one person through at a time. Samuel stepped through first, followed by the rest of the group, before the door boomed closed once they'd all crossed the threshold.

"It's so dark," Alice said. She squinted at the shadows.

"They haven't shot us yet," Samuel said, "so at least there's that."

"Come on," Charles said. He walked toward a faint lantern deep inside the cave.

"Charles von Atlier," boomed a deep voice from nowhere and every-where. "Halt and state your purpose."

Charles's silhouette froze in front of Jacob and slowly turned toward the voice. It spoke from above them, somewhere in the shadows.

Charles crossed his arms slowly before he asked, "Who here knows that name?"

"State your purpose."

"What is this?" Samuel whispered. His hand settled on the hilt of his sword.

"Protocol. Keep your hand off your sword lest they take it from you."

Jacob didn't know if Charles meant Samuel's sword or his hand, but they both sounded bad.

"I am Charles von Atlier, smith and tinker of Ancora, survivor of the Scorpion's Trial, ally to the Steamsworn, and I seek only rest and refuge for my friends."

A shadow moved close to the doors, and Jacob almost yelped when a cloaked man stepped into the dim lantern light. His cloak bore the color of stone, leaving him invisible until he moved. "Then enter our city of Cave, tinker, and journey well."

"Can I ask you a question, Cave Guardian?"

The cloaked form nodded at Charles.

"Does The Rock Inn still exist here?"

"It does."

"Do they still offer transportation? We had to flee Ancora with no mount."

The cloaked man pulled his hood back and Jacob stared slack-jawed. The man's eyes were slightly canted, and his gaze was intense as he looked over everyone in their party. His skin was darker than any Jacob had seen before, even more so than that of the travelers from Dauschen. Jacob had heard stories of people born to the Deadlands, but this man's skin rivaled the night sky.

"Stop staring," Alice said as she jabbed Jacob with her elbow. "You're being rude."

"I just … I didn't mean … He's … I …" Jacob fumbled for words, and then for an apology, but the cloaked man only laughed.

"Do not worry, little one. The first time I saw hair as fiery as your friend's, I stared at it for half a day." He paused before adding, "And half a night, but that's a different story."

The Cave Guardian turned back to Charles. "As to your original question, they do offer transportation when it's available. Sadly, many of their best transports died while the hordes made way to Ancora. Many of their masters died too."

"Red Death?" Charles asked.

"Some," the guardian said with a nod. "Many more were lost to the Mantises, and a few to Sky Needles."

"Sky Needles?" Charles said as he frowned. "We didn't see any of those blasted things in Ancora."

"Thank the Steamsworn, Charles von Atlier. Their archers brought down a great many beasts on the other side of the horn. Travel well."

The guardian pulled his hood up, leaving his face in shadows before he turned and retreated to the doors. Jacob blinked, and the man seemed to vanish.

Charles patted his shoulder and said, "Let's go."

✧   ✧   ✧

"WHAT ARE THE STEAMSWORN?" JACOB asked after they turned the second corner by a lantern and could no longer see the doors at the entrance. "They're mentioned in the book a little bit, but not in much detail."

Charles glanced back at Jacob. "Some people call them the Noble Mechs," he said as he squinted into the darkness ahead of them. "Not unlike the Spider Knights in their oaths." The old man looked around the floor. "They used to keep torches down here."

"Knights of the Deadlands," Samuel said. "That's what I've heard some of the old men call them."

Charles grunted. "Well, we're certainly not young anymore."

Jacob stepped forward and the floor sank slightly. A moment later, a light sprang to life farther down the hall, and then another and another, until the length of the hall was bathed in dim torchlight.

"Not bad," Charles said. "Not bad at all. The city is just up ahead."

"City?" Alice asked. "You mean there's an entire city inside the caves?"

"Yes indeed."

The world grew louder the closer they got to the city. A door waited around a slight bend, ringed in a yellow-orange glow. Muffled voices whispered from the other side, along with a raucous laughter and the sounds of a hammer on steel.

Charles pulled the door open and smiled as he ushered the other three through the archway. "Welcome to Cave."

CHAPTER FORTY

TOWERING STREETLAMPS CAPPED WITH WIDE copper reflectors lit the town, casting a golden glow on the traffic bustling up one street and down another. People laughed and talked as they moved between the carriages, shops, and inns, and across carefully laid cobblestones nicer than anything Jacob had seen in the Lowlands.

The street was an odd contrast with the buildings. Some sort of gray moss speckled almost every surface, and it made the city look more run-down than it really was. Jacob wrinkled his nose when the air shifted, lifting his hair. A subtle, distinct stench, like sewage and rotting food mixed with long-unwashed pets reached them, but it passed as the wind died.

"What is this place?" Alice asked. Jacob understood the awe in her voice completely.

"A long time ago, they called it the City of the Cave," Charles said, leading them down the street. "In time, it became known simply as Cave." He sniffed. "Haven't improved the smell much."

"Has it been improved at all?" Samuel asked. He frowned and stuck his tongue out like he was trying to rid himself of a bad taste.

"You get used to it," Charles said as he started down the street. "Five minutes here and you won't notice a bit."

"Unless that five minutes involves a fair amount of drink, I'm quite sure I'll still notice."

"For a Spider Knight, you do like to complain," Charles said. He glanced over his shoulder and winked.

Two kids wandered by in clothes that didn't look unlike Jacob's. They pointed at Samuel. Jacob didn't have to hear what they were saying to have a pretty good guess what it was.

"They're starting to notice your armor," Jacob said. The group rounded a corner. The next street was just as busy as the first.

"Not to worry," Charles said. "They're probably wondering if they can steal it and sell it for scrap. It's a good alloy, and it fetches a fair price at any smith willing to take salvage."

"Salvage?" Samuel asked. "I'm still alive and wearing it."

Charles cocked an eyebrow. "Probably a good reason to keep your guard up, yes?"

"I can't believe we're underground," Alice said. She looked up at a tall marble building with a thin dome near the top of the cave. "Is that a church?"

"Is indeed," Charles said. "No self-respecting den of thieves would have a city without a church. Or so I hear."

Buskers stood outside the white steps that led to high, sharp gothic doors. One of them held a lute and picked an intricate melody that Jacob could barely make out over the noise of the street. The other seemed to be telling stories, and whatever they were seemed to have the children enthralled. A tired-looking mother in a gray dress with a bronze cane dropped a coin into the man's cup.

By the time Jacob turned his attention back to Charles, he almost walked right into the old man.

"Here we are!" Charles walked up a short flight of dark wooden stairs to a modest-looking door. Above the windowless doors, spelled out in smooth river stones, was "The Rock Inn."

Samuel stepped forward and pulled the door open, holding it while Charles and Alice and Jacob filtered by. Jacob had expected a loud, raucous room like the bar they'd seen at the Wild Horse Inn. This was nothing like it.

Booths lived in shadow all around the small bar. The only light came from small flickering candles mounted outside the benches. A few loud men sat at the bar in the center, yelling about some brawl on which they'd lost a bet. One bore a deep scar across his left cheek, and the other was dressed in finery to rival that of the wealthiest Highlanders.

A lute and an old drum arrangement stood in the corner, but they were silent, waiting for a musician to return to the darkness of the Rock Inn.

They all followed Charles as he wove between a few awkwardly placed wood tables, and eventually pulled out one of the backless stools at the bar.

"Smart layout," Samuel said as he glanced back toward the door. "A raid would either have to go around the tables or push them out of the way."

"You'll see a lot of common sense prevention here," Charles said. "They don't have a police force like they do in Ancora. It's more of a public-enforced system of … guidelines."

"Maybe they can hire a Spider Knight for that," the hooded man beside Charles said. His voice was deep and wore the same kind of cloak as the guardian at the gate.

"I doubt you could convince *him* to do that," Charles said as he sat down. "He's a rather stubborn Highlander these days."

"Hey now," Samuel said, pulling out his own seat.

"No disrespect meant," the guardian said. He pulled his hood back. His skin was lighter than the man they'd met at the gate, but still darker than anyone Jacob had met from Ancora. His eyes were canted slightly too. Jacob could tell he was well muscled, the way the cloak spread around the guardian's shoulders. The man eyed Alice and Jacob for a moment before turning his attention back to Charles. "So it's true. Charles von Atlier has returned to Cave."

"What business is it of yours?" Samuel asked, the irritation in his voice palpable as he bit off the words.

"My name is Drakkar, Spider Knight. It is my business because you told my brother of it."

"The Gate Guardian?" Charles asked.

"Yes."

Charles nodded. "We didn't catch his name."

"You never will," Drakkar said, turning his pewter stein on the bar top. "He took the oath to guard the entrance to our city many years ago, and he will be Nameless until his death."

"So his name is Nameless?" Alice said. "Even that's still a name. You can't *really* go nameless."

Drakkar blinked and frowned at Alice. He tipped his stein at her before lifting the lid and taking a deep swallow. "In a way, I suppose you are correct. All Gate Guardians take the Oath of the Nameless. It has been that way since the Melding."

"Melding?" Alice said as she leaned back to get a better view of Drakkar. "What's the Melding?"

"Did you not learn of it in school?"

Alice and Jacob exchanged a glance and shook their heads.

Drakkar's brow furrowed before he took a deep breath. "Many years ago—centuries, in fact—there were far more races of men than you know today." Drakkar pointed at Alice. "You consider Ancorans a race, and Bollwerks, and Dauschens. They were once many people."

"How many?" Alice asked, sitting up straighter.

"I know not, child, but many."

"What changed in the Melding?" Jacob asked, his own curiosity piqued by Alice's interest.

"Some men say the races were erased by Ancorans and Bollwerks marrying the wrong people. Those men are fools. We do not know everything about the cities lost to time."

"We don't know much at all," Charles said with a short huff.

"We can guess, tinker. When the old cities fell, the people scattered. They loved and married and bore children in new settlements. Most would have been a mixture of a dozen races, and given enough time, those men and women became a new whole."

"What happened to all the stories from those races?" Alice asked. "It's sad to think they're all gone now."

"Oh no, child." The guardian adjusted his cloak as he turned to Alice. "The stories of those lost races are *our* stories. Each one lives on in us. We are them, and they are us. They'll never be gone. All who walk the guardian's path learn this truth. Every man our brother, every woman our sister."

No one said anything for a moment. Charles broke the silence. "What do you have to offer?" he asked as he picked up a chopstick from the bar and spun it between his fingers. "We'll need to resupply. Some of our food was lost to the underground river in our escape."

"A friend of the guardians owns Traveler's Cove in the far east of town. He can get you anything you need."

"For a price," Samuel muttered.

"Nothing's free," Jacob said before Drakkar had a chance to respond.

"Unless you steal it," Samuel said.

Jacob frowned at the Spider Knight. He had nothing but respect for Samuel, and for him to say something cruel hurt. "It's not like I had a choice."

"Hush," Charles said. "Choose your words more carefully, Samuel. You sound like one of Parliament's judgmental mouthpieces."

Samuel stared at Charles, wide-eyed. "I didn't mean … I'm sorry."

"And Jacob. Don't admit to thievery in this place, whatever you do."

Drakkar nodded. "They will take more than your hands in this place. It has been that way since the founding of Cave."

"I thought Cave was full of thieves."

"True," Drakkar said, "but thieves do not steal from each other. They are bound by oaths here. If you find the thieves along the trade routes, however, be wary."

Charles rubbed his beard before he crossed his arms and sighed. "What do you have in the way of transportation? We can pay, mind you.

"We were able to save several Walkers, but they will be very expensive. You may prefer to take the Rhinos."

"Rhinos?" Jacob asked.

"Carriage beetles without the carriage," Charles said. "You know we're traveling to the Deadlands, Drakkar. I'm not sure riding a black mount is advisable in that kind of heat."

Jacob watched Charles lift the medal out of his vest. It was the same medal he'd shown in Ancora to get into the tower.

"Are you sure you can't find another way?"

Drakkar leaned forward and smiled. His teeth were brilliant white. "Steamsworn. I would not have guessed that."

"An old pledge from an old war, Drakkar. I'm still all me, no mechanical bits."

"It is an honor, nonetheless. Let me speak to the proprietor of the Traveler's Cove. I suspect I can play upon his sympathies for the Steamsworn."

"Thank you," Charles said as he hid the medal beneath his leather vest once more. "Do you have any idea what the supplies might cost? We need rooms for the night too."

"Allow me to negotiate on your behalf," Drakkar said as he motioned to the bartender. The bartender nodded, acknowledging Drakkar before he turned to help another patron. "The bartender is the innkeeper here, and I know him quite well. I am sure I can save you a great deal of gold."

"Do I even want to know the price for that?"

"It is a small price." Drakkar laid his fingertips on the edge of the bar and turned his head toward Charles. "You will join me in my house for a meal, and I will travel with you."

"Why?" Samuel said, blurting out the question.

Drakkar smiled. "I would enjoy seeing Bollwerk again. If war ravages the Deadlands, the old city will be at its center. The people of Bollwerk took me in and gave me a home when I had none. I owe them much."

"We'd be honored to have your company," Charles said as he held his fist out to Drakkar.

The guardian wrapped his hand around Charles's fist and looked the old man in the eyes. "You have my pledge for this journey, Steamsworn. I will protect you as I would protect my own kin. May we live in peace, or die defending it." He released his grip and picked up his stein again.

Jacob watched the guardian for a moment. He seemed kind and strong, yet he seemed so different from the people Jacob knew. The man was utterly intimidating. If they could trust him, he'd be a powerful ally.

Jacob exchanged a glance with Alice. She shrugged, and he knew exactly how she felt.

"We'd be honored to have you along," Charles said. He nodded to Drakkar. The guardian mirrored the gesture before Charles turned back to Jacob and Alice and Samuel. "You three better get some sleep tonight. In the morning, we make for the Deadlands."

Note from Eric R. Asher

Thank you for spending time with Jacob and Alice! I've been blown away by the reader response to this series, and am so grateful to you all. The next book of Jacob and Alice's adventures is called Steamforged, and it's available now.

If you'd like an email when I release a new book, sign up for my mailing list (www.ericrasher.com). Emails only go out about once per month and your information is closely guarded by a ravenous Pilly.

Also, follow me on BookBub (bookbub.com/authors/eric-r-asher), and you'll always get an email for special sales.

Thanks for reading!
Eric

Please enjoy the following excerpt from

Steamforged

The Steamborn series, book #2

By Eric R. Asher

*There are old wounds in the forgotten places of the world, and
some are soaked in blood.*

*Jacob and his allies flee into the Deadlands after the fall of Ancora.
Charles, the enigmatic smith, hopes to find answers in the desert
city of Bollwerk that could prevent a war.*

*Their enemies are many, and here Jacob will learn the cost of life in
the Deadlands.*

JACOB WATCHED DRAKKAR cinch a belt beneath the Walker, securing yet another leather saddlebag to the creature's back. The Walker didn't seem to mind. Its forty legs twitched, running from its head back down to its armored tail while its face remained buried in a trough of Sweet-Flies.

Walkers didn't have fangs to impale things with so much as they had built-in spears in their front legs. Drakkar simply pushed those venomous barbs to the side when the Walker grew too curious. The bug's antennae flattened out and then sprang back into the air when it started feasting again.

"Can I help with anything?" Jacob asked when Drakkar stood up and patted the Walker's head.

"I believe we are almost ready." Drakkar smiled at Jacob, and his teeth were a brilliant contrast to his dark skin. "Once Charles returns with Samuel and Alice, I see no reason to linger."

Jacob stepped up on some wooden crates stashed at the edge of the stables. It let him peek through the iron-barred windows where he could see the sweeping grasslands outside the city of Cave. He'd spotted a small cluster of Red Deaths earlier in the day, but nothing moved in the fields now except for a handful of giant Pill-Bugs.

Jacob unwrapped a packet of butcher paper and popped a square of jerky in his mouth. It was chewy, and a bit too salty, but surprisingly not bad at all. "This is really from a Pill-Bug?" Jacob asked, turning back to Drakkar.

"You sound surprised. Do you not eat insects in Ancora any longer?"

"We do, but not that often. Alice sure likes her Sweetwing Tea." Jacob frowned and scraped his tongue across his teeth while he watched the Walker take another mouthful of Sweet-Flies. "How are you going to keep him fed on the trip?"

"George?" Drakkar asked as he patted the Walker's head again. "He does not need much food. Though he was born in the desert, I do worry about him dehydrating more than starving. This feast will last him many days."

"I can't believe you call it George."

"It is a good, strong name, and a name that does not frighten our Ancoran guests. Would you prefer Impaler or Venom Sword? Those are traditional Bollwerk names."

If Drakkar knew about Bollwerk, he might know about some of the other things Jacob had read about in *The Dead Scourge*. "Drakkar?"

"Hmm?" the guardian said, glancing over his shoulder.

"Have you ever met the Forgotten?"

Drakkar laughed under his breath. "You reveal too much of your intention with your questions. I doubt your tinker and your knight would appreciate that."

Jacob crossed his arms. He hadn't given away anything as far as *he* was concerned. "Well, have you?"

"I have met many people, Jacob from Ancora, as I suspect you will too. I am sure some of those people were, and will be, the Forgotten."

The door behind Jacob creaked open, and Charles stepped into the room with the Walker. George's antennae shot straight up and then relaxed as another mouthful of Sweet-Flies made a sickening crunch in the trough.

Jacob wanted to prod Drakkar for more information, but the more he thought about it, the guardian was probably right about Charles not liking his constant questioning of the man. Maybe he *had* revealed too much. He shook his head to rid himself of the thought.

"What has you so deep in thought?" Charles asked. He paused in front of Jacob, set a large saddlebag beside the Walker, and then dropped it with a grunt.

"It may have been my fault. I mentioned the fact you and the knight may not appreciate his rather revealing line of questions."

Charles blew out a breath through his nose. "You can trust Drakkar, Jacob. Ask him anything you wish, but be wary of men we don't know, especially men who are not pledged to the Steamsworn." Charles rubbed his hands together and looked at Drakkar. "I suppose he already told you about *The Dead Scourge?*"

Jacob's hand flew to his backpack on instinct alone. He had the book with him. It was a rare time he didn't have the book if he had his backpack.

"Not so directly, but his questions of the Forgotten and the lost city of Oase raised my suspicion."

"I didn't say that."

Charles smiled at Jacob and began stuffing his saddlebag into the larger bags on the Walker's back. "Some people are very good at learning what you said, without you saying it."

"Why *do* you seek the Forgotten?" Drakkar asked. He picked up Charles's saddlebag with little effort. Where the old man had struggled to lift it high enough to get it into the Walker's bags, Drakkar moved it like a small sack of potatoes. "Most Ancorans would prefer a great distance between themselves and the men they betrayed." He deftly tied the saddlebags closed.

Charles eyed Drakkar like he was measuring fuel for a Burner. Jacob could almost see the gears turning in the old man's head, choosing each word with great care.

"The invaders?" Charles said.

Drakkar nodded.

"They were driven into Ancora using sound."

"What?" Drakkar asked with a small frown. "That is madness."

Charles shook his head. "You've heard of the amplifiers of Ancora, yes? They use them so one man can speak and most of the city can hear him. It's the same idea."

"I have seen them, in fact. We guardians visit many towns."

The thought of invisible, stealthy guardians creeping through the city sent a shiver down Jacob's back.

"It's the same basic principal," Charles said. "Transmitters were mounted in Ancora, with receivers and repeaters set into a select number of bugs."

Drakkar stared at Charles. "That is not possible."

"I know the men who helped refine the technology."

Jacob thought that was an interesting thing to say. He knew Charles had invented the technology, but he hadn't heard Charles say it had been refined.

The door to the stable flew open and cracked against the wall. The sudden sound made George rear up and hiss at the newcomers. The Walker was intimidating, but Drakkar just shouted at him and pulled on his leg.

"Hey!" he said, yanking on George's leg again. The Walker swung around and looked ready to strike before Drakkar stuffed a Sweet-Fly directly into its mouth. George's antennae twitched, and the Walker dove face-first into the trough once more.

"Umm, sorry," Alice said. She carefully eased the door closed behind Samuel. "I thought the door would be heavier."

"It's heavy," Charles said, "just has some excellent hinges."

"Not such a great doorstop," Samuel said as he made his way to the far side of the Walker and set his precariously stacked armload of boxes and parcels down.

"Were that true," Drakkar said, picking up his conversation with Charles, "someone would have had to place the device on the invaders."

"Talking about the transmitters?" Samuel asked. He slid some of the twine-wrapped parcels into a nearly empty saddlebag.

"Yes," Drakkar said. "Did you see them with your own eyes? It sounds more like some ancient magic than something a man could build."

"Trust me," Alice said. "They work just fine. Besides, it could have been a woman."

Drakkar grinned at her. "I meant no disrespect. I only meant man as in human hands. I would not dare to cross such a capable person."

Alice narrowed her eyes. "I'm not entirely sure if you meant what you said, but I hope you did."

Drakkar nodded. "Ah, that would be an insult to the guardians, my young friend."

"What? Why?"

"They never lie," Samuel said. "Or so the stories say."

"They never lie unless it's convenient," Charles said. He picked up the holster for his air cannon. "That's what the stories *should* say."

"That's true for anyone," Jacob said. He helped Alice load her bags onto the Walker.

Drakkar watched him for a moment. "You are not wrong, Steamborn. You are not wrong."

That wasn't the first time Jacob had been called a Steamborn, but it was the first time he thought it was said with respect.

"Looks like that's everything," Alice said as she fastened the heavy brass buckle on the saddlebag.

Drakkar looked out the window. "The sun is just breaking the mountaintops. We should be able to make Bollwerk before night falls."

"We don't have the gear for a night in the desert," Charles said. "We have to make it. If we freeze to death before someone has a chance to shoot us, we'll feel mighty stupid."

"I still don't see how a *desert* can be cold," Jacob said.

"That's because you never paid attention to Miss Penny," Alice said. She pushed Jacob out of the way and hopped onto the saddle farthest from George's head.

"Still doesn't make sense," Jacob grumbled.

Drakkar motioned for him to come closer. "Help me with the stable door."

Jacob and Drakkar pulled from the south end of the door while Samuel pushed from the north. George the Walker's antennae shot straight up as his body curled and twisted and turned in the ever-widening strip of light.

"That should be enough," Drakkar said. "Alice, I would suggest you duck when George—"

Alice yelped as the Walker shot through the gap in a blur of rolling legs, barely ducking the top of the stone doorway.

"Yes, well, when George does that."

Steamforged

The Steamborn series, book #2

Available now!

Also by Eric R. Asher

Shop ebooks, audiobooks, and paperbacks at ericrasherstore.com

The Theme Park at the End of the World

The Steamborn Series

Steamborn
Steamforged
Steamsworn
Skyborn
Skyforged
Skysworn
Stormborn
Stormforged
Stormsworn

The Vesik Series
(Recommended for Ages 17+)

Days Gone Bad
Wolves and the River of Stone
Winter's Demon
This Broken World
Destroyer Rising
Rattle the Bones
Witch Queen's War
Forgotten Ghosts
The Book of the Ghost
The Book of the Claw
The Book of the Sea
The Book of the Staff
The Book of the Rune

The Book of the Sails
The Book of the Wing
The Book of the Blade
The Book of the Fang
The Book of the Reaper
Dreams of the Forgotten Dead
Garden Gnome Graves

The Vesik Series Box Sets

Box Set One (Books 1-3)
Box Set Two (Books 4-6)
Box Set Three (Books 7-8)
Box Set Four: The Books of the Dead Part 1
Box Set Five: The Books of the Dead Part 2

Mason Dixon: Monster Hunter

Episode One
Episode Two
Episode Three
Episode Four

Want to receive an email when one of Eric's books releases?
Visit ericrasher.com to get started.

About the Author

Eric is a former bookseller, cellist, and comic seller currently living in Saint Louis, Missouri. A lifelong enthusiast of books, music, toys, and games, he discovered a love for the written word after being dragged to the library by his parents at a young age. When he is not writing, you can usually find him reading, gaming, or buried beneath a small avalanche of Transformers. For more about Eric, see: www.ericrasher.com

Enjoy this book? You can make a big difference.

If you've enjoyed this book, I would be very grateful if you could take a minute to leave a review on the platform of your choice. It can be as short as you like. Thank you for spending time with Jacob and Alice.

9 781964 216003